Doan on New York...

"It's a tough town, have you noticed? It's like, in San Francisco being weird is not only all right, it's your duty as a citizen to be weird, to keep the theme park entertaining for the tourists. When we were in L.A., being weird was *so wrong*, because it wasn't good box office. And I've figured out that here, being weird is good, just as long as you can sell it. There! Our national character in a nutshell."

Applause for this divine new series:

Death Wore the Emperor's New Clothes

Orland Outland

BERKLEY PRIME CRIME, NEW YORK

DEATH WORE THE EMPEROR'S NEW CLOTHES

A Berkley Prime Crime Book / published by arrangement with the author

PRINTING HISTORY
Berkley Prime Crime edition / December 1999

All rights reserved.
Copyright © 1999 by Orland Outland.
This book may not be reproduced in whole or in part, by mimeograph or any other means, without permission.
For information address: The Berkley Publishing Group, a division of Penguin Putnam Inc., 375 Hudson Street, New York, New York 10014.

The Penguin Putnam Inc. World Wide Web site address is
http://www.penguinputnam.com

ISBN: 0-425-17263-5

Berkley Prime Crime Books are published by The Berkley Publishing Group, a division of Penguin Putnam Inc., 375 Hudson Street, New York, New York 10014.
The name BERKLEY PRIME CRIME and the BERKLEY PRIME CRIME design are trademarks belonging to Penguin Putnam Inc.

PRINTED IN THE UNITED STATES OF AMERICA

10 9 8 7 6 5 4 3 2 1

Death Wore the Emperor's New Clothes

one

~~~~~~

Doan moved through Williams Sonoma with the practiced air of a professional chef. He glided past the big-ticket items, the best of which he'd already acquired—the copper pots and pans from France, the knives from Germany, the Mixmaster—and lingered over the little items, another one of which always seemed to be needed to put the finishing touches on his kitchen. He admired the Swiss melon ballers, the silver tea infuser . . . "Ooh!" he said out loud, admiring a platinum vegetable peeler.

This went into the basket atop the chocolate-covered Arabica beans; he'd bought the Jamaica Blue Mountain ones last time but the scene with Tim had not been pretty. "Thirty-five bucks for chocolate-covered coffee beans! Doan, what were you thinking!" Doan's boyfriend, Tim, had an unfortunate predilection for saving money, which was good because it meant Tim had a tendency to end up with money in the bank at the end of the year, but bad because it meant he thought Doan should be in the same situation. Thus, Doan had economized today, buying the chocolate-covered coffee beans that only cost half as much as the last batch.

He picked up the item he'd actually come for and made

for the checkout. There was no way he'd been willing to
go home last time with both the large *and* the small mad-
eleine pans on the same day, so the small one had had to
wait for today. He had to grudgingly admit that Tim had a
point about his extravagance; after all, he had spent so
much time equipping the kitchen he hadn't really even
cooked anything yet. "I love to cook!" he told Tim the
day he brought home enough small appliances to run an
intimate restaurant, but truth be told, now that he had acquired enough money to go out to dinner on a nightly basis,
he rarely cooked when he could dine out. That had now
gone on for some time, but Tim had finally laid down the
law, inasmuch as anyone could with Doan—they would
either stop going out, or Doan would stop purchasing so
many unused kitchen implements. Since these purchases
had become the high point of his shopping day, Doan had
resolved to start cooking again—"to economize," he said
aloud, fooling nobody but himself.

Doan had finally put his glittering kitchen to use today,
serving up cornbread madeleines with Tim's morning coffee. "See!" Doan crowed, "I'm cooking!" Tim had rolled
his eyes and given up.

"Hello, Mr. McCandler." The checkout girl smiled. Uh-
oh, Doan thought, they know me by name. Maybe I *am*
spending too much money here. He smiled and exchanged
pleasantries with her, handing over his MasterCard debit
card without looking at the total on the register, reveling
momentarily in the fluffy joy of knowing he could afford
it, whatever it cost.

This had only recently become the case. As a youth he
had enjoyed the privileges of travel and ease accorded to
beautiful young gay boys in the big city who are willing to
hang off the arm of those less physically but more finan-
cially endowed, but those privileges had ended abruptly
when he found himself inordinately attracted to women's
clothing. He had no desire to be a drag queen, to bury
himself under a hurricane of hair, a crayon box of makeup,
and a meteor shower's worth of glitter. Women's clothes
were just more fun, more attractive, than men's clothes. He
grew his hair long but wore no makeup; naturally slim and
with feline features to begin with, he soon looked to most

eyes like a woman, all the more so because he wasn't trying very hard. No longer the boy on whom older men could project their fantasies of gilded youth, nor the drag queen of some men's fetish fantasy, Doan found himself out on his own but with tastes acquired during his years of indolence that he would never lose. He spent the next ten years living as well as possible on as little as possible while working hardly at all, at least not at a "real" job; then he had befriended Binky Van de Kamp, with whom he stumbled into a series of adventures that culminated with their forming a detective agency, solving a big case, and collecting both a fortune in fees and a boyfriend for Doan in the form of handsome and hunky entertainment writer Tim O'Neill.

"The Avalanche," as they referred to the cash that had rolled in, had come six months ago. Binky's own appetite for luxury items rivaled Doan's; she had grown up in privileged splendor in Connecticut but had turned her back on the family and their plans for her in order to live footloose here in San Francisco, subsisting on the occasionally necessary menial employment and a modest trust fund, both of which she had left behind when The Avalanche had come. The detective agency had become a going concern, but neither of them spent much time working there, preferring instead to hire competent people to do the work while they themselves kept busy spending the windfall from the big case that had started it all.

Just as he got out of the store, his cell phone rang; he pulled it out of his purse and slid the earpiece up. "Hello?"

"Hey, where are you?" It was Binky.

"Out running some errands."

"Uh-oh. Not Williams Sonoma again."

"Maybe," he said defensively.

"I thought you and Tim—"

"Tim O'Neill is not my husband," Doan stated authoritatively. "We don't even live together! Yet. Maybe never if he keeps nagging me about what *I'm* doing with *my* money."

"He just has your best interests at heart."

"No doubt. And remember what happened to the last one who tried that with me." Binky remembered very well; at the end of their first adventure Doan had found love with

Binky's friend K.C., who had made the foolish mistake of
trying to reform Doan. Doan had lived with K.C. for all of
a month before flying out the door in a hysterical frenzy
and never returning.

"Hmm, yes, you don't like to be told what to do, even
if it's what's best for you. But I've seen your kitchen,
Doan—what could possibly be left for you to buy?"

"Why, my dear, that's the wonderful thing about shopping for kitchen gadgets—there is *no end* to the little gee-
gaws you can pick up!"

Binky sighed. "Doesn't that tell you something?"

"What?"

"That you have bought *everything,* Doan, that you can
buy. All the clothes, all the furniture, all the gizmos. That
you have shopped yourself out so thoroughly that all that's
left for you to do is go buy a platinum vegetable peeler."

"They have those! How did you know!"

"Oh, my god, I can't believe it. That was a joke!"

"Sorry, hon, nothing so ludicrous someone hasn't already done it."

"I mean, I know I haven't exactly been a frugal person
either. . . ." Doan bit his tongue so as not to shout *Amen
to that!* Binky had spent as much money on facials and
waxings and tints and pedicures as Doan had dropped at
Williams Sonoma and Sur le Table.

"Well, word on the street is that you have your own
Aveda rep," he couldn't resist sniping.

"I just . . . I just don't think this is a good time to piss
Tim off."

"Whyever would this be a worse time than any other?"

"Plans for lunch?"

"Uh-oh. It's complicated, I can smell it. I'll meet you in
half an hour."

Café Flore at lunchtime on a weekday was wedged full,
proving that San Francisco really was Doan and Binky's
kind of town, because nobody else who lived here seemed
to work, either. There was the usual assorted crowd: rent
boys just rising for breakfast and not removing their shades
for anyone or anything; gay men on HIV disability taking
their time over the paper and a frittata; the self-employed

stopping in for a latte and a bit of social; always at least one person waiting for a blind date. . . . One could linger forever over a mineral water if need be, which made it precisely the kind of place that had attracted Binky and Doan in their lean years, and while they could afford to eat real meals now, places to linger were still as precious as gems.

"So what's the deal?" Doan asked once they were settled at a table in the September sun.

"Well, I'm not sure. The first thing I noticed was that Tim and Luke have been spending a lot of time on the phone together—haven't you noticed?"

"No, but then Tim's always on the phone to somebody. And he and I are still in our own places, whereas your and Luke's separate apartments are really just a polite fiction now, seeing how much time he spends at your place. . . ." Doan's eyes widened. "Maybe they're having an affair!"

Binky nearly choked on her latte. "God forbid! No, I don't think it's *that* serious. But there's something mysterious going on, and I can't say I like it."

"Maybe they're plotting something wonderfully romantic," Doan suggested. "A trip to Italy or something."

"First they're cheating on us and now they're sweeping us off our feet. Wonderful thinking, Doan. What makes you so sure it has anything to do with us at all?"

"Well, what else could it be? I mean, Tim's an entertainment writer and Luke's a homicide cop. The only thing that could bring them together, besides us, would be a celebrity murder. . . ."

Binky fished an airline ticket jacket out of her purse. "Here. Look at this."

Doan examined the contents: the stubs from round-trip tickets from San Francisco to New York City for Luke and Tim. "They went to New York a week ago. . . . Tim never told me he was going! Why would he do that?"

"Afraid what would happen to the rest of your funds if you discovered Madison Avenue," Binky couldn't help thinking out loud.

Doan scowled. "Thank you. No, this is *weird.* I mean, it's one thing to talk about things on the phone, another to take a transcontinental trip and not even tell us. Look, they went one day and came back the next . . . that must have been the day Tim told me he had to go to L.A." He frowned. "An outright lie, obviously. Hey!" he shouted indignantly. "They went first class! Fine nerve, telling *me* to economize."

"Doan, you well know having to fly coach on a cross-country trip is cruel and unusual punishment. So what do we do? Confront them, or wait for them to explain things?"

"Hmm. I hate surprises. But I hate arguments even more. Oh, this is awful!"

"I say we wait until Sunday; that's only two days away. If they don't spit it out by the end of dinner, we tell them we know they're up to something."

Doan sighed. "O.K. All I can say is that it better be good!"

The two couples had made a practice of meeting for Sunday brunch; this weekend they took the ferry to Sausalito and ate on the waterfront with a smashing view of San Francisco.

Doan had been fit to burst all through the meal, and only several strategic kicks under the table from Binky had kept him from demanding an explanation. But when Luke ordered a bottle of Veuve Clicquot at the end of the meal, they knew something was up.

"Shall I?" he asked Tim, who nodded. "We have an announcement."

"We've been waiting for it," Binky said sweetly.

"Yes, put us out of our mystery," Doan demanded.

Tim and Luke laughed. "Guess we couldn't keep the secret forever from two such excellent detectives."

"Flattery later, facts now," Doan pressed.

"Okay, okay. It's just that this is something very big that will change all our lives. You guys have heard of Andrew Weatherall, haven't you?"

Doan and Binky glared at him. "Duh!" Doan said, offended. It was simply impossible to be a gay man, as Doan was, or a voracious reader of fluffy "profile" magazines, as Binky was, and not have heard of Andrew Weatherall. While there were a handful of gay billionaires floating around, Weatherall was the only one who'd been officially and openly gay long before he was officially and openly stinking rich.

Andrew Weatherall had been a male secretary with a knack for computers just as the PC revolution was getting under steam. He had a marvelous knack for mastering any program that came along, even if it was something related to a field he'd never worked in before—for instance, Weatherall had learned Lotus 1-2-3 before he'd ever worked in anything related to corporate finance; he'd mastered dBase III only weeks after hardly being able to guess what a database might be for. He made a few weak stabs at learning to program, but never really got into it—"too much work for too little gain," he had famously said. And yet in a weird way, he was a savant. "It's easy," he explained years later to the *New York Times*. "A computer program is a system. Once you learn the basic rules of the system, your knowledge is portable. All word processing programs have to do certain things, so once you learn how to do them in one program, you can figure out how to do them in another." Well, *he* could, anyway. One day, like the apple hitting Newton on the head, Weatherall realized something—all these little software companies, known only to nerds and techies and power users like himself, were all going to be very big companies, once computers became more affordable. And that would mean that anybody putting a little money in, say, Microsoft or Sun or Oracle today, would have a whole hell of a lot of money tomorrow.

He moved into a studio apartment, sold his car, and worked like a dog, sometimes even at two full-time jobs, putting practically every penny into stocks, completely ignoring all advice to diversify his portfolio or put money into blue chips or other "safe" investments. Six years later, his net worth was approximately $40 million. Now, for most anyone else, that would have been the signal to cash out and retire, but Weatherall had more ambitious plans in mind. Some crazy thing called the Internet and the World Wide Web had come along; Weatherall had spent a day on the Web using Mosaic, one of the first Web browsers, and the next day he was a venture capitalist, liquidating his tiny shares in today's big boys to capture huge shares of tomorrow's big boys. When his genius for picking stocks became apparent, he quickly capitalized on that to begin the Weatherall Fund, a high-risk, high-reward mutual fund that churned out amazing profits. When *Fortune*'s 1998 list of the richest Americans came out, there was Andrew Weatherall, clocking in at $7.6 billion and rising exponentially.

It was not his wealth that had made him famous (a few billion in itself no longer being enough to attract attention in America), but his outspokenness. When Congress had passed the Defense of Marriage Act, denying federal recognition to gay marriages, Weatherall had taken out a full-page ad in the *New York Times* decrying everything from the "Orwellian use of language in the bill's title" to Congress's inability to focus on anything other than regulating other people's sex lives. "Here we have a Congress," Weatherall wrote quotably, "which year after year cannot pass any kind of campaign finance reform, but which can set a land speed record when it comes time to regulate other people's morality. We have a bunch of Republicans who prate about the glory of states' rights until the day that one state decides to legalize gay marriage, at which time federal power suddenly becomes a marvelous thing."

The 1996 Republican convention was substantially more moderate than its 1992 predecessor in part because Weatherall had threatened to give $10 million to the Democratic party every time a "right-wing kook" took the podium (the Democrats managed to collect $30 million from him, Republicans being unable to keep all the kooks at bay). At a luncheon for tycoons whose purpose was to heap plaudits on retired General Colin Powell (and hear his well-compensated nuggets of wisdom), Weatherall took the opportunity to excoriate the general for his stand on gays in the military, "especially for using the very rhetoric about 'good order and discipline' that was used in his own time to prevent the integration of African Americans into the armed forces." When the right had put out newspaper ads saying that homosexuals could become heterosexual through praying to Jesus, Weatherall had wondered aloud if any paper in the country would have printed an ad telling Jews or Muslims that they could save themselves from hell by becoming Christians. Needless to say, Andrew Weatherall had become the Gore Vidal of tycoons, always good for a juicy quote on a slow news day.

"We love him," Doan said enthusiastically. "He is our friend."

"Would you like to meet him?" Tim asked.

"Would I! Wait a minute, how do you know . . . oh, wait a minute . . . your trip to New York! Binky, they met Andrew Weatherall!"

Tim and Luke exchanged glances. "How'd you know about that?" Luke asked.

"Hello, we're detectives," Binky said cuttingly. "And your partners, by the way, who resented being kept in the dark."

Luke winced. "Ow. I'm sorry. But Andrew insisted on absolute secrecy."

"Ooh, it's *Andrew* now!" Doan mocked. "And just what were you doing lunching with *Andrew*?"

"He offered us both jobs," Tim said, cutting to the chase. "Working for him in New York City."

Binky and Doan were silent with shock. "But we haven't accepted," Luke appended hastily. "We told him we needed to talk it over with our partners."

"What kind of jobs?" Binky asked, reeling from the news.

"Well . . ." Tim and Luke began together. "You tell them," Luke deferred.

"He just bought a magazine group," Tim explained, "and he contacted me about a job as editor of one of the mags. Coincidentally, he mentioned on the phone that he was looking for a new head of security, so I asked Luke if he was interested, and he was, so we both went to New York, he liked us both, we liked him, and . . . here we are."

"He wants to meet the two of you," Luke continued.

"Really?" Doan said. "Whatever for?"

"We told him it was unthinkable for us to relocate without taking our partners with us, and that the two of you had a thriving business here. He said, maybe I can find positions for them, or something."

"Wow!" Doan said, already won over and turning to the more skeptical Binky. "Can you believe it?"

"I'll believe it when I see it," Binky said darkly, still

resenting the underhandedness of the whole thing.

Luke took her hand. "I know you don't like the fact that I took things this far without talking to you. But there just didn't seem to be a point in mentioning it unless I thought it was really going to go somewhere. I thought, I'll see how the interview goes and while he chews on whether or not to hire one or both of us, I'll tell Binky."

"But he works fast," Tim said, "that's the way his industry moves. By the end of lunch we both had firm job offers." He turned to Doan. "Would you consider moving to New York?"

"Would I!" Doan said delightedly, but then he looked at Binky and his face fell. "Well, I mean, if Binky goes. We're partners in this business, so we'd both have to agree to . . . close it or whatever."

"I think Weatherall would buy you out," Tim said. "That was the impression that I got."

"You mean . . . cash? A lump sum?" Doan was dizzy with the thought.

"And what would we do?" Binky asked. "Become bored housewives while you two worked?"

"That's why Weatherall wants to meet you," Luke said. "To see what you could do in his organization."

"Oh, come on, Binky," Doan pleaded. "At the very least we get a free trip to New York and we get to meet *Andrew Weatherall!*"

Binky sighed, outnumbered and overwhelmed. "Okay, let's meet him and see what happens."

"Yay!" Doan cheered, signaling for the waiter. "Another bottle of champagne, please." He turned to his friends. "Courtesy of Andrew Weatherall!"

That night in Binky's apartment, Luke came to bed to find Binky with the covers pulled up to her chin. "Are you still mad?"

"Well, Luke, look at it from my perspective. Doan and I finally hit on a money-making business that hardly requires our labors, and now you're telling me to drop it all and move to New York. I mean, I love New York, but what the hell am I going to do there if this guy Weatherall and I don't get along?"

Luke got into bed and wrapped his arms around Binky. "Look, if he doesn't have anything for you, I won't take the job. Fair?"

"But then what about Tim and Doan? If we stay here and they go, I'll be ... well, Doan is my best friend, you know."

"I know."

"It's almost like I have to go already, because if he decided to stay for me, that ruins Tim's chances, and I've screwed things up for everyone."

Luke gave her a squeeze. "Binky, nothing's going to get screwed up. I have a good job, Tim makes a good income. . . ."

"Yeah, but neither of you is ever going to get this kind of opportunity again, especially not here." She thought a moment. "How much would this job pay you?"

"About two hundred grand a year, plus bonuses indexed to the success of the Weatherall Fund, which, I'm told, at the current rate of return will make the salary more of a rainy day fund."

"Oh, my god!"

"He's well known for being extremely generous to all his employees. He told Tim and me that being at the bottom of the corporate food chain for so long taught him the value of properly compensating good employees."

"You could never make that much money as a cop."

"No, I couldn't."

Binky sighed. "And I'm just like Doan, I'd rather spend it than save it. Which leaves you to provide for our old age."

"Hey, be careful, you just implied you're going to be sticking around for a while."

Binky smiled. "Yeah, that's what I'm counting on." She rolled over and nestled her head on Luke's broad chest. "I hope this all works out."

"Listen, I only spent two hours with the guy, but I can tell you something—Andrew Weatherall has a way of making things work out."

Binky and Doan had fully expected to be carted across the country in first class, but Weatherall had gone one step further in the courtship, sending his own private jet to pick them up. An attendant (male, cute, gay; Binky speculated on what services Weatherall got on long trips) kept them liquored up the whole way, with a never-empty tray of exquisite little snackies on the table in front of their swiveling, reclining chairs.

"Can we have some more of those shrimp thingies?" Doan asked the steward. "I love this. Can we afford one of these?"

"I think a private jet runs about five million bucks these days."

"Oh. Ow! Oh well. God, this is even better than flying first class! We don't even have to share a bathroom with coach!"

"Mmm." Binky looked out the window.

"Binky?"

"Yes?"

"Are you okay?"

"Well, Doan, I'll tell you that on the flight back."

"Hmm. Fair enough." There had been no tense scene at Tim O'Neill's house that Sunday night. Doan loved San Francisco, but he'd seen it and done it. An urban creature, he would be happy anywhere there was a subway, a Macy's, a gourmet grocery store, and a housecleaning service. Doan knew that this was a great opportunity for Tim; the editorship of *Edgy Hipster* magazine did not come along every month (actually, under the syndicate's previous owner, it had tended to come along once every year). He felt no qualms about shuttering the detective agency, especially if there was a handsome sum involved. Doan would never admit to Binky, but had to admit to himself, that he had pretty much shopped out San Francisco. The platinum vegetable peeler, he was sure, was a sign from God it was time to move on to bigger and better things. New York was surely an inexhaustible trove of things to purchase, and he did not share Binky's desire to be doing something productive. Doan felt that just being what he was, was a significant contribution to mankind.

The car met them on the tarmac and they and their luggage were whisked to the Regal Royal, a luxury hotel on Central Park that Weatherall had purchased during the recession for a relative song and which now poured still more cash into his coffers. Their suite was packed with shockingly large floral arrangements, gift baskets, and a bottle of Perrier-Jouët on ice. Doan raided the gift basket and made up a plate while Binky poured the champagne.

"Wow, New York City!" Doan enthused, looking out over the park. "I never thought I'd live here."

"No, why not?" Binky asked, perusing the pile of PR info on Weatherall's conglomerate that had been placed on the coffee table for them at his request.

"Too expensive. I mean, as far as rents go, San Francisco is just as bad now, but still. I think I sat down and did the math one day; I decided that I'd have to have $100,000 a year, after taxes, to be happy in New York. I mean, you've got to get out of town in August, and winter here means snow—yuck! Gotta leave town when that hits. There's no Fast Pass, so public transportation means a dollar fifty every time you go anywhere and no round-trip transfers, either. Then you have to bribe your building super, at least at Christmas and probably again in summer when your air conditioning goes out. And of course there's so much more entertainment—all those plays, but the tickets are so expensive! No, I never would move here without an honest-to-god *pile* of money."

"And you expect to get a pile out of Weatherall?"

Doan shrugged. "He can afford it. What's a couple million to him? Tim says the magazine syndicate spends a million bucks a year just on hired cars."

"He also said Weatherall was going to change that."

"Yeah, so he can afford to buy us out!" Doan concluded brightly. "Oh, Binky, come on. We really weren't doing that much detecting, you have to admit."

"Well, no, but still . . ."

"I know, you had an identity and you were a business owner and it was all very respectable blah blah blah. Well, you'll have an identity as an employee of Andrew Weatherall, that's for sure!"

"Right, as what? His social secretary?"

The phone rang. "Hello?" Doan answered it. "Yes, we are. Now? Well, yes, that's fine." He hung up. "Speak of the devil, that was his secretary wanting to know if we were available to see him."

"Now?"

"Now. Let's see what our destiny has in store, shall we?"

They had expected the sort of faceless pomo office building most billionaires take in stride as the place they would spend most of their waking hours, but such was not for Andrew Weatherall. According to the literature Binky had perused in the limo, Weatherall had purchased a great old seven-story building in Silicon Alley ("I don't want to walk out of my office and see suits everywhere I look") that used to be a garment factory, and had it done over from head to toe, laying down exquisite wooden floors over miles of computer wiring, putting in an efficient HVAC system but insisting that the windows open ("they don't open downtown because they don't want 'em jumping"), putting in an employee cafeteria that one cheeky restaurant critic actually finagled her way into and wrote up (she gave it three stars), a state-of-the-art gym in the basement, and even a child care center ("way in the back where I can't hear 'em screaming all day").

The limo driver must have made a discreet call, because a beaming black woman in an Armani suit was out in front of the Weatherall building to greet them. "Mr. McCandler, Ms. Van de Kamp, welcome to Weatherall and Associates. I'm Mrs. Keith, Mr. Weatherall's executive assistant. Mr. Weatherall is expecting you."

They were whisked inside with barely time to inventory the lobby; Binky caught a flash of large, comfy chairs on Oriental carpets and huge floral bouquets on glass-topped recess-lit tables. The elevator was paneled in rich dark wood and fitted with brass rails and fixtures; Mrs. Keith made small talk on the way up, asking them about their hotel and their flight. The elevator opened on the top floor and she led them past several desks where assistants (Weatherall had three) were fielding calls or peering intently into computer screens. She opened the double doors at the end of the room and escorted them in.

They were dazzled by the light bouncing off the buildings across the way, filling Weatherall's office. Doan could make out a form at the window but couldn't discern any features.

"Hello?" Binky asked, and Weatherall turned around to see them squinting.

"Oh, I'm sorry" were his first words, as he pressed a button on his desk. The windows polarized, cutting the glare dramatically but still leaving the room bright. The man came forward and offered his hand. "I'm Andrew Weatherall."

Weatherall was just under six foot, his hair, just graying at the temples, cut short to accommodate the fact that his hairline was slightly receding (to their delight, Binky and Doan would later find that comb-overs were expressly forbidden in the Weatherall and Associates employee manual). He was handsome in an odd-duck sort of way, obviously quite fit, judging from his jawline and the firm handshake he offered, with arresting brown eyes that seemed to fix you with their complete attention and demand the same in return. "Miss Van de Kamp." He smiled, riveting Binky with his magnetism. "I should have expected that Luke's companion would be beautiful, but not this beautiful."

"Such flattery," Binky laughed, secretly pleased; somehow it had come out of Weatherall sounding courtly rather than corny—must be all that money, she thought.

"Not at all. I've taken the liberty of doing some research on you, and I must say, it's very impressive. I hope you don't mind; my prying goes wide but not deep."

"No, not at all."

Weatherall picked a folder up off his desk. "I'll tell you now I don't really give a shit about educational credentials so don't worry that you didn't go to college; I didn't either." He smiled, sharing a conspiratorial look. "And I do tend to favor the self-educated here, I'll admit. Oh, and I curse a lot, too, hope you don't mind that," he added absently, already back to the folder.

"Hell, no."

"You recently spurned an inheritance, I understand."

"Well, yes, but only because it came with strings attached and I didn't need it anymore."

"All the same. Most people don't turn down free money." He regarded her closely.

"That was my point," Binky said. "It wasn't exactly free."

He smiled. "I see. Please," he said, realizing they were all standing. "Sit down." They all took comfy seats around his small conference table. Weatherall leaned forward and eyed Binky. "I have a place for you. Well, it's not a place, more a role, really, you'll create the place. You were raised in Connecticut?"

"Yes, I was."

"Miss Porter's School and all that?"

"Yes."

"Family well connected socially?"

"I suppose they still are. We don't speak."

"Ah. No matter. My point is, you're used to dealing with people with lots of money. Ladies who lunch and fill the idle hours on various boards and committees, doing good or at least appearing to do so in the papers."

"Well, I wouldn't say I was *used* to them. . . ."

"But they don't faze you, do they? You worked undercover for Mary Duveen, the She-Devil of Hollywood, and I understand she was very pleased with you until she discovered your motivation in working for her."

"It was an easy job," Binky admitted.

"Hmm. Listen." He leaned back in his chair. "Here is what I need. I am a gay man, Ms. Van de Kamp. I will never have children, not biologically and almost undoubtedly not by adoption. I don't like the idea that I could drop dead tomorrow and have to watch from above as a bunch of fucking lawyers—excuse my French—motion and plea and carry and bill and bill and bill until the whole huge pile of money is gone down their disgusting greedy gullets. I want to give my money away, but in pieces," he said, holding up a hand. "If I were to give it all away today, I would be powerless, and I need power. I have goals that can only be fulfilled through the sort of power that money brings in spades. However, I've got about eight billion dollars" (both Doan and Binky successfully repressed the urge to gasp at this point) "and I could stand to wave bye-bye to a billion without feeling a pinch.

"Now, the lawyers tell me that to set up a tax-deductible trust I need to come up with a charter and a board of directors blah blah BLAH, and I'll tell you something: I'd rather pay the goddamn taxes and give it away to whomever I feel like than to turn it over to some board who could end up doing God knows what once I'm gone. So here's what I'm doing. I'm putting a billion bucks in the bank, calling it the Weatherall Foundation, and looking for someone to help me give it away. Namely, you."

Binky was stunned. "Me?"

"Yes, you, for several reasons. First, I want Luke Faraglione as my head of security and I have to give you a job. Second, after investigating you and reading your profile, I think you're exactly the kind of person who can, first, deal with the sort of people who are going to try to convince you that the money should go to them, and second, weed out the scam artists, and third, not take any shit from anybody. I have a reputation to uphold"—he smiled—"as a big-mouthed, opinionated bastard who could give a damn what people think, and I want my foundation to reflect that," he finished, inviting her to join him in his smile, which she did.

"I want to do good," he continued, "and I know places I can do good. But the fact is, if I gave more than a million dollars to an organization that feeds people with AIDS, well, they'd just turn into a giant bureaucracy and I'd be feeding people with M.S.W.'s instead, and that is not my goal. I am a busy man, obviously, managing all the money I manage, and I don't have time to pick over all these little virtuous organizations that want money. You see," he added, smiling, "I am not asking you to stop being a detective; you are perfect for the job precisely because you are a good detective—what I want you to do is investigate to find out who deserves the money and who doesn't. Are you interested?"

Binky could not believe her ears. Here she was, only days ago protesting that she felt useless, and now here she was, being handed the opportunity to wield *a billion dollars* in the name of good! "It sounds too good to be true—" she began, but Weatherall cut her off.

"It's not. I have my pet charities, and I expect you to have yours. I expect you to keep me posted on who you're giving the money to, how much and, most importantly, why. I guarantee you the job for a year at, oh, I don't know, two fifty? And if I don't like what you're doing, I'll fire you at the end of the year. Deal?'' He extended his hand.

''I . . . yes!''

''Yay!'' Weatherall cheered, suddenly becoming another person, now a happy boy who'd gotten his way. ''So you will all be members of our happy family.''

''Ahem,'' Doan said. ''Hem.''

Weatherall remembered Doan. ''I'm sorry, Mr. Mc-Candler. I didn't mean to ignore you. I tend to focus on one goal and ignore everything else until''—he smiled winningly at Binky—''I get my way. I will of course buy out your detective agency; a million dollars apiece?''

''And what would I do for you?'' Doan asked.

Weatherall frowned, looking over Doan's much thinner file. ''Well, I don't know yet, exactly.'' He looked up and smiled brightly. ''But everything's gone so well for everyone else involved, I'm sure something will turn up!'' He stood up and they followed suit. ''My next meeting awaits me. I look forward to having you all over to dinner at my house when you're all settled.'' The door opened magically. ''Mrs. Keith will help you with everything you need.''

''I have a list of apartments you might like to see,'' she said, steering them out of Weatherall's office as another assistant led in the next appointment.

In the car, Binky bubbled over all the way back to the hotel. ''Oh, Doan, I was so wrong! This is all going to turn out wonderfully!'' Then, noticing Doan's unusually long period of silence, she asked, ''What's wrong?''

''Oh, nothing.''

''Yes there is, spit it out.''

''Nothing! I didn't expect anything and I didn't get anything, so there it is.''

''So why are you so obviously unhappy?''

Doan shrugged. ''I don't know. It's never bothered me *before* to know I wasn't and never would be a productive member of society, but . . . damn! You're going to run a foundation, Tim's running a magazine, Luke's a big cheese.

In six months you'll all be . . . *yuppies!* You'll all have absolutely no use for the likes of me."

"Doan. That is totally untrue. Like Andrew said—"

"Oh, it's *Andrew* already for you too!"

"Like he said, he just doesn't have a role for you yet."

"Hmph."

"I mean, you don't have a résumé, or a file, whatever, you don't have what someone like . . . Mr. Weatherall can just look at and say, 'He goes here.' You never wanted the kind of job that would get you that kind of résumé!"

"I know." Doan sighed. "I guess I'm just jealous. All this time I thought you were just as reckless and heedless as I was and suddenly I see you've been preparing for this great role all your life."

"Right, preparing to throw money around like it was water, that's what we do best! Doan, you could work with me, we could—"

"I could work in an office, reading letters—'Please give me some money'—evaluating some proposal to build a bridge made out of matchsticks over the East River? And how long would it be before I ran screaming out of *that* particular position?"

Binky said nothing. It was true. The world of Andrew Weatherall was a practical one; it offered little opportunity for a frivolous decorative object like Doan. "So what are you saying?"

"You mean, am I going to stop the rest of you from becoming fabulously successful? No, dear," he said, putting a hand on Binky's arm. "Of course not. I'll just"— he sighed—"just have to become one of those ladies who lunch that Weatherall was talking about, find some museum board to wheedle my way onto." He smiled. "Don't worry about me, I'll make out just fine."

Binky was dying to call Luke but didn't want to gloat any further in front of Doan, so she decided to take a walk and let Doan and Tim talk in private.

"Baby, I'm sorry," Tim said after Doan recapped the day's events.

"No, no," Doan said, his customary cheer restored after all of an hour of most un-Doan-like depression. "It's fine.

I'll have plenty of money, I can find plenty to do. Start a salon, you know, take up starving artists or some such, become the next Peggy Guggenheim.''

"Peggy Guggenheim slept with all her artists," Tim reminded Doan. "I hope you don't get to feeling *that* lonely while I'm at work.''

"Oh. Well, I'll think of something. The important thing is, we are all going to be together and wealthy and happy and successful in our new home.''

"That's my Doan," Tim said warmly, "always landing on his feet.''

"Well, that's what they say, you know—the higher the altitude from which you throw the cat, the more time it's got to right itself.''

"And you're feeling thrown from a pretty high altitude right now, eh?''

"I'll be fine. You go on back to your back issues of *Edgy Hipster* and try to come up with a phrase for next season's clothes that doesn't include the word *revolutionary,* I dare you.''

Tim laughed. "Okay, baby. You go out and spend some of that money, okay?''

"Will do," Doan said, hanging up. Treating me like a child! he thought indignantly. Telling me to go suck my lollipop! Still, Doan thought, that great big Armani boutique *is* just on the other side of the park. . . .

Binky took to the streets, chatting merrily with Luke on her cell phone. "It's unbelievable, Luke, I've basically got carte blanche to give away this money. I mean, it's all invested in the Weatherall Fund so even if I just gave away the earnings on the principal we're still talking a hundred fifty, two hundred million dollars!''

"You're going to have a lot of new friends," Luke said, laughing.

"Yeah, a lot of *greedy* new friends. Guess it's unlisted phone numbers for us from now on.''

"You always had an unlisted number," Luke reminded her, "So those men couldn't call you back after the first . . . date.''

"Hush," Binky said. "My past is behind me. I am an

upstanding social lioness now, dispensing my bounty with
a fair and even hand.''

''Oh, brother.''

Binky laughed. ''Don't worry, I won't get all East Side
on you. I'll never forget I'm still the girl from the typing
pool. And I'll never let *you* forget you used to walk a beat.''

''I'm so glad this is all turning out. How'd Doan make
out?''

She sighed. ''Oh, Doan. I don't know what we'll do with
him. Andrew didn't even have a *file* on him, let alone a job
for him.''

''Hey, it's New York City. If there isn't anything for
Doan to do in that town, I'll eat my hat.''

''You're right. He'll be fine. We'll all be fine! Oh, Luke,
I'm so happy. This job is just what I wanted, and I didn't
even know I wanted it until I got it.''

''Lady, never say I didn't promise you the moon.''

She laughed. ''And deliver.''

She hung up and kept walking, because she could. New
York was so *flat*! she marveled. A long brisk walk in San
Francisco almost inevitably ended with the walker having
scaled numerous hills, but here you could just go and go
and go. . . . Another thing she loved was the foot traffic.
There were *so many* pedestrians here, it made the balance
of power tilt in favor of the walker and not, as it did back
in S.F., the car. In San Francisco, indeed in all of California,
pedestrians were viewed basically like orange safety
cones—you were supposed to go around them, but if you
hit one, well, so it goes. Here there was a critical mass that
protected you like a cocoon—after all, to hit one pedestrian
was an accident, two a tragedy, three indisputably a felony.
She didn't know any of these people and none of them
knew her, but there they were, looking out for each other
just by virtue of being in the same crosswalk.

San Francisco was cosmopolitan, indisputably, but not
metropolitan; the subways here didn't shutter up at night
nor did the sidewalks grow deserted. All night you could
find a bag of Pepperidge Farm cookies at some little corner
store, or get a pastry hot out of the oven just before dawn,
and there was always, always, something to do or see. A
play that wasn't *The Phantom of the Opera*! As many fa-

mous people seen in one day here as *lived* in San Francisco! As it was for many people, San Francisco had been home for Binky in a way the place she'd grown up in had never been, but like many people, she knew you couldn't live at home forever.

She looked up at the tall buildings, momentarily unashamed of her rube-like appearance. ''I love this town,'' she sighed. And she had the feeling it was going to love her back.

two

~~~~~

Binky had expected that her first day would be a quiet one, enabling her to set up her desk, get to know her new assistant better, orient herself to the rest of the Weatherall and Associates building (she had a plum office on the sixth floor, overlooking the garden park Weatherall had had installed in the lot behind the building), meet the other big shots, go over Weatherall's notes on his pet charities, and the rest of the usual orderly, first-day-on-the-job tasks.

None of that was to be. Two months had elapsed since her first meeting with Weatherall, enough time to get all four of our heroes settled into comfy new digs in Manhattan, but also enough time for word to get around the world of professional importuners that a huge new gravy train had just pulled into town, which could dispense half a million dollars *a day* without blinking, let alone touching capital. When Binky walked in she found a gaggle of people outside the Weatherall and Associates building, held back from the doors by police barricades, waving their petitions at her as if she were an Eastern potentate of yore. "Binky!" one of them shouted, and she turned to see who knew her name—a big mistake, as everyone else suddenly picked up the refrain. "Binky! Binky! Binky!" they shouted, with an occasional "Betty!" or "Betsy!" from those whose hearing wasn't that good or who would always willfully mishear a strange name and convert it into a familiar one.

In the safety of the lobby, she ran into Luke, who was trying to control the mob outside. He smiled ruefully at her. "Did you have to bring all your friends to see me on my first day?" For this Monday was his first day as well, and he looked as likely to settle into his job in an orderly manner as Binky was.

"My fan club," she apologized. "You don't want me to let them down, do you?"

"Why can't they just stay home and write you, begging for autographed eight-by-ten glossies?"

"If only that was all they wanted," she sighed.

Upstairs it seemed quieter. Her new assistant, Chloe, was at her desk, dressed in something black that probably would have raised eyebrows anywhere but at Weatherall and Associates. Binky had received résumés by the carton for the job; working for Weatherall in any capacity meant bonuses and profit sharing, which meant even an assistant could clock out of the firm in a few years with a million or more in hand. But Chloe's résumé had been the one to arrest Binky's attention—listed under "Experience" in the same form that others would list their jobs, Chloe had listed her "situations," as she'd called them in the interview. "4/94 to 5/96—Model. Underate, slunk around, pretended to be on heroin for so long I got so many invitations to do it I finally ended up a junkie. Crowning moment: cover shoot for *Edgy Hipster* with Ewan McGregor. 5/95 to 5/96—Girlfriend to Rock Star. Responsibilities included attending countless dreary music awards shows, picking up the drugs for the after party while he was onstage, doing my impression of Nancy Spungen to entertain his friends. Crowning moment: Bruce Springsteen kissing me on the cheek after I accidentally hit him with a bottle meant for boyfriend. Education: flunked out of Bennington, and that's no mean feat, I tell you." Binky had interviewed Chloe and found in her exactly the qualities Weatherall had found in Binky—an absolute unflappability in someone completely unimpressed by any living famous person.

Chloe jumped up as soon as Binky came in. "Good

morning," Binky said. "Thank God it's not as bad up here as it is down there."

"Oh, yes it is," Chloe said, pointing to the console. "It just got to be so bad I put them all on hold. *And none of them are hanging up,*" she finished darkly. "I tried taking messages for about half an hour," she said, waving around a pile of about three dozen pink slips, "but then I gave up. You can fire me if you want to."

"No, that won't be necessary," Binky said. "I would have done the same thing. Do I have voice mail?"

"You sure do, but your box is full. It only holds 256 messages."

Binky sighed. "Okay, then just put the phone to voice mail and let them get the 'box full' message for a while. In the meantime, can you listen to the ones in there now and see if there's anybody I really, really would want to talk to?"

"You sure you don't want me to help you with the mail first?"

"Uh-oh. Is it bad?"

"Oh, yeah." Chloe opened the door to Binky's office; on her desk were stacks of unopened mail and there were at least three sacks of mail on the floor. Binky sighed. "Okay, let's start in on this. You open 'em up and if they're clearly crackpots, just throw 'em in the trash."

"No generic thanks-but-no-thanks notes?"

"I think even a postcard back to everyone who wants a piece of this money would bankrupt the foundation. No, just get a . . . a Dumpster, I guess."

As the morning went by, the flowers started piling up. Chloe would read the cards attached out loud—" 'Congratulations on your new position, your friends at the American Ballet Theater.' Lilies, with the pollen thingies cut out, that was nice of them. 'Our best wishes for you, Binky, your friends at the Metropolitan Museum of Art.' You got a lot of friends now, don't you? 'Our condolences on the loss of your wife.' Oops, that was misdelivered. I'll call them."

"Don't bother, just let them pick it up in half an hour when they deliver the next load."

Binky found herself amazed at the desperation that would

drive people to write some of the letters she got. " 'Dear Andrew Weatherall Foundation,' " Chloe read aloud. "I am writing you to ask you, no, to beg you, to pay off my charge card bills. I am a compulsive gambler, an alcoholic, and a shopaholic, and my addictions have left me with several hundred thousand dollars in charge card bills. Now I am dying of cirrhosis of the liver and my wife is going to have to pay the bills. I cannot go through bankruptcy as I already did that several years ago. Please, please help us.' Jesus."

Binky shuddered. "Don't read me any more of those. Just toss them, okay?"

Chloe nodded. "This could turn out to be a very depressing job."

Binky looked around at the pile, which they'd barely dented. "We're going to either have to hire more help or just start throwing this stuff out unread."

Chloe sighed. "It's lunchtime, you mind if I get a sandwich?"

Binky looked at her watch, amazed. "God, no. I need to eat, too." She grabbed her purse and made for the front door, then stopped to call Luke first. "Are they still out there?"

"No. I told them Binky has left the building."

"Thank God."

"Rough morning?"

"You wouldn't believe it."

"Yeah, I would." Luke sighed.

"Uh-oh. What's wrong?"

"Nothing serious. Are we on for dinner tonight?"

"Absolutely, it's a date. We'll swap war stories."

Outside Binky found a car and driver waiting for her, the driver standing around waiting for her exit from the building. "Miss Van de Kamp?" he asked.

"Yes."

He tipped his cap and opened the car door for her and she got in automatically. Only when she shut the door did she realize she wasn't in the car alone. "Oh, I'm sorry!" she said impulsively, moving to get out.

"No, Binky, don't apologize," the man said. "Don't *ever* apologize." He extended his hand. "I'm Will Pow-

ers.'' Binky shook his hand, sizing him up. He was handsome, in the sort of injection-molded way that played well
on TV, tan and blond with blue eyes and a toothy white
smile and the sort of plastic coiffure Binky thought of as
''anchor-banker hair.'' His suit was well tailored but a dull,
corporate navy blue, with a red power tie to match.

''Pleased to meet you, and what are you doing in my
car?''

''Oh, this isn't your car, it's mine. Of course, working
for Weatherall and Associates, it seems natural to you that
there should be a car and driver outside awaiting your every
whim,'' he said with a bland smile that left Binky wondering if he was being sarcastic or not. ''I projected that
you would need to escape the office during your first day,
what with the avalanche of needy people awaiting you on
your desk. And I wanted to introduce myself.''

''Stop the car,'' she commanded the driver, knocking on
the partition.

''I just ask you to hear me out. I am not, repeat *not,* here
to ask you for money.''

''What do you want?'' she asked coldly, folding her
arms and flopping back into her seat in frustration.

''I know about the foundation, and about the awesome
burden that's being placed on your shoulders—all those
people out there, all those agencies, all those little theaters
and big theaters and dance troupes and children's after-
school recreational activities. And there you are, making
decisions that are going to *alter the lives of every person
whose proposal sits on your desk.*''

Binky got nauseous at the thought, but there was no denying it. A word from her would change a life, save a
widow from her husband's profligacy, or cut a promising
young actor's career short.

''I see it's hitting you,'' Will went on. ''All that
power . . .'' he said, his envy clear in his voice, snapping
her back to reality.

''And what does all that power have to do with you?''

''I want to help you handle it, Binky. That's what I do.
I help powerful people handle their awesome responsibilities.''

''How?''

"Well, I have a huge business myself. I give seminars, sell books and tapes and posters and other motivational materials. And most people who want a piece of what I know have to pay four hundred dollars or more to come to one of my seminars. But for *a select few,* I offer one-on-one counseling. Absolutely free."

"Why?"

"Because it's excellent publicity. When I can give a potential client of my seminars, a potential buyer of my books, a testimonial from a Fortune 500 executive, a nationally prominent politician, they look at that and say, Hey! This guy knows what he's doing!"

"And all I have to do is endorse your product," Binky said sardonically.

Will threw up his hands. "If it works for you. Only if it works for you. Binky, I want you to attend one of my seminars, *absolutely free.* It's a four-hundred-dollar value. . . ." Binky couldn't believe there was actually a person who sounded in person exactly like a television commercial, but here he was. She accepted the brochure he handed her and got out of the car, finding herself back in front of Weatherall and Associates.

Will leaned out of the car. "Binky, it's been a pleasure meeting you, and I'll see you at the seminar." He shut the door and the car sped away.

Binky went back inside, having decided that she'd seen enough of the outside world for a while. The cafeteria, to her delight, offered her the choice of either a lavish buffet or a menu from which she could take her pleasure. The buffet offered immediate gratification and she went down the line, loading up on lobster salad, mashed potatoes (carbos in a crisis, was her motto), and a generously cut piece of chocolate mousse torte. A waiter took the tray from her at the end of the line and she followed him.

"Oh, Binky, over here!" Andrew called to her from where he was eating with a handful of men.

The waiter automatically turned in Weatherall's direction and placed Binky's plates on the white tablecloth, whisking away the tray. Another waiter appeared and filled her water glass, another offered up a tray with iced tea, Coke, and 7 Up all ready for her. The luxury of it all quickly soothed her nerves, as did the food, which was incredible; even the potatoes weren't just mashed potatoes but garlic mashed potatoes with chives.

After a round of introductions to Weatherall's young, fresh-faced financial whiz kids, he asked her, "So how's the first day?"

"Hectic," she answered truthfully. "I don't honestly know if Chloe and I alone can deal with all the calls and all the mail. . . ." she opened hesitantly, but Weatherall cut her off.

"Of course not. I went to check out your office this morning to make sure everything was in order before your arrival, and I saw the piles of mail. There's no room here to put any more lower-level employees, but if you want, we have another building downtown where dreary work goes on, human resources and accounting and all that. You can commandeer some empty offices down there and get people to take phone messages and open mail, that sort of thing."

"Thank you," Binky said, plainly relieved. "You wouldn't believe what some people would do to get ahold of me."

Weatherall laughed, his eyes twinkling. "Oh, yes, I would! Believe me, once I decided to give away a bunch of money, I knew the only way to keep Mrs. Keith from quitting was to put the onus of the whole operation onto someone else, with my hands strictly off! I hope you don't think I've buffaloed you into something," he added.

"Oh, no, I'm sure it'll be wonderful, once . . . well, once I can get someone else to sift through all the *crap.*"

Weatherall nodded. "Yes, I know. 'Dear Mr. Weatherall, my daughter needs a new car for her sixteenth birthday or she's going to join the Hare Krishnas. Please help me,' blah blah blah."

"This guy even tricked me into getting into his *car* just a half hour ago. I thought it was one of yours. Wanted me to endorse some seminar on helping powerful people deal with their burdens or some such."

Weatherall started, as if stung. "Who was it?"

"Well, I . . . He gave me this brochure. . . ." She handed him the brochure.

Weatherall looked at it for a moment and nodded. "I knew it," he said calmly, but then suddenly he smashed his fist down on the table with a *bang!* "I knew it!" he shouted, prompting a temporary calm in the cafeteria, but conversation quickly resumed albeit at a quieter volume—the rest of the occupants were used to Weatherall's bursts of rage. "It's that goddamn Will Powers, acting on orders from his puppet master, Herbert Kildare."

Binky knew vaguely who Kildare was—a big media baron like Ted Turner or one of those guys, someone with his fingers in a lot of pies, but to be honest she was not one to follow the world of high finance too closely. "Oh," she said noncommittally.

"That man," Weatherall said, turning red with the effort it took him not to bang his fist on the table again, "is the devil on earth. Okay, Jesse Helms is the devil on earth, but that man is second in command. Herbert Kildare has done more to undermine me than any other man alive. He's allied himself with every right-wing kook in America, his newspaper chain excoriates me at every opportunity, and now he's added a news channel to his family of cable TV networks, which he will also no doubt use to beat on me."

"Oh, he's a hard-line anti-Commie and all that?" Binky asked, trying to sound as if she knew what Weatherall meant.

Weatherall laughed bitterly. "Anti-Commie? Yeah, unless the Commie is the one with the money. He's bent over backward to keep his papers and his news network from criticizing China because he knows there's so damn much money to be made there."

"So why is he out to get you?"

"Because I'm his worst nightmare, a liberal gay man with billions of dollars and therefore someone with a lot of opportunities to sound off and throw my weight around, and when I do, it's usually to the detriment of greedy bullies like Herbert Kildare. You know the magazine chain I just bought? That includes *Edgy Hipster*, where our friend Tim O'Neill is now the editor? I paid a hell of a lot more for that than I should have, to prevent Kildare from getting it. The man already has too much influence on our culture as it is; I don't need him taking over some of the most important magazines in the nation." Weatherall's eyes suddenly lit up. "I want you to go."

"What?"

"I want you to go to Will Powers's seminar. I'm betting Kildare put him up to inviting you to try and get inside my empire. So I want you to go and play along, and see what you can learn about *his* empire in the process." Weatherall smiled. "I know you've recently given up the detecting game, but would you mind?"

Binky thought about it. She had been undercover before, and done rather well at it—and unlike that case, this one wouldn't involve the dreaded fate of becoming a secretary again. "I'll think about it. I mean, I'll go, but how far I'll go is another matter." A confabulation with Tim O'Neill was clearly in order; as a bona fide media type, Tim would know all about Kildare and whether he really was the portrait of evil that Weatherall was painting or just a bitter business rival.

Weatherall beamed at her and patted her on the back. "That's all I ask."

Luke had been similarly overwhelmed on his first day as Weatherall and Associates' security chief. There was so much involved it staggered him—security for both Andrew's person and his home, for starters; then security for the office building, which meant keeping everyone from crackheads to reporters from rifling through employees' desks, and ensuring that HVAC repair people, for example, were escorted at all times by a security guard; and security for the tangle of computers that made up the heart of Weatherall's business, which meant protecting the computers both physically and cyberspatially. Fortunately he'd found a reliable underling in the person of the supervisor of the security guards, who'd managed to contain the mob outside the building begging for Binky's intercedence, and he could spend the morning with Weatherall getting to know the operation.

Some things soon became obvious—for instance, Weatherall hadn't become a multibillionaire by playing it safe. The man was not only investing in stocks, he'd moved into venture capital. Luke had sat in on a meeting with Weath-

erall and his "cowboys," a group of men and women
Weatherall's age or younger who had equally brilliant
grasps of both finance and technology. They listened to a
pitch from a pair of guys who wanted to offer a "build-your-
own radio station" software package/Internet site; if you
bought the software you could log on to the site and pick
from thousands of songs, selecting your own playlist to listen to on your computer, to run as "musical hold" on a
PBX system, and more. Weatherall's people peppered them
with questions about royalties, copy protection technologies, market research, costs, and so on and so on. Weatherall concluded the meeting by drawing up a contract buying
51 percent of the company and infusing it with capital.

Just as the meeting was ending, a red light started flash-
ing on the ceiling of the conference room. Luke had been
warned about this, notified in advance that there was no
need to panic when Weatherall and the cowboys suddenly
bolted for the door at the sight of the light. Known as the
"sheep alert," it sent everybody to a phone or a trading
post. "Sheep are running!" Weatherall shouted gleefully,
dashing down the hall. "Baa! Baaaaa!"

"Sheep alerts" were triggered by a sophisticated computer program. They were Weatherall's way of taking
advantage of less technologically sophisticated investors—
when, for instance, Intel announced that its earnings would
be less than anticipated, the tendency of many institutional
investors ("the sheep") was to sell off all the tech stocks
in their portfolio, hardware or software, as if bad news for
one leading tech stock was inevitably bad news for all of
them. Weatherall knew this was foolishness, and all it did
was temporarily depress the prices of perfectly healthy
companies—at which point Weatherall and Associates
would rush in and buy the suddenly improperly devalued
stocks at a bargain price. Everything at the company
stopped during a sheep alert as even secretaries (who, after
all, being Weatherall employees had rather healthy portfo-
lios) decided what to buy on sale and how much. "It's like
the wedding dress sale at Filene's Basement!" one woman
enthused.

Luke took this time as an opportunity to meet one of his
employees. Down in the basement, Kevin Stocker was un-

perturbed by the sheep alert. Surrounded in the dark room by his glowing monitors, he was obliviously playing a video game while the rest of the building went frantic. "Mr. Stocker?"

"Please, I haven't been called that since my last court appearance." The boy got up and shook Luke's hand. He was indeed a boy, nineteen years old, according to his file. He checked Luke out with piercingly intelligent eyes and nodded, having somehow already decided that Luke was all right. "You're my new boss."

"That's me. So why aren't you on the terminal, buying up stocks on sale?"

"I don't have to. I wrote the sheep alert program, so when it flashes the lights upstairs it also automatically activates my 'buy' program, which selects the companies taking the most unwarrantedly large dip in price and adds them to my portfolio."

"Very scientific. But not much fun."

"Oh, I have fun." He picked up a remote and clicked on a monitor. Luke found himself watching security camera shots of people upstairs darting around frantically, the scene changing every five seconds. He was disconcerted to see a shot of Binky, sitting at her desk unaware of the chaos outside.

"Oh, sorry. That's your girlfriend, isn't it?" Luke didn't bother to ask how the kid knew, instead deciding that the kid probably knew more than anybody other than Weatherall. "I'll take her office off the program."

"Thank you. I wouldn't want your curiosity getting you into any more trouble." He said it with a gleam in his eye and Kevin took it the way it was intended. At fourteen, he'd been arrested in a scene out of *War Games* by a phalanx of CIA, FBI, and Secret Service men after he'd successfully broken into computers at the Pentagon, the White House, and, most dangerously for himself, the NSA. Although he hadn't stolen or damaged anything, breaking in just for the challenge, at fifteen he'd found himself the center of a show trial designed to "make an example" of him. Weatherall, ever alert to both talent and injustice, had hired top-notch legal talent (and publicists) and young Kevin had found himself saved from jail on the condition that he never do it again, and use his powers from now on only for the good of the Establishment, at least inasmuch as Andrew Weatherall could be called the Establishment.

"So now that you're on the good guys' side, who's the biggest threat to Weatherall's operation?"

"That's easy," Kevin said. "Herbert Kildare."

"The media mogul?"

"The very same."

"I don't get it. Weatherall is high technology and Kildare is newspapers, magazines, TV stations."

"And the two are becoming one. The *New York Times* national edition is beamed by satellite to California where it's printed for West Coast subscribers. CNN is owned by Time Warner, so stories from *Time* and *Fortune* are getting sent around the world. Weatherall is investing in Internet technology that's going to obsolete current newspaper production methods—soon *Times* subscribers will dial in on their dirt-cheap computers, get a list of appealing stories, select the ones they want to read, and their dirt-cheap printers will run them off a newspaper tailored to their desires. There's nothing a classic union-buster like Kildare would love more than to eliminate the blue-collar element from the newspaper production process, but every time one of these new technologies is created, guess who's already gone and bought 51 percent of the company?"

Luke nodded. "Andrew. And from what I know of Kildare, he'd do anything to block him from getting any more powerful."

"Our Mr. Weatherall has a social agenda, and the billions to see it through," Kevin nodded.

Luke wasn't the least bit surprised to hear of a business rivalry between Kildare and Weatherall. The two men had their similarities—both started from scratch, neither attended college, each heard again and again that his ambitions were actually folly. Kildare had started with one Auckland tabloid, then added what became his flagship paper—the *London Daily Beast*. With that, he practically changed the meaning of the word *tabloid* single-handedly. If titties and sex scandals sold papers, then by God, Kildare would print them. Any member of the household of the Royal Family even *mentioning* Kildare's rag would lose his head; the paper was known to pay millions for stories from disgruntled former imperial employees. Kildare had expanded from this base into an international network of newspapers, including New York's own tabloid, the *New York Beast*, which, while omitting the titty pages of its slutty British sister publication, nonetheless managed to find the cheesiest stories in the city for its covers and the most salacious gossip for its columns, all the while running an editorial page notoriously prudish and arch-conservative. And now he had his own cable TV news network, KNN, ads for which constantly trumpeted its "objectivity" in the face of the rest of the "liberal media." KNN was actually about as objective as Rush Limbaugh, and the network had already gotten a reputation for killing stories that displeased the leaders of totalitarian regimes with whom he was eager to do business.

Kildare was exactly the sort of businessman Weatherall would rant about in the media when given the opportunity—the amoral vampire who would buy any politician, trounce any civil liberty, flout any journalistic standard in the pursuit of money or, more importantly now, power.

"So Kildare plays dirty pool, and Weatherall has good reason to suspect him of trying pretty much anything to get his hands on this technology."

"That's not all, though—it's personal. Kildare is obsessed with the holy rollers, loves 'em. Has 'em over for dinner all the time. He's not a religious man, it's not about that at all. But he knows these guys have figured out a way to build a power base, a political power base, on the backs of angry, frustrated, fearful people—"

"The kind of people who read Herbert Kildare's newspapers."

"You got it. Kildare gives these right-wing kooks a forum in his papers and in return they use their power over their masses to help him elect the puppets who will do his bidding come time to, say, pass a tax break on newsprint or authorize the money to put up a satellite that will beam KNN into strong-man markets that currently block those damned liberal networks like CNN. And so Weatherall is always calling Kildare on his shit, loudly and in public. It's very embarrassing for a man like Kildare, who likes to work behind the scenes.''

"And being gay, Weatherall probably feels he has a personal stake in preventing the right-wingers from getting too much media power.''

"You bet. When you think of all the gay billionaires—Barry Diller, David Geffen, that whole crowd—only Andrew has been out longer than he's been rich. He's really got that gay identity thing going, you know? It means something to him, ethnically, to be gay. He doesn't distance himself from the community like most of those rich business gay guys. And of course Kildare's got all those guys like Thom Wont, the columnist at the *New York Beast*. You ever read him?''

"I've never read the *Beast*,'' Luke admitted.

Kevin laughed. "Man, I have—he went after me ass over teakettle when I was in the headlines. 'Amoral youth run amok thanks to liberal public schools and the decline of the family, which of course is the product of all that sex people keep having, especially those sinful homosexuals.' Guy always brings everything around to queers, somehow. Makes you wonder. Anyway, he's always running columns on Weatherall, calling him the Pied Piper and saying anyone who invests in his mutual fund is 'arming the Visigoths for their assault on civilization.' '' Kevin chuckled. "I read it every day; lets me know there's someone out there who's crazier than I am.''

Luke pondered this. "So do we know of any attempts by Kildare to breach security here?''

"Oh sure. I mean, they aren't exactly wearing his livery, you know, but Kildare's from New Zealand, and he likes to hire yobbos from the old homestead for the dirty work, know what I mean? So you catch someone busting into a building in Santa Clara where one of Weatherall's hush-hush projects is going on, and he gets hauled into the police station and sits there saying, 'I dinna ken ya' or something, well, you do the math.''

"What about computer attacks? Viruses, hackers, all that.''

Kevin smiled confidently. "That's where I come in. Nobody puts as much as a single floppy disk into a computer here but I don't know about it and everything on it. I'm the man, okay? I violate my probation and hang out with my old hacker and phone phreaker friends, keep up with the latest developments. Even though I'm on the other side of the equation, they let me because they think Weatherall's a cool guy, getting me out of jail and all, and just between you and me he's saved some of those guys' bacon, too, they just didn't get the publicity I got. But I know some of these guys, no matter what Andrew's done for them, Kildare offers them enough money, they'll do their damndest to bust my chops. But fear not"—he grinned—"I'm still the best. You just gotta hold up your end of the deal—see, some guy gets in here at three A.M. and gets into the cold room, where the actual heart of the network is, he can sit at a terminal there and with the right codes he can mess shit up, you know? I keep 'em out my way and you keep 'em out yours, and we're all okay, all still making money, still kicking Herbert Kildare's ass."

"You seem to take some satisfaction from that thought."

Kevin nodded. "My dad was a union man all his life. UAW. Then GM closed down the plant, hell, the whole town, and that was that. He shot himself. Anyway, it wasn't Herbert Kildare who did it, you know, but it was his type. Some fuckin' vampire who doesn't care who gets killed as long as he's making the big bucks. Andrew's not like that. Like this charity thing your girlfriend's doing—a billion dollars! He's just *giving away* a billion dollars! Bill Gates is sitting on something like forty billion and what's he giving away? He's giving schools old Microsoft software that he can write off! What's with that? Andrew's cool." Kevin nodded. "Andrew's cool. I'm gonna make sure Andrew stays cool."

This day was also Tim's first day as editor at *Edgy Hipster*. The magazine was one of a half dozen or so that Weatherall had acquired with the purchase of Imminent Publications. All of Imminent's magazines were glossy, high-profile, dollar-a-word publications—*Edgy Hipster*, *YB*, *Moda*, *Manhattan*, and, to the glee of all the participants in our heroes' last adventure, *Pendennis*. Tim could feel the tension in the building as he entered; it was the first day for

a number of new editors handpicked by Weatherall to replace the former regime, and nobody but the new bosses
were sure they'd still have jobs at the end of the day.

Edgy Hipster had started in the early eighties as a small,
"what's trendy downtown" magazine read by a handful of
fashion models, graphic designers, window dressers, and
other people obsessed with public prettiness. It had been
purchased in the grunge era by Imminent and remolded into
a glossy national mag to appeal to young male consumers
who wanted to read about music but found *Rolling Stone*
tired, who were interested in fashion but found *YB* too suit-
and-tie-oriented, who wanted to read about models but
weren't going to be caught dead with a women's magazine.
Over the years *Edgy Hipster* went back and forth between
catering to a coffeehouse crowd, who had some interest in
politics, wanted to hear from sexy girls with brains, and
had few prejudices against gays, and a frat-house crowd,
who had no interest in politics, liked big tits, and hated
fags. A gay writer could find himself unable to get a rejec-
tion letter from one editor, then get a monthly gig from the
next editor, only to find himself out on the street again with
the third. Of course, even during its "straightest" phases
the mag, like all glossies, was well-populated behind the
scenes by gay men, many of whom were publicly rejoicing
at the advent of Tim O'Neill.

Edgy Hipster had always been positioned as a "feeder"
magazine for *YB*, rarely referred to even on its cover by its
full title, *Young Bastard*. Readers of *EH* were usually in
college for a liberal arts major, just out of school in their
first corporate jobs where they were still swearing they
wouldn't be co-opted, or doing the coffee slinger by day/
band front man by night thing; whereas *YB*'s demographics
were the business major, the just out of college and dying
to be co-opted types, the predigital class of entrepreneurs,
and of course the former *Edgy Hipster* readers who were
now well on their way to corporate dronehood. *YB* had seen
glory days in the eighties as young bastards reveled in the
perks of being absurdly prosperous twenty-something investment bankers and brokers (cigars, cocaine, Armani),
dipped disastrously during the recession, and had seen its
advertising pages surge again in the late nineties as young

bastards reveled in the perks of being absurdly prosperous twenty-something digerati (cigars, cocaine, Hugo Boss). *YB* had been one of the first men's fashion magazines and was notorious for its original publisher's longstanding dictum to keep the magazine from becoming "too faggy," which he was sure would have scared away the rich, young, red suspender–wearing, Rush Limbaugh–loving demographic he and his advertisers craved.

Weatherall had as of yet made no dramatic changes at *YB*, nor at *Moda*, the women's fashion magazine, though he had plans for *Manhattan* as well as, of course, *Pendennis*. *Manhattan* had been given a dramatic facelift by Imminent, who had converted it from a twee publication full of twenty-thousand-word essays on "Fall" printed in spidery, unreadable type, to a more dishy "who's hot" magazine. Weatherall had mentioned to Tim his plans to finish the overhaul of *Manhattan* begun by Imminent, who had left the fiction section of the magazine essentially untouched. Publication of a short story in *Manhattan* was considered to be the coup de grace that established one in the literary firmament, but a recent scandal had shaken the magazine and indeed the literary world to its foundations. The mag had printed yet another one of the same kind of stories it had been printing for twenty years now. This particular story had opened with "Margaret goes to the mall. She walks around and stares at the things she could buy. She does not know what she wants." Margaret went on for several thousand words not knowing what she wanted until suddenly a butterfly floated into her car and she experienced a flutter of emotion, as small as the butterfly but a flutter of emotion at last nonetheless.

Nothing unusual in such a story running in *Manhattan*. The controversy had come about when the author of the story, Max Jacobs, had then turned around and penned a blistering article for *New York* magazine about how he had studied the "formula" required to compose a winning *Manhattan* story and executed it successfully. "The story must be written in the third person, present tense, in cool, glossy, short-sentenced prose that reveals the main character's emotionally stunted nature and takes a shot at commercialism along the way, ending with a tiny epiphany.

Only a tiny epiphany is allowed in a *Manhattan* story,"
he'd written, "as only tiny emotions can be handled by the
brittle characters who populate them. Any great, overpowering emotion would smash up both them and the
blown-glass prose they dwell in." A delighted Tim had
contacted Jacobs and asked him to write for the new *Edgy
Hipster*.

Tim's first order of business on this day was meeting the
staff, which he had decided to do en masse rather than one-
on-one. He had spent enough time at *Confidential* in L.A.
to know that starting with individual meetings would only
be giving each person an opportunity to air grievances
against the others (such grievance airing being a certainty
in any environment full of creative people under pressure).
He had arranged for a lavish breakfast buffet in the main
conference room, partly to assuage rumors about Weatherall's plans for ruthless cost-cutting, and also to load them
up on carbos and fats and thus ensure a placid group, at
least temporarily.

"Hello, everyone," Tim said, entering the room unan-
nounced and informally. They took their seats almost like
schoolchildren and he smiled. "I'm Tim O'Neill and I'm
the new editor. I'll be meeting with all of you individually
as the day goes by but for now I wanted to give you all
the same basic information at once. First off, I know you've
heard rumors about cost-cutting under Mr. Weatherall, and
that will definitely be occurring, *but,*" he said hastily, "not
in the form of any mass firings. Andrew is concerned about
some of the bigger bills, like the hired car expenses." A
few knowing smiles around the table; previous editors had
been known to abuse the hired cars, meant to take them to
and from home and meetings, by using them to transport
large parties to Southampton or Fire Island.

"What I really want to talk about today is my vision for
the magazine. I don't really think the magazine is on a bad
track right now, but I do want to expand the axis beyond
New York and L.A.—there are a lot of college towns out
there where some interesting stuff is happening musically,
there's a lot going on in Miami and Chicago. I don't want
the magazine to be predictable, I don't want someone to
pick it up and see the guy from Bush or Blur on the cover

and say, oh of course. I don't want people on the cover who are on the cover of every other magazine in the world.''

A man in horn rims and a bowling shirt raised his hand and spoke up in an arrogant, grating voice. ''But who's going to buy the magazine if there's a bunch of nobodies on the cover?''

''They won't be nobodies once we're finished with them,'' Tim said, and a couple of people who'd frowned while Horn Rims had spoken now smiled and nodded, glad to see him get his comeuppance. ''I want to be the cutting edge, not the trailing edge. Lead, not follow. I want to put Billy Crudup on the cover—is he the star of a big Hollywood movie? No, not yet—but he will be. And he's gorgeous.'' Tim smiled. ''I'm not stupid; I want to sell magazines, too. I just don't want to do the same stories everyone else is doing. I don't want the same old 'how to' pieces, either, you know, how to buy a suit, how to order wine—let *YB* run that stuff. I've got this great piece already lined up, from this guy who was a five-time *Jeopardy!* winner, on how to get on and win on *Jeopardy!* It's great stuff.

''And fiction—I want to start running fiction.'' This caused considerable rustling. ''One piece every issue, by someone hot, or about to be hot. Nick Hornby has a new book out, and an excerpt from it ran as a story in *Esquire*— it should have run in *Edgy Hipster*; it's people who read our mag who read *High Fidelity*.'' Tim was getting excited now and he felt at least part of the room pulling with him. ''Max Jacobs? The guy who tricked *Manhattan*? He's doing a piece for us. You see where I'm going?'' Heads bobbed.

Horn Rims raised a hand again. ''And what about fashion? I haven't heard you mention fashion.''

Tim nodded. ''I think we're doing just fine on that count.''

''But if you start running all this other stuff,'' Horn Rims pressed, ''you only have so many ad pages and something's got to give. What are you going to get rid of? What about—''

Tim ducked as a shoe suddenly came out of nowhere and flew past his head. The room exploded in laughter, everyone cracking up except Horn Rims, who got up and left the room. "I have work to do," he said, red-faced.

A woman next to Tim put a hand on his arm. "Nobody was trying to kill you—it's just that, well, that was David. We call him the 'shoe editor.' Every damn issue, every damn meeting, he gets up and says, 'What about shoes? There's nothing in this issue about shoes! You can't do a fashion magazine without shoes!' His next question was going to be about that. Thus, the shoe, from an anonymous donor."

Tim knew he shouldn't laugh at one of his employees behind his back, but it was hard not to. "Well, I'll speak to him later and he can air his concerns in private. Anyway, I think you all get a general idea of where I'm coming from, and I'll let you know right now I hate long meetings, so this one is officially over; I for one am going to eat some of this food."

A burst of applause greeted Tim, and the staff started introducing themselves one by one. While the official meeting was over, nobody left and Tim soon found himself in a bull session with staffers throwing around pet ideas that previous editors hadn't wanted to hear, or didn't like. When Tim finally left for his office, he was as happy as a clam about the job.

Later that afternoon, his assistant buzzed him. "Doan for you."

"Thanks. Hey, baby."

"Hey, you. How's your first day?"

"Great. This is going to be the greatest job ever."

"Good," Doan said.

Tim sensed something odd in Doan's voice. "Just good?"

"Oh, great, fabulous, et cetera, et cetera. Really, I'm happy for you, and Binky, and Luke. And I'm sure I'll find something I can do in this town."

Tim sighed. He felt guilty all of a sudden; he had sucked Doan out of his old existence where he'd had, if not any enormous responsibilities, at least an identity as a detective. "Well, how'd the volunteering idea go?"

"Not well," Doan said. "Let's not speak of it."

"Oh. Okay." Tim's phone buzzed. "Oh, God, I've got to take this. Can we talk tonight?"

"Yeah, sure. I'm making a nice roast chicken with little baby potatoes and baby carrots and baby onions, with your favorite dressing, and gravy, too."

"Mmm. I can't wait. I love you."

"I love you, too," Doan said, warming up at the thought of a succulent dinner with his mate. "I'll see you tonight."

But Doan did not see Tim that night, nor for several nights to come. Tim soon realized it had been foolish of him to think he was going to get out at six o'clock or even seven when he was not just taking over but making over a magazine. Doan had been very "that's all right" on the phone when Tim had called and begged off; he'd just call Binky to see if she wanted to come over and help him eat the succulent fowl. But Binky and Luke were out celebrating their own first day at work, and Doan found himself sitting in his well-appointed kitchen, staring morosely at his Lenox plate, thinking about that scene in *Rear Window* where the woman pretends to have a dinner companion and then finally slumps dramatically onto the table in tears, no longer able to maintain the charade.

Decorating had consumed a good deal of the first hectic weeks in the city, during which time Doan had been just as busy as the rest of his compatriots, but once all that was done, he found himself with a sudden glut of time. New York had not been as kind to Doan as San Francisco had been; the two cities had very different temperaments. In San Francisco, when asked, "What do you do?" one could simply say, "I'm an artist," and that was the end of it; you were accepted as "one of us," a creative soul drawn to the city. But in New York, your answer only provoked a slew of other questions: "What are you working on? What gallery are you at? Who's your agent? How much did you make at your last show?" Everything in New York, Doan was realizing, was about career, and here he was without one. In San Francisco one could just *be;* in New York one was expected to *do.*

His attempts at doing had been cruelly rebuffed, but then, how could he have known about the byzantine politics of the charitable world? Doan had fully expected that a nice little donation of ten thousand dollars or so would get him a seat on the board of the Whitney or the Met; he would never speak to anyone, not even Tim, *not even Binky,* of the humiliation he'd suffered at the hands of an Upper East Side doyenne on a museum board who'd agreed to meet with him thinking that when he'd said "large donation" he'd meant millions. She'd cattily sent him to the volunteer coordinator, a far more kindly old bird who seemed at a complete loss at the sight of Doan, looking so feminine and yet . . . something not right . . . maybe the dear girl needed some of those estrogen pills the doctor gave me. . . .

So Doan spent his days wandering the streets. Even shopping had paled for him—Macy's was an inferno of tourists pawing over piles of Tommy Hilfiger, quacking loudly in indiscernable languages and celebrating their cultures by shoving their way to the front of the line; he'd been literally knocked over in Bloomie's by an aggressive shopper who'd suspected him of reaching for the last of the Prada handbags on the sale table. Even the good people at the Armani boutique had raised eyebrows at him, despite his careful selection of a top-of-the-line Armani suit to go shopping in—the old birds at the museum might not be so quick, but *these queens* knew a man in a dress when they saw one.

Doan didn't even see Tim that night; his boyfriend was home late and up again early and Doan slept the sleep of the dead. When he woke up the next morning, he was, he suspected, depressed—he'd never been in that state of mind in his life, but he had to wonder if that wasn't the reason he suddenly had absolutely no interest in getting out of bed. But then Regis and Kathie Lee came on and he couldn't find the clicker, so he had to bolt up out of bed to turn off the TV before La Gifford's smug chirpings could push him over the edge of the windowsill.

Like many a bored housewife before him, Doan decided it was time to get a job. He'd had all sorts of jobs before becoming a detective—DJ, record store clerk, even Binky's part-time maid. None of those would do now, of course— N.Y.C. was chock-a-block with DJs and Doan knew no one of any importance who could help him get a gig (connections being more important than talent in a glutted marketplace). Still, he was not a depressive by disposition, and just the thought of finding something smart to wear and hitting the bricks to see what might happen cheered him up.

He was not long out of his Chelsea apartment when he found a nearby street blocked off for some kind of filming. That was the great thing about New York, he thought, its clear advantage over San Francisco—there may not always be something to do in either place, but in New York there was always something to *see*. Upon investigation he found not a film shoot but a fashion shoot; models were lounging about in front of smart brownstones, smoking and waiting for something to happen. Only a handful of spectators, mostly tourists, watched the proceedings, a mere fashion shoot being far too blasé an incident to captivate a New Yorker. Doan could hear an argument going on between the photographer (readily identifiable in his bush jacket) and a wildly gesticulating man. Doan recognized the man immediately: the unruly curly hair pushed back with a woman's headband, the drapy black clothes, and, of course, the voice—high, nasal, and bitingly sarcastic. Doan had seen Jacob Mannheim on *Style with Elsa Klensch* more times than he could count. Mannheim was one of his favorite designers, right up there with Armani, Galliano, McQueen, Gaultier, and John Bartlett.

Doan examined the clothes on the models, and was surprised to find himself unimpressed. Everything was so beige! Doan was just over thirty now, old enough to have harrowing aesthetic memories of the seventies, when ''earth tones'' had cast an almost Orwellian bleakness over every home and apartment built, furnished, and carpeted in that era. Armani could do beige, because of the fabrics and the cuts, but most anyone else was asking for trouble. This was *Jacob Mannheim*! Doan said to himself, appalled. He shook his head sadly and was horrified to find himself getting caught doing it by Mannheim himself. They made eye contact and it seemed to Doan that in a second Mannheim knew exactly what he was thinking—it was odd, it was the sort of immediate connection Doan associated with cruising, though there was no sexual attraction whatever between the two men. Mannheim came over to Doan at the barricade, clearly evaluating him, recognizing him as a man and yet, not a "drag queen," as Doan was forever pointing out to people ("I don't wear makeup, I don't wear falsies, I don't tease up my hair—I'm just a man in a dress!").

Sometimes in life you get lucky, and find a kindred spirit. The more offbeat you are, the less likely you are to find such a fellow being, but it seemed to both Jacob and Doan in that moment that both of them had gotten lucky. "It's all wrong, isn't it?" was the first thing Jacob said to Doan.

"It's all wrong for *you*," Doan said. "It's all . . . it's so . . . I hate to say it."

Jacob sighed. "Say it. I know."

"It's so Randall Reid," Doan said, naming the famously "clean" designer who almost never left the neutral range of the Pantone palette.

Jacob flinched. "Ow. Ow! That old queen," he spat. "You know why he does everything in 'blah'? Because that's what happens to your creativity when you're a big ol' closet case!"

Doan nodded. "Let a little color into your life and the next thing you know you'll be publicly announcing your love for Keanu."

"I swear to you I didn't try to copy him. I was just so *depressed* when I designed these clothes. I just wanted everything *black,* you know, but black is so *done*. And nobody in my studio said a word to me; they all said, 'Oh yes, Jacob, fabulous fabulous.' Then I see all the clothes together and I think, Oh shit, it is *so* Randall Reid!"

Doan knew opportunity when he saw it—more, he knew *destiny* when he saw it. Catching the SoMa Killer had meant he should become a detective, and being confided in by Jacob Mannheim meant only one thing.

"You need me," Doan announced.

"What?"

"You need me! You are surrounded by yes-men. This never would have happened if I'd been around."

Jacob eyed him. "And your qualifications?"

Doan spread his arms. "Look at me!"

Jacob thought about it for a moment. There was something about Doan, all right. Fashion sense, that was primo; Doan certainly had that. Honesty, too; he spoke like someone with nothing to lose. Jacob recognized someone who really didn't *care* what people thought—a kindred spirit, in short.

"I can't type, I can't sew, but I've got a hell of an eye. I don't honestly know what I'd do for you but you need me around for a while. I don't need the money," Doan said hastily, "I have my own and my boyfriend makes good money, too. But I just moved here, I sold my detective agency back in San Francisco, and I am *bored!*"

Jacob's eyes widened. "Detective agency? San Francisco? You're not Tim O'Neill's boyfriend, are you?"

It was Doan's turn to face his new acquaintance with widened eyes. "How did you know?"

Jacob laughed delightedly, spinning around and clapping his hands. "My dear, *everybody* knows about your little posse. Haven't you seen the latest issue of *New York*? Oh, no, I guess not, I keep forgetting I get an advance copy. Well, it'll be out in a few days." He pulled the barricade back with surprising strength and put an arm around Doan. "I think you should see this magazine right away, dearie, and then it's off to work for you."

"I'm hired?" Doan asked delightedly.

"Hell, yes. You're my Vice President in Charge of Inspiration!"

three

~~~

Binky and Doan hadn't seen each other for at least ten days by the time they got together that weekend—a record time apart. They almost couldn't believe their own ears as they apologized to each other ("I've been so busy!"); both were learning that when people from New York talked about "the pace," they were serious. Without even trying, they'd seen their lives of carefree indolence disappear, replaced by a whirlwind of work and social engagements that left nothing like the daily hours they'd had back in San Francisco for loitering aimlessly in each other's company.

So they had firmly set aside that Saturday as a day for doing what they had always thought of as the right and natural thing to do with a Saturday—lolling around eating pastry and drinking champagne. Binky brought the Veuve Clicquot and Doan had risen early and cabbed it over to Gramercy Park, where a little patisserie offered the most scrumptious pastry-wrapped apples in the world (Doan's first priority upon landing in N.Y.C. had been to scour the town for the best baked goods). Doan and Tim's apartment had a pleasant little terrace, and after setting up their food on an attractive Italian hand-painted platter and pouring the champagne into Waterford stems, they regarded the tableau momentarily and sighed. They'd always lived well, but there was admittedly something less stressful about being able to actually pay for it, rather than being cruelly forced to charge it.

"Where's Tim?" Binky asked.

"At his new home. He even talked about putting a cot in there, but I put my foot down. It's bad enough I only get to see him asleep; imagine not seeing him at all!"

Binky nodded. "Luke's been logging a lot of hours, too. I have to hand it to him—he really didn't know diddly about technology but he's learning fast. Remember that hacker kid? The big federal trial? Saturation coverage on CNN? He works for Andrew, as his systems security consultant! And he's teaching Luke about computer stuff. So it's like Luke's got a full-time job and school on top of that."

"And how's the foundation going?"

"Good, actually. I have some people opening mail for me—I mean, that's all they do, open mail! And cull out the really hopeless requests." Binky smiled. "Can you keep a secret?"

"Hell, no!"

"Well, I mean a *real* secret. Like a major, big, hush-hush secret."

"You're killing me. Spill it."

"Guess who I'm having lunch with next week? Someone who wants to talk to me about one of her pet projects." Binky waited for Doan to egg her on but to no avail; he only sat there frowning, arms folded, looking at his watch. "Okay. *Mrs. Henry M. Boston, Junior.*"

Now Doan was impressed; it was not every day that one got to meet anyone connected with one of America's oldest liberal Democratic families. HMB Jr. had been the hunkiest and most eligible bachelor in Manhattan, and there were more than a few less-than-idle threats made by single women about slit wrists when he married Lisa Crane. "Oh, my god! Is *he* coming?"

"No. I mean, I don't think so. But that would be pretty smart of her, wouldn't it? Have him show up at the end of lunch to pick her up, wow me with star power?"

"Oh, my god, you'd love that—it'd be your chance to

go down in history as the queen of all homewreckers!''

Binky laughed. ''I am very happy with what I've got, thanks. Luke is the stud for me, I've concluded pretty definitely.''

''About time,'' Doan said, thinking of the rocky romantic road Luke had faced in their previous exploits to bring Binky to this sensible position.

''But I'm not saying I wouldn't want to . . . shake his hand,'' she added, laughing.

Doan nodded. ''Uh-*huh.*''

There was a pause, and Binky said gingerly, ''So have you been keeping busy?''

''Oh, yes,'' Doan said airily. ''I have a job.''

''Oh, that's great!'' Binky said, meaning it. Truth be told, part of why she hadn't seen Doan in a while was guilt—her life was becoming more fabulous and interesting every day, while Doan had been relegated to the sidelines. Of course, that hadn't stopped her from trumpeting her lunch with Mrs. HMB Jr., but then, that was the kind of dish she was not constitutionally capable of repressing. ''What are you doing?''

''Oh, I'm helping out this fashion designer I met,'' Doan said airily, deciding to string Binky along.

''Doing what?''

''This and that, you know, picking up scraps off the design floor, sweeping out the showroom . . .''

''Oh . . .'' Binky said, at a loss for words.

Doan laughed. ''I'm kidding! I'm working for Jacob Mannheim!'' He pulled out his new card from his shirtwaist pocket and handed it over to her.

''Jesus, Doan, vice president! In charge of . . . inspiration?''

''Yeah, don't you love it? I read magazines, I go to lunch, I hang out with Jacob and look over his shoulder. They all hate me, it's like I'm Yoko to his John. But they're all a bunch of toadies and yes-queens so he needs me around to slap him sometimes. I love it.''

Binky impulsively got up and squeezed Doan. ''I am so happy. And so relieved! I—we all—felt so guilty, bringing you here and leaving you with nothing to do. Now you're going to be more famous than all of us put together!''

Doan's eyes twinkled. "I wouldn't count on that, dearie." He opened his Jacob Mannheim leather valise and pulled out Jacob's advance copy of *New York* magazine. "I think you'd better take a look at this."

Binky nearly choked on her pastry. There on the cover was a photo of her, looking surprised, taken at night outside the Weatherall Building. "BILLION-DOLLAR BABY," the headline shouted. "Nobody had heard of Binky Van de Kamp before last month. Now everybody wants to be friends with the woman in charge of handing out Andrew Weatherall's fortune."

"Have a drink, dear," Doan said solicitously, taking the magazine out of her hand and filling her glass.

Binky knocked off the glass in one gulp, burped, and held it out for more.

"It's really not a bad article," Doan said, flipping through the mag. "From what I've read of it so far."

"Nobody called me about it!"

"Well, the article says they tried repeatedly, but couldn't leave a message with your voice-mail box. And that they sent you telegrams, e-mail, messenger packs . . ."

"Which all got lost in the million other pieces of shit sitting in an office downtown." She sighed. "Oh well, better them lost than Mrs. HMB. Read it to me."

Doan eagerly took a sip of champagne, cleared his throat, and began. " 'BILLION-DOLLAR BABY. What's a girl from Miss Porter's do with her education? If she's Binky Van de Kamp—yes, of the Connecticut Van de Kamps, heirs to the plumbing fortune . . .' Plumbing?" Doan asked.

"Toilets. Very discreet of them not to mention it."

"Very discreet of *you* not to mention it all these years. So Henry James of you, keeping your undecorative source of wealth hidden so long."

"Not *my* wealth," Binky insisted. "Go on."

" ' . . . You turn your back on the family, move to San Francisco, work at an amazing assortment of odd jobs, from police typist to department store perfume spritzer . . .' "

"A job I had for all of an hour and a half. Damn, they've really done their homework!"

" ' . . . open a detective agency with your friend Doan McCandler'—that's the only mention of me—'and find fame and fortune cracking one of the decade's biggest cases, the Jeff Breeze murder. But how would any of this qualify you to be selected by eccentric gay billionaire Andrew Weatherall as the person to give away his money?' ''

'' 'Eccentric gay billionaire,' he'll love that.''

''Then it goes on to talk about Andrew and how he got his money, then about how you and Luke and Tim were all hired as a package deal, and it's got some not-very-nice quotes about your qualifications from professional foundation-running–type people who sound like they think they should have gotten the job. Let's see . . . 'But Van de Kamp's background may actually make her the ideal person for the job, combining an upper-class upbringing that will enable her to hold her own amongst the social lionesses of New York's fundraising world, and a history of handling and consorting with lowlifes and murderers that has probably well armed her against the onslaught of need and desire that has poured into Weatherall's offices since the announcement of the foundation.' So it's not really so much about you as it is about Weatherall and the money. But I think you come out of it rather well.''

Binky sighed. ''It could have been worse, I suppose. Is this out on the stands?''

''Monday. I have an advance copy, now that I'm a Manhattan insider and all that.''

They laughed. ''Oh, Doan, I don't know. I mean, it's a great job, or at least it's going to be, once I get a handle on it. But this''—she indicated the magazine—''isn't helping. It's just going to make my life worse for a while. Now I'll probably have people stop me in the *grocery store* to ask for money.''

''But it's your fifteen minutes!'' Doan said, as if there could be any question of the desirability of that time slot's arrival. ''I wish I were on the cover of *New York*.''

''I imagine you will be, Doan.'' Binky petted him. ''I give it six months.''

Doan sighed, took another pastry, and leaned back in his chair. The terrace faced west over the rest of Chelsea and the piers, and images of old movies leapt unbidden to mind. ''Someday, all this will be mine, eh?'' He shuddered. ''Well, as long as I don't have to be Judy Garland to get it.'' He brightened. ''I love this city! You know, everything is going better than we could have ever imagined.''

''Yes,'' Binky admitted, brightening automatically under the influence of Doan's relentless cheer. So she'd be harassed for a while; so she would have to go to this dumb Will Powers thing for Andrew . . . no matter. Here she was, only weeks into her new life and already at the top of the heap. She smiled. ''Yes, everything is going to turn out just fine.''

Monday found Binky and Tim in a Lincoln Town Car, being whisked off to Will Powers's seminar. Tim had been about as enthusiastic as Binky at the prospect, but Andrew had asked him as a ''*personal* favor'' to go, with an eye to writing it up ''in that inimitable Tim O'Neill style'' for *Edgy Hipster*. Tim might have pled with his new boss to get out of it, had it not been for Binky's assault on his eastern front.

''Don't make me go there alone,'' she pleaded. ''That Ken doll has designs on me and I need protection.''

''Just tell Luke you've got a masher on your hands and I'm sure he'd be delighted to beat the crap out of him.''

''I wish he wanted *sex*,'' Binky sighed, causing Tim's eyebrow to rise. ''No, I mean, I don't want sex with him, well, you'll see him in a few minutes and you'll know sex with him probably isn't anatomically possible so I won't waste time protesting now. I mean he wants my *soul*! He wants me to endorse his stupid seminars. And he's . . . well, he's persuasive. You'll see,'' she said with a sigh as the car pulled up to the hotel.

Outside the ballroom, a huge banner was strung up: WILL POWERS SAYS: YOU CAN RATIONALIZE ANYTHING! For a moment Tim thought this was some kind of protest, until they got to the registration desk and he realized to his horror that this was indeed the name of the seminar.

''Oh, my god,'' he groaned.

''You see why I didn't want to go alone?'' Binky triumphed.

They were issued their badges and escorted to prime seating near the front of the ballroom. Tim flipped through the materials they'd been handed—a ''workbook'' with "exercises" that Powers would assign, and a set of flash cards that reminded Tim eerily of Jenny Holzer "Truisms," right down to the Helvetica bold type:

IT WILL COST JOBS

was one.

I DESERVE IT

was another. He particularly liked

I HAVE TO DO THIS FOR ME

It was soon apparent this was to be a theatrical performance: instead of a podium and the usual blah-blah introductions, the room was abruptly plunged into darkness, with the exception of the stage lights. Music rose up out of the sound system, stormy and beautiful, the opening to Mozart's Twentieth Piano Concerto. Then a voice, which Binky recognized as Will Powers's.

"They say that you can't do it. And when you prove you can, they say that you shouldn't do it. And when you prove that you should do it, they say that you mustn't. *I say,*" he boomed along with the suddenly crashing music, *"you can. You should. You must."* And the curtains opened to reveal a lone man in a blue suit, head down, hands clasped in front of him. Thunderous applause ensued; Binky looked around to check out the crowd, most of whom looked not unlike Will Powers—suits, Devo plastic hair, even the attractive faces had sort of a Scotchgard sheen on them that discouraged thoughts about them of a sexual nature.

Head still bent, Powers raised a hand and the hall quieted. "I want to talk to you today about your future," he said. "I want to ask you, Who controls your future? Do you? *Do* you?" He looked up at last. "I do. *I control my future.* Do you want to know how I do it? Because there is nothing to stop me."

He started to pace around the stage now, like a TV minister. "I want to tell you a story. Once upon a time, there was a large corporation, let's call it the Three Initial Corporation. Now, TIC was doing quite well for its shareholders, making a very nice return on investment. Then, one day, a group of employees sued the company. They said they'd gotten cancer from working with hazardous materials at a TIC plant. Of course, TIC had very good lawyers, and they were able to get out of paying these employees any money, but unfortunately, the case attracted quite a lot of media attention, and politicians got involved, and the next thing you know Congress was talking about making TIC clean up this plant. This would have been *very bad news* for the shareholders, since this cleanup was going to cost somewhere around a billion dollars. Yes, a billion dollars! So what did TIC do? Well, sir, one of their executives was a Will Powers seminar graduate, and he came to me.

"And I told him, You know what? You don't have to clean up this plant. You can get out of it. I said to him, 'Now, my friend, you know and I know that the real brunt of this cleanup will fall on the shareholders. But I want you to simply *forget* that. Yes, forget it! I want you to think about the employees, those poor thousands who will get thrown out of work if TCI goes bankrupt cleaning up this factory. You need to go in front of the media and say *not* that it will cost shareholders money, but that *it will cost jobs.* I want you to all raise up your flash card and say it along with me."

"It will cost jobs!" the room echoed.

"Excellent. Now, I told him, you have to not just say this, you have to *believe* this. I want you to go in front of the camera and believe with all your heart that you are fighting this cleanup because it will cost jobs! Now, we all know that any time any corporation wants to fight anything that's going to cost them profits, they never say that—they say 'it will cost jobs,' don't they? Don't they?"

The assembled businessmen looked around nervously. Was it safe? Were they with their own kind; could they admit the truth?

"SAY IT AGAIN!" Powers shouted as the phrase showed up as a supertitle over the stage. He pointed up at it. "IT . . . WILL . . . COST . . . JOBS!"

"IT WILL COST JOBS!" the room roared, the audience suddenly believing it with all their heart, delighted that they had suddenly been admitted to a secret society, where the unsaid could be said!

"Yes!" Powers was pacing the stage now like a madman. Suddenly a picture of O. J. Simpson was flashed above Powers's head. He faced the picture. "Did O. J. Simpson kill his wife?"

"Yes!" they shouted.

"And did he get away with it?"

"Yes!"

He whipped around to the audience. "Why?"

The room was quiet. *"Why?"* Powers shouted. "Because *he convinced himself that he didn't do it!"* A sigh went through the room. Anything was possible. . . .

"Do you see where I'm leading you? You *can* rationalize anything! You can, if you just *believe it!* Now, some of you have an advantage over the rest of us, because you work in advertising, where convincing people of things that aren't true is your livelihood." A guilty chuckle from corners of the room. "What does the Lexus ad say? This classically trained English twit actor gets on there and he *oozes* into your ear, and what does he say?"

The next flash card was supertitled over the stage and the crowd shouted along:

YOU DESERVE ALL THIS LUXURY!

"That's right!" Powers smiled. "You may have spent your day poisoning Third World countries—we're not allowed to call them that anymore, are we? Poisoning 'developing nations,' then, or laying off ten thousand people to get the stock price up just in time for your options to come due, or kissing some dictator's ass to get a factory built in his country using slave labor . . ." The room shifted uncomfortably at this and Tim wondered for one wild moment if Powers hadn't tricked them all, if he wasn't really some plant from whatever Left was left, but then Powers smiled. "But *it doesn't matter!* You watch TV and the commercial tells you, 'You worked so hard today, you *deserve* this car.' *And you believe it!* So," he said, going from a shout to a whisper, "why should the advertising guys have all the fun? Why should the only things you believe be what they tell you to believe to sell you stuff? Why can't you make up your own beliefs? Say you meet some hot chick, and you're saddled with a sagging old wife and a pair of miserable grunge kiddies who you've hardly ever seen. Do you leave the wife because the babe is hotter? No! You leave for 'personal development.' You leave because . . .''

He waited, arms folded. No supertitle came along to help the hapless rationalizers. Finally one courageous young man flipped through his cards and raised his hand.

''Yes?'' Powers said. ''Because?''

''I . . . I have to do this for me?'' he asked timidly.

''*Yes!*'' Powers shouted, and the room erupted into applause. ''I HAVE TO DO THIS FOR ME!''

''I know what I have to do for me,'' Tim said to Binky. ''Get the hell out of here.''

''Will it cost jobs? As in, ours?''

''Do you care at this point?''

''Hell, no,'' Binky said, getting up. She was appalled to see the faces on the way out—Nuremberg faces, freed of their guilt and their sin and unchained to kill, kill, kill!

Out in the lobby, Binky leaned against a pillar for support. ''I wish I still smoked.''

''I wish I still got stoned,'' Tim added.

''There *is* an open bar,'' an older gentleman advised them in a plummy accent, extending a well-manicured hand toward the hotel bar.

''Thank you,'' Binky said, grabbing Tim and heading that way. Suddenly she remembered her manners and turned around. ''Will you join us?''

''I'd be delighted.'' His hand against his solar plexus, he extended an elbow; Binky laughed but accepted the invitation.

''How did you enjoy the seminar?'' he asked when they were seated.

''We hated it,'' Binky said. ''Were you there?''

''I . . . have seen Mr. Powers in action before.''

''Then you know what we're talking about,'' Binky went on, knocking back her martini as her new gentleman friend signaled for another. Tim said nothing as he nursed his scotch—there was something about this guy, something familiar . . . he knew he could place him in just a second. . . .

"I think Mr. Powers is an excellent showman," the stranger continued. "He gives the people what they want."

"Yeah," Binky said, "absolution for their sins."

The man chuckled. "If the Pope doesn't fill the need anymore, somebody has to, no?"

"Especially if there's a great deal of money to be made at it," Tim said.

"Ah, but didn't the Catholic church build its real estate portfolio on the funds raised selling indulgences?"

"Sounds like you don't need Will Powers to teach you how to rationalize," Tim said, feeling like he was coming closer to knowing the answer—this guy was someone he didn't like, he could remember that much.

He smiled. "No, I don't. It's the generation that came after mine that needs it," he said thoughtfully. "They were all hippies once, you know, supposed to change the world for the better. Now they tell themselves that since they saved the world, it's their right to destroy a little piece of it to feather their nests . . . but it eats at them, their youthful idealism; makes them feel *bad*," he said in a dead-on California accent. "For a while that's all they needed—they could rape and pillage all they wanted, as long as they felt *bad* about it for a minute. Now they've got another generation coming up behind them, judging them, their own children reminding them of what they used to believe. Now when they feel bad it's harder to leave that feeling behind. So," he concluded breezily, "now they need Will Powers, to make it all better. To keep them from having to feel bad at all in the first place."

Binky was already half drunk on her martini. "Who are you?"

He smiled. "My goodness, I haven't introduced myself, have I? I'm Herbert Kildare."

"I knew it!" Tim shouted, having figured that out just before Kildare said it.

"Uh-oh," Binky said.

"Oh, don't be alarmed, I don't bite. Though I'm sure that's not what Mr. Weatherall told you."

"Weatherall?" Binky said, dumbfounded. "You know who we are?"

Amused, Kildare raised an eyebrow. "I thought the sort of people who would work for Andrew would bolt in horror from Will Powers's little pep talk, so I waited for you in the lobby. I have had the pleasure of reading about you, Miss Van de Kamp, in *New York* magazine and recognized you from the cover. And, of course, even if I hadn't made the effort to keep up on goings-on in our fair city, your names *are* on your name tags."

Tim sighed and pulled his tag off. "You make a lot of money off these seminars."

Kildare nodded. "Yes, I do. Mr. Powers sold quite a large piece of his operation to me, in an effort to take it global. Which I believe he will be able to do quite well, at least in Protestant countries like your own, and mine—countries where it is good to grow rich but not good to enjoy it." Kildare signaled across the room. "Mr. O'Neill, I'd like you to meet someone."

Tim had no problem placing this man. Tim could sit at a table with Herbert Kildare, whom he was already finding fascinating and certainly more worthy of a profile than Will Powers—though God knows Weatherall would explode at the thought—but it was quite another to have a drink with Peter Cures. If there was any man alive who already knew everything Will Powers had to teach, it was this man. Cures had risen through the ranks of the Republican party as a media savant whose gifts of rationalization (called "spin" in politics but still the same thing) had assured the election of one president, two senators, and seven representatives, all supremely unqualified if not outright crazy. Cures was a master of the "attack ad"; his most infamous had featured a dead ringer look-alike of a Democratic senator in scrubs in an operating room, about to perform an abortion. The voice-over had labeled the senator "the abortion lobby's best friend," microscopic type had referenced several of the senator's votes against draconian antiabortion legislation proposed by the usual fringe comb-over–sporting loonies, but it had been the look of evil glee on the senator's—er, actor's—face as he prepared to perform the abortion that had cause the most outrage (and lost the Democrat his seat). Now Cures was running Kildare News Network, whose ads trumpeted its "objective" reporting but which actually skewed farther right than any mainstream news organization would ever have dared to skew left.

Tim got up. "Gotta go."

Kildare put a gentle hand on Tim's. "Please sit for a moment. I am sure Mr. Cures is distasteful to you; he is to most people, I suppose." Cures's face fell at his boss's dig at him but he said nothing; Tim suspected it wasn't the first time this had happened. "But he does what he does very well." Kildare turned his gaze directly onto Tim—no whimsy in his voice this time, no gentle musings, but a direct stare that meant business and had caused tougher nuts than Tim O'Neill to crack. "I have been watching you, Mr. O'Neill, for some time. I have quite a large stake in several entertainment companies, so of course I am always interested in what is reported about them and their products in the media. You are an excellent writer, and always fair. And usually right."

Cures spoke up. "KNN is about to—" But he froze suddenly; Tim realized that Kildare had merely lifted a finger but it had been enough.

"KNN," Kildare continued, "needs to expand its entertainment coverage. We've got our hard news format in place, our seasoned political reporters, our legal analysts and court watchers . . . now we need the 'back of the book' " This was the publishing industry term for the mishmash of reviews and gossip once relegated to the back of the magazine; the term is still used even though the same material now comprises the bulk of most magazines' features and cover articles. "I am offering you the job of vice president of KNN's Entertainment News division, with a salary of $2.5 million a year, *generous* stock options in Kildare Worldwide—generous enough even to beat Weatherall's package—and any other perks you might request."

"I'm not interested," Tim said. But he looked over at Binky, who was being completely ignored by the two men—used, no doubt, to women at meetings as the people who took notes and fetched things. *Play it cool,* Binky mouthed silently, unbeknownst to Kildare and Cures, and Tim changed his mind about getting up and walking out.

"Of course not," Kildare said, surprising him. "As far as you are concerned, I am evil personified. Look around

me: people like Will Powers and Peter Cures doing my
bidding" (Cures turned purple but swallowed his rage
along with most of his drink) "my right-wing newspaper,
my right-wing news network, my right-wing friends and
allies. All very convenient for my business interests, especially through twelve years of Republican presidents and
seven of a Democrat who might as well be, but it's not
enough. I've been paying attention to America, you know.
You're becoming a more . . . European country. Better ed-
ucated, thus more enlightened, more tolerant, more sophisticated in your tastes and opinions. It's almost time for me
to leave my old friends on the right behind; their power is
waning in this country. But first, I need to make new
friends—I need to prepare the way for Kildare Worldwide's
millennial change of heart. Black people, brown people,
gay people, women; they're the readers and consumers who
will be my heart's desire in a few years. I am not evil, after
all, you see—just pragmatic."

Tim nodded. "And what happens to Cures and company
when you make your big switch?"

"Mr. Cures will retire comfortably, perhaps find a job
as a pundit on some TV politics talk show; they're always
looking for some radical right-winger for 'balance'—at
least that's what they say when they mean 'controversy to
ensure ratings.' But enough of that." Kildare rose and
Cures rose with him. "Think about what I've said. Andrew
Weatherall is going to self-destruct, you know. He is a brilliant young man, but too angry—the markets don't like
volatility, and they will punish him. And Mr. Weatherall is
not so all-powerful as you might think. He has enemies,
many enemies, beyond me—more powerful, perhaps, even
than I," he mused before shaking his head. "No matter.
We shall leave you. Think on it." He turned to Binky.
"Miss Van de Kamp, I wish you joy in your role as Lady
Bountiful." He took her hand and kissed it. "I imagine the
Kildare Children's Trust should not expect any checks from
your office, nonetheless it is a good thing you do and I
wish you well. Good day." And they were gone.

Tim looked at Binky; Binky looked at Tim. "Waiter!"
they shouted simultaneously.

Binky's third martini and Tim's second scotch soothed

several million jangled nerve endings. "He is something, isn't he?" Tim marveled.

"You like him," Binky said.

"Well, no, I don't . . . but he interests me." He shrugged. "The writer's flaw, you know—always looking for an interesting subject, and Herbert Kildare is one hell of an interesting subject. I could see a book about the two of them," Tim mused, "Weatherall and Kildare, so alike yet so dissimilar, so hell-bent on power yet such different uses for it. . . . Hey, why'd you tell me to play it cool, anyway?"

"Well, Andrew sent us here to see what we could learn, and Kildare seemed pretty expansive today. I thought, Let him talk, the more he talks the more we have to take back to Andrew."

Tim smiled. "Damn, you really *are* a detective!"

Binky laughed. "Well, not anymore. Though, you know, once you get in the habit . . . kind of like being a writer looking for interesting subjects," she needled him.

"Touché. Too bad he *is* evil, for all his protestations. I wouldn't mind running an entertainment news division. . . ."

"Get thee behind me, Herbert," Binky warned him.

"Yeah, yeah." Tim sighed. "I guess we ought to go back and let Andrew know what he's up against."

"I have the feeling he already knows. That's why he's so damn mad."

Luke had just crawled into bed next to a sleeping Binky at around midnight (young Kevin becoming a more animated teacher the later the hour wore on), when the phone rang. Binky grumbled in her sleep. "Hello, this is Binky, how may I help . . . mmgph." Clearly a relic of her previous incarnation as a secretary, Luke thought with a smile as he answered the phone.

"Sorry to disturb you, Mr. Faraglione," said Gary, Luke's right-hand man in charge of physical security.

"No problem," Luke responded, wondering if he should tell the man to call him Luke and then deciding against it—like himself, Gary was a former cop and needed a chain of command to feel secure. "What is it?"

"It's Mr. Weatherall. We, uh, can't locate him."

Luke sat up. "What do you mean?" It was Security's job to stay, if not with, at least close to Weatherall, for a variety of reasons—the garden-variety worries about kidnapping, which any billionaire faced, but also the daily ration of death threats Weatherall got for his pronouncements on politics and society.

"He got away from us," Gary admitted sheepishly. "We had him at Yankee Stadium and we lost him."

"Yankee Stadium?" Luke asked. "What was he doing there?"

"Oh, Mr. Weatherall's a great baseball fan. He goes to quite a lot of Yankees home games. Has seats right behind the Yankees' dugout. Anyway, he went to the bathroom and never came back."

"Shit," Luke said, reaching for his pants. "You tried his cell phone?"

"Oh, yes, sir. No answer."

"All right. Did you try Mrs. Keith?"

"Sir?"

"Mrs. Keith. His secretary. Did you call her?"

"Well, no, I didn't think she would . . . ah, shit. Yeah, if he took a powder she might know something we don't, is that what you're saying?"

"You got it. Okay, Gary, I'll call her. I'll call you back; I assume you're at the office?"

"Yes sir. In case a ransom demand comes in or . . . whatever."

"Good. Stay there." He hung up and fished his wallet out of his pants, pulling out of it one of the most top-secret documents at Weatherall and Associates: a list of home and cell numbers for the key players. He dialed Mrs. Keith.

She answered on the first ring. "Hello?" Luke had a great deal of respect for Mrs. Keith already. A no-nonsense black woman who had no qualms about playing the "big black mama" if it got her what she wanted from you, she'd been with Weatherall for years now and was rumored to be worth nearly $100 million herself, thanks to Weatherall's generous compensation package. Her knowledge of the company, and Weatherall, was frighteningly encyclopedic.

"Mrs. Keith, it's Luke Faraglione. Sorry to disturb you

at home, but our security detail has . . . lost Mr. Weatherall.''

''Tonight was the Yankees game, wasn't it?'' she asked
calmly.

''Well, yes. And the detail lost him at the stadium. . . .''

She sighed. ''I have told him he mustn't do this, but he
. . . well, I'll get him to call you. Are you at home?''

''Yes. Thank you.'' He hung up and a minute later, the
phone rang.

''Luke, it's Andrew Weatherall. Sorry about that, but I
had to . . . meet somebody, and—''

Luke cut him off. ''Mr. Weatherall, if you do this again,
I will resign. Your security detail is there to provide security, and if you don't trust them to accompany you to a
meeting, you need to fire them and hire new people.''

''You're right,'' Weatherall said, surprisingly sheepish.
Luke got the impression Mrs. Keith had already given him
a tongue-lashing that had softened him up for Luke's assault. ''I have good people and . . . I need to trust them. It's
just that this is a very delicate matter.''

''Well, then, entrust me with it and when you need to
make these 'delicate' assignations, I will accompany you.
But at least *one* person on your security detail has to go
with you. It's not enough just to tell Mrs. Keith where
you'll be.''

''Yes, Mrs. Keith has reminded me what could happen
to the markets in five minutes were I to disappear during
the trading day.'' He sighed. ''Can you hold on a minute?''

''Of course.'' Luke waited on hold for a few seconds
before Weatherall came back on.

''Please meet me at the corner of Sixty-fourth and Madison. I have someone for you to meet.''

He met Andrew at the appointed place, realizing too late
that he should have told Weatherall that a dark street corner
was no place for a billionaire to be standing at one in the
morning. ''Come on,'' Weatherall said. He led Luke into a
doorman building and up to the penthouse apartment. Andrew called out ''We're home'' as they walked in. A tall,
young, handsome man came out of the kitchen in shorts
and a T-shirt and Luke almost passed out.

''Holy shit,'' he whispered.

Weatherall smiled. "Luke Faraglione, may I introduce you to Mark Bowers . . . my boyfriend."

Late the next day, Luke ran into Tim in the halls of Weatherall and Associates. "Hey," Tim said, "how's it going? I'm just dropping off some notes for Andrew on that Will Powers seminar I went to with Binky."

"I'm not doing bad. You?"

"Okay. Heard you got a scare last night."

"Uh-oh, it's public knowledge?"

"Nah. From you to Binky to Doan to me."

Luke heaved a sigh of relief. "Good."

"Big secret?" Tim held his hands up. "I won't press if it's confidential."

Luke thought about it for a moment. He liked Tim, though they hadn't socialized outside their respective couples. "Do you follow baseball?" he asked dubiously. Luke was about the most tolerant person on earth, but his experience with gay men had taught him that quite a few of them would snap "I hate sports" at the very mention of the subject, so he was going out on a limb with Tim.

"Yeah, love it. Why?"

"Do you know who Mark Bowers is?"

"God, yeah. The Commander. Best pitcher in baseball right now."

Luke nodded. "You wanna go get a drink?"

The more Luke thought about it that day, the more it made sense. At twenty-eight, Mark Bowers was indeed the best pitcher in baseball today, though only a few years earlier nobody had heard of him. As a minor league player, he'd gotten a reputation as being "difficult"—moody, temperamental, and, worst of all, unable to prevent those moods from affecting his game. He could pitch a perfect game one week . . . then be pulled in the second inning for his next three games. If he ever hit a player unintentionally, he wouldn't just stand there like most pitchers, but would instead raise his hands and make eye contact with the hit player to make damn sure the man knew it was an accident . . . then he would trash the locker room in a fit of volcanic rage. Anybody with less natural talent would have been cut years earlier, but Bowers had the benefit of coaches who wouldn't give up on him.

Then, four years ago, things had begun to change. Who knew besides Bowers what had happened, but suddenly he'd grown up and taken charge of his talent and his career. A perfect game was followed by a no-hitter, followed by a one-hitter. Bowers won twenty games and suddenly the majors beckoned. He had the great good fortune of ending up with the Yankees, a team on which he wouldn't be the only person with a temper or a dark past, a team that offered redemption to exactly such players, if they had the stuff. And Bowers had the stuff.

As a troubled minor leaguer, he'd barely bothered to do more than show up for practice and throw balls. But now he was a demon—working out in the weight room in the off season to build strength, practicing his bunting, and running wind sprints like a madman. Reporters had asked him, why are you bothering, you're an AL player, you don't have to hit the ball or run the bases. Bowers had responded, "I may not be an AL player forever, and besides, I think the designated hitter rule sucks and I hope they get rid of it. If you're a ball player, you should be able to hit the ball. That simple. Besides, we're going to the World Series this year and if I'm pitching in an NL park, I'm going to need to hit the ball and make it to first base." And with that, Bowers earned the respect of his teammates and the fear of his opponents.

He'd always had a wicked fastball, but now he'd added a fair curveball, a good splitter, and a frightening knuckleball. He'd become a team leader, because of his talent, his dedication, and his fearlessness. His catcher had said of him one day, "He's the man. He's got the pitches, he's got the attitude, he brings the team up with him. He's the fuckin' commander around here." The name had stuck.

"So how did he end up dating Andrew Weatherall?" Tim asked over beers.

"Andrew said he'd first heard of him two years ago, when he made headlines by turning down a lucrative Nike deal."

Tim nodded. "I remember that. Big news."

And indeed it had been; Bowers's publicly stated reason

for turning down the deal had been widely quoted: "Well, first of all, I'd only endorse products I use, and I don't wear Nikes. Secondly, I think it's important for us all to take a look at the economics of this product—people in the Far East making a dollar to make a shoe that costs a dollar in materials that retails for $150 in the States, where they're marketed to inner-city kids who are made to feel like their only escape is sports and that if they want to escape through sports, they're going to need Nikes, so they'd better spend their minimum-wage incomes on these overpriced shoes."

"He didn't get any other endorsement contracts, did he?" Tim asked.

"I think he's got something with Met-RX or EAS or one of those sports nutrition companies, but that's not exactly paying for that penthouse apartment."

Tim nodded. "So Weatherall hears the sound of a kindred spirit and asks him out on a date? Pretty cheeky."

"Well, I guess Andrew was a little more discreet than that. Sent him a note congratulating him on his position, told him if he wanted any financial advice to just ask for it . . . kind of a gamble, but I guess his gaydar told him something might be up with Bowers. Who sends him a note back, saying thanks, would you like to get together for coffee?"

Tim laughed. "And how does a major league pitcher go out on a date with a famous billionaire and not see it in the papers the next day?"

"Exactly why Weatherall ditched the security detail last night. They've been going out for two years now, and nobody's the wiser except Mrs. Keith and Mark Bowers's mom."

Tim shook his head. "Amazing. I'm happy for both of them, though. But Jesus, that's gotta be tough—being a gay sports hero. One whiff of it in the press, and he's outta there."

"Especially if anyone were to find out he was not only gay, but consorting with Andrew Weatherall, sworn enemy of the Moral Majority."

Tim smiled. "Looks like you've got your hands full."

Luke shrugged. "You'd be amazed how well they've

handled it. I mean, it's sad; they can't go out to dinner, or see a movie. . . ."

"Remind you of anyone?"

Luke was blank for a moment before he got it. "Oh, yeah, Jeff Breeze and Tyler," he said, referring to their last case. "No, this is different. Weatherall *owns* an island in the Caribbean, and they fly in, separately, during the winter when Bowers isn't playing ball, and spend what I gathered from their chemistry last night are some pretty wild times together."

Tim shivered. "Just imagine what the *New York Beast* would do if they got wind of it. Herbert Kildare would love the chance to spit in Weatherall's soup."

"That's why this is a confidential conversation, bud. The fewer people who know, the better."

Tim appraised Luke. "You didn't have to tell *me* about it. I appreciate the trust."

Luke nodded. "You're a straight arrow, Tim." He didn't elaborate that he missed the camaraderie of the police force, that the only men he knew in New York were his subordinates and his boss. He could see already that there were going to be times when this job would be a bitch, and he wanted someone to talk to. Binky was there, sure, but she was a woman, you know?

Tim clinked his bottle against Luke's. He said nothing of what he was thinking. It *was* good to have a friend, he thought, someone in the organization he could trust implicitly, someone whose personal life was so tied up with his own. He knew it was harder for straight guys to vocalize these needs, and that this shared secret was Luke's overture of friendship to him. He was glad to have it.

He looked up at the TV. "Hey, look, it's Mark Bowers."

Luke turned around to see Bowers's face above the shoulder of ESPN's *SportsCenter* anchor. "Hey, turn it up, would you?" he asked the bartender.

The anchor had just started the story. ". . . In a surprise deal, the Yankees star pitcher has been traded. The Yankees will receive three of the Wizards' minor league pitchers and power hitter Rich Mayfair in exchange for Bowers. Bowers could not be reached for comment, but sources say he is 'shocked' by the deal."

"Oh, Jesus," Luke said, his blood running cold.

"What?" Tim asked. "From the look on your face I'd say this is no ordinary trade."

"Hell, no. He's been traded to the Windy City Wizards. Do you know who owns the Wizards?"

"Oh, Jesus," Tim echoed. "Maybe it's just a coincidence. . . ."

"Yeah, right," Luke said darkly. "The Yankees have just handed their ace, who happens to be Andrew Weatherall's boyfriend, over to a team owned by *Herbert Kildare* and it's a coincidence."

"This is not good, is it?"

Luke's phone rang. "Guess who," he said. "Hello? Yes, sir, I've just seen it. No, absolutely not. No. Well, if you think that will help . . . yes. Yes, sir." He hung up. "Damn."

"Weatherall?"

"He wants me to investigate. See how the hell Kildare managed to get Bowers out of the Yankees' stable and if he knows about the relationship." Luke sighed and got up. "Back to work."

"I'll make some calls, if you want," Tim said. "I know a couple gay reporters at the *Times* who might know someone who knows someone, et cetera."

"Yeah, thanks, that'd be great. Just . . . be discreet. Let's not tip our hand if we don't have to. Maybe we're incredibly lucky and this *is* a coincidence."

Doan was just over thirty years old now, and had rarely enjoyed anything that could be labeled "work." He'd had a reasonably good time at the detective agency, as long as nobody confronted him with horrifying matters like filing corporate tax returns or calculating payroll deductions or anything else related to the nuts and bolts of "running a business." Binky was as wont as he was, when sitting down with a calculator, to come out off by several thousand dollars, whether tabulating accounts or balancing a checkbook, and they had both been secretly relieved to sell the business, truth be told. Now Binky's only relation to money was spending her own and giving away someone else's, both of which suited her just fine. And Doan was finally doing what it seemed he'd been born to do.

His job as vice president of inspiration at Jacob Mannheim's airy loft headquarters consisted basically of hanging out with Jacob—going over patterns, poring over *WWD*, and dishing other designers (Jacob confessed his long-standing crush on Marc Jacobs while Doan admitted to an irrepressible lust for Todd Oldham that could easily jeopardize his marriage should the opportunity to act on it come up), and working on his most important task, dismantling Jacob's entourage of hangers-on, wanna-bes, and yes-queens. These hapless toadies had originally made the dreadful mistake of underestimating Doan, assuming him to be simply another addition to the carnival. Imagine their surprise when Doan, taking his imperial title quite seriously, started *scheduling Jacob's time,* including time for design during which interruption was not to be brooked for even the juiciest bit of dish. And none of them would ever forget the night they were advised upon arrival at Balthazar that orders had come down that they would not be able to put their evening's entertainment on Mr. Mannheim's account!

Doan's new job had the added bonus of bringing him closer to Tim. They found themselves both coming home late (Mannheim being an inveterate night owl who was now home by midnight only because Doan was practically locking him in at that hour), and enjoying take-out Chinese and long walks through their Chelsea neighborhood, as chock-a-block with people at two A.M. as the busiest San Francisco street would be at nine P.M. Doan suspected that Tim *respected* him more now; the title in and of itself would have meant nothing, but Tim knew that Doan was capable of marshaling mighty forces when necessary to get his way, and he was glad to see that his partner had found a creative home for those energies.

The morning after the Commander's surprise trade, Doan was in his office, flipping through the advance copies of the fashion mags, when Jacob burst in dramatically. "Have you seen the *Beast*?" he asked breathlessly.

"God no, Tim would kill me if I spent four bits on that rag. Why?"

"Read this." Jacob folded the tabloid back so Doan could read the paper's notorious gossip column.

"Hmm, hmm, let's see, guest gives Kathie Lee a black eye—wish I'd seen that; new book alleges Liz Smith takes marching orders from Pat Kingsley—I'm shocked, *shocked!* Oh, here we are. 'Fashion designer Randall Reid is allegedly fit to be tied after his peek at Jacob Mannheim's new line for spring.' Oh, dear. 'The designer feels that Mannheim has basically designed a Randall Reid collection in a bid to siphon off some of the customers who have kept Reid profitable through boom and bust.' Uh-oh."

"We have to get over there *today* and see the old witch," Mannheim said, running a hand through his unruly dark locks. "I can't have that old queen accusing me of ripping *him* off. Going to see him is something I can do to get that item contradicted in tomorrow's paper." He clutched at Doan. "And you have to go with me."

Doan gulped. "Me?"

"This job ain't all cake and roses, honey. How are your diplomatic skills?"

"Lousy," Doan confessed.

"Good. Because I may be ready to grovel if he's going to be gracious, but if he gets the least bit nasty, the gloves are *off.*"

An earnest call from Mannheim got them a grudging audience at lunchtime. They took a humble cab to the exquisite building that housed Randall Reid, Inc.

Hard as he looked, Doan could find absolutely no direct lighting anywhere in the lobby of RRI. Mannheim in black and, more so, Doan in a splashy dress from his beloved Todd Oldham were out of place amidst the uniform beiges and neutrals of the furniture, the fixtures, the carpets, the walls, and the employees of RRI. It was all very "clean," Doan had to admit. And excruciatingly boring.

A tall blonde with severely pulled-back hair approached them. "Mr. Reid will see you now."

She led them into a palatial office, a far cry from Mannheim's creatively messy studio. Randall Reid was not at his desk but at a conference table, laid out with a lunch prepared by his personal chef and served on the best china and silver in the Randall Reid Home Collection. "Hello, Jacob," Reid said, not getting up from his lunch as he smoothed the napkin tucked into his collar. "You remember Rhianna." Seated next to him, her napkin in her lap, Reid's auburn-haired wife nodded vacantly.

Doan perused the couple. Randall Reid was one of those American incongruities, a man everyone knew was gay yet who, because he never said he was, was allowed benefits in our society unavailable to its more honest members. Ask any gay man who had been in New York since the early eighties and you would hear stories about Randall at Studio 54, Randall at Fire Island, Randall in the back room of the Mine Shaft . . . no matter. At the height of the AIDS epidemic, Randall Reid had found himself in a particularly sticky situation. Several prominent fashion designers had died of the disease and Reid was finding it difficult to get financing for his expansionist plans—the money men were loath to invest in yet another *fegelah* who would soon be dead. Then, on a trip to Atlanta, Randall had found Rhianna, a compliant young woman whom some suspected of an unsurpassable idiocy, but whom others found to be a clever girl who had married well without ever having the worry of her gravy train's pulling out of town with some other, more buxom caboose in tow. She filled her newly prosperous idle hours pursuing her hobby of painting, putting out a book of watercolors of staircases called, with an imagination on a par with that of the material, *Staircases*.

The money men knew Reid was gay. And yet, once he married, it was all right; he had magically "reformed" in the hands of a good woman, their curative prescription for all homosexuals. Moreover, with Rhianna at his side, Reid found himself able to avail himself not only of deeper dippings into conservative heterosexual money bags, but of social invitations previously unavailable to a, um, "bachelor," invitations that led to commissions for haute couture outfits for the Upper East Siders among whom he was now accepted.

Randall and Rhianna ate their lunch complacently while Doan and Mannheim sat across from them, watching them eat. They were not offered so much as a glass of water as Mannheim poured out his apologies, insisting that the col-

lection was a mistake and that he'd been led astray by people who no longer worked for him. "But I have Doan
now," Mannheim beamed, patting Doan's hand, "and
things will be different."

Reid seemed to notice Doan for the first time. His bland,
Addison DeWittish eyes seemed to pop open in horror. A
drag queen! And he's *clashing with the furniture*!

"Oh, and I suppose you'll be putting *sequins* in your
next collection," Reid drawled.

"Now, wait a minute . . ." Mannheim began, but that
was it for Doan, who burst in.

"No, actually, it's going to be quite a splash. We're taking Chelsea to America."

"We are?" Mannheim asked.

Doan kicked him discreetly. "Yes. Big Chelsea muscle
boys with nipple rings and boots and floppy hats and tight
everything, only you needn't worry, it won't be like your
underwear collection, all homoerotic without ever acknowledging that you're getting rich off the very people you *spit
on* every day. No, we're going to put a lot of *big-muscle
fags* up there onstage and take America by storm!"

Reid was frozen in his tracks. Rhianna had never, *ever*
seen anyone treat her husband so scornfully and simply sat
there as a large piece of quiche fell off her fork and onto
her lap.

"That's right," Mannheim said, suddenly no longer interested in apologizing. "We're going to be *so openly gay*
that nobody could *ever* confuse my collection with yours
again!"

And he got up and whirled out of the room, Doan right
behind him. But on second thought, Doan whirled right
back and seized a plate of finger sandwiches. "And thank
you for lunch." He smiled sweetly.

Out on the street Mannheim hooted. "Oh-my-god, what did
you *do* in there!"

"I lost my temper, that's what," Doan huffed, making a
face as he ate a sandwich. "Needs salt. I couldn't take it!
There he was, eating in front of us like some . . . Eastern
pasha, not so much as a cracker to spare, raising his eyebrow at *me,* making . . . jokes about *sequins,* like he was

some truck-driving straight man, and I'm sorry, I cracked.''

"Oh, no, don't apologize. It was worth it to see the looks on their faces!" Mannheim sobered. "But you know what this means, don't you?"

"No, what?"

"I have to get back to the studio! I have a collection to design!''

"You're serious."

"Weren't you?"

"Well . . ."

"Come on, Doan! Hello! Vice President of Inspiration, you just gave me my first big inspiration! Oh, they'll *all* make rib-knit T-shirts, but none of them would *dare* to come right out and say, We're gay and ninety percent of the men who buy these are gay men. Well, I am gay, and I don't care who knows it, unlike a certain old biddy who probably hasn't had sex with a man in *years* for fear the boy will somehow manage to get photos and ruin him! And haven't you noticed that all the models these days are so damn *skinny?* Yeah, heroin chic is over but the damage remains. It's time for big strapping *hunks* again!" Mannheim whooped a second time. "In fact, I am going to do this collection for spring. I'm going to *throw out* those damn neutrals that got me in trouble with Miss Thing in the first place. But I'll have to hurry . . . we have to get back so I can get started! And you have to help me. Oh, Doan, I am so psyched! I am so ready to do this. This collection is going to make John Bartlett look like Brooks Brothers! Come on!"

Doan sighed and followed behind. "I've created a monster," he murmured.

four

~~~~~

Binky couldn't believe a month had already passed since she'd started her job. She had to admit she was proud of herself; she'd gotten a handle on the huge influx of mail and managed to find a couple of additional permanent foundation employees out of the dozens of temps who'd been recruited to open and sort mail. Chloe spent most of her days sorting voice and e-mail messages, deleting anything that would only waste Binky's time. Her assistant's brief stint as a celebutante had proved invaluable; Chloe knew the names of the "right" people and ensured that Binky didn't slight them.

Binky had to admit a pang of envy when she watched Chloe at work—after all, the girl's job was not unlike her own dream job, the one she'd had for all too short a time while working undercover in Mary Duveen's office during their last investigation. For basically, Chloe spent her days reading *New York*, the *New York Observer*, the *New Yorker*, and the *New York Times* and painting her nails while listening to messages on the speakerphone and occasionally reaching over to press 2 for save or 3 for delete with a free knuckle.

But those days of ease were behind Binky now; she reminded herself that she'd wanted to become a productive member of society and, well, here she was, about to go in front of the cameras and name the first beneficiaries of Andrew Weatherall's awesome munificence. The press conference had been set up for her by the ever-efficient Mrs. Keith, who was an old hand at it after years of helping Andrew publicize his fulminations. All Binky had to do was look poised and confident and not stumble over her words. She reminded herself that she'd even won a prize at Miss Porter's school in an oratory contest and if those old birds couldn't intimidate her, CNN certainly wasn't going to do the trick.

A conference room at the Regal Royal Hotel had been set aside for the event, and Binky arrived early just to make sure that nothing happened to make her late—an ingrained habit in a lifelong rider of public transportation, even though she now had a town car at her beck and call. In the space of minutes she regretted her promptness, as she was seized upon by various social butterflies who thought, mistakenly, that her U background would make her sympathetic to their various causes. Still, these women had one value to her—it was hard to feel foolish with a name like Binky when one was surrounded by women named Sugar and Tiger.

The whole gang had turned up to lend her emotional support. Luke breezed in first and kissed her on the cheek. "Hey, Binks, sorry I couldn't bring you down here."

She kissed him back full on the lips, to the envy of many a trophy wife in attendance—it was one thing to have the consolation of money when one was married to a man whose daily evildoings had given him the visage of a reptile, but to see someone who had money *and* a hunk like Luke Faraglione was more than certain green-eyed monsters could handle. "No problem. You're here, and you're not late."

Luke grinned. "I *couldn't* be late, actually. I had to escort Andrew."

Binky laughed. "Well, at least you're honest." Weatherall was going to make one of his "little statements" before Binky read out the grants.

"At least? Is that the complete list of my assets?" Luke

was feeling frisky; seeing his mate as the center of attention was having the effect of making her all the more attractive.

"Oh, you want a list? How do I love thee?" Binky put a hand on Luke's chest and looked up adoringly at her six-foot-four-inch lover.

"And in public, too," Andrew murmured behind her. "This could be your *next* magazine cover, my dear. Are you ready?"

Weatherall escorted Binky away as Tim and Doan joined Luke. "Are we on time?" Doan asked breathlessly.

"Early, actually. Hey," Luke said, nodding to Tim.

"Hey, how's it going?"

Doan eyed the men but said nothing. He'd noticed the burgeoning friendship and approved, even as it set off an automatic note of panic. We're one happy family, he thought. That means it's all settled! Binky is married to Luke and I'm married to Tim and Luke and Tim are becoming bosom buddies—my single life is over! Not that he minded—and not that he could imagine any better husband than brilliant, gorgeous, lusty Tim O'Neill. It was probably just what Binky had gone through with Sam Braverman in their last adventure, a little note of panic at the end of irresponsible youth.

"Oh, hello, Doan!" A woman Doan did not recognize approached him.

"I'm sorry, have we met?"

The woman was first pained, then angry, then resumed her mask of pleasantry, but it was too late. "Oh, I'm sure you've met so many people lately you can't remember them all." She extended her hand. "I'm Muffy Fforbes-Hamilton. We met at the Whitney?"

The light went on in Doan's head. Muffy here was one of the princesses that had led Doan to visualize the Upper East Side as one giant iceberg, forbidding and desolate. She had practically laughed Doan out of her office at the Whitney when he'd tried to get involved with the Friends of the Museum. "Oh, yes," he said with distant politesse. "How are you?"

She leaned forward confidentially. "I'm so sorry we got off on the wrong foot. Really, it was my mistake. If I'd known who you were . . ."

"Who I am?" Doan asked, baiting the hook.

"Why, yes. Jacob Mannheim's vice president of inspiration and your, your, your *friend* is Tim O'Neill," she finished, not recognizing the subject of her sentence behind Doan.

That was the last straw for Doan, who had lived in San Francisco too long to put up with lovers being called "friends" by people who knew better but who simply wished to edit out the details of any relationship they either couldn't understand or didn't want to picture. "This is my *friend* Tim O'Neill right here," he said, putting a hand on Tim's forearm. Conveniently, Luke was on his other side and he put his other hand on Luke's shoulder. "And this is my other *friend,* Luke Faraglione."

She paled as Luke and Tim worked overtime to keep straight faces. "Oh. Well," she said, automatically brightening as she dismissed all these details as secondary to her goal, "I hope you'll call me and we can find a place for you at the Whitney."

"Why don't you call *me,*" Doan said wickedly.

She knew she was being cruelly beaten but the glittering prize of any association with Jacob Mannheim was irresistible. The autosmile returned. "I certainly will." And she was gone.

"You are *evil,*" Tim said admiringly.

Doan smiled. "Only when properly inspired." He turned to Luke. "I'm sorry, but I had to do that to her. After all, you are my *friend,* aren't you?"

Luke chuckled. "Just don't let this get back to Binky or we're all in trouble."

Doan fumed. "I can't believe the nerve! She treated me like *shit* when I went to see her, practically laughed at me, and now she has the gall to come begging! 'If I'd known who you were . . .' As if it were perfectly all right to treat people like that if they weren't associated with someone famous!"

"She didn't say no to you that day at the museum, did she?" Tim said.

"What do you mean?"

"What exactly did she say to you that day?"

"Oh, that they had more people who wanted to be on

the board than they could accommodate but that she'd certainly get back to me. Why?''

"Just research, for a piece I'm thinking about. It's interesting here, have you noticed? Nobody ever says, 'Screw you.' They say, 'We'll get back to you.' Because this is a town where somebody who's nobody can be somebody the next day, and where are you tomorrow if yesterday you just blew off today's hottest somebody? This way they can say they've been *so busy* and *really* meant to get back to you and what do you know, here they are! Amazing coincidence . . .''

Doan nodded grimly. "We certainly are in a whole new world, aren't we?''

There was a great commotion at the front of the room as Andrew took the podium. The threesome moved around the crush of cameras to get a better view as Andrew began.

"John D. Rockefeller was the richest man in the world. He ran over everyone who got in his way and some who were just standing on the sidewalk. But he left behind a massive legacy of charitable works. All those old robber barons did, you know; I sometimes think they really believed in the heaven and hell they used as a carrot and stick to keep their minions happy in this world. Nobody believes in heaven and hell anymore, or justice, or compassion. Bill Gates is the richest man in the world, and he's holding on to every nickel until he decides to go into 'philanthropy mode.' Spoken like a man with a heart of gold. . . .'' A few chuckles from the media. "Ted Turner gave away a billion dollars—in fact, he's the one who inspired me to do it. But for God's sake, Ted, not to the UN! The whole enchilada is just going to pay for a lot of diplomatic parking spots and catered conferences. And my good friend Herbert Kildare doesn't have *any* plans to go into such a mode, as far as I know, not that I would be granted much inside information into his operations.'' A few more chuckles. "I suppose his children's fund makes for good photo ops on KNN, though.

"Anyway. I'm not here to bash the other rich guys. I'm here to make sure that you're here, basically, but today is really more Binky's day. I put my billion dollars in her hand and from the list of grants that are being handed out

today, I must say I am pleased with her performance.''
Weatherall turned to Binky and clapped and the Weatherall
and Associates employees in attendance did the same. ''I
have suggested a few of the grants myself, which ones will
be apparent to all the Weatherall watchers in the media, but
most of them are Binky's decisions. And with that, I introduce to you, Binky Van de Kamp.''

A good deal of applause and Binky took the podium.
''Thank you. One of the first things Andrew said to me
when we talked about my taking the job was that he had
little patience with agencies that spent more of the benefi-
cence they received on social workers than on social work,
and I agreed wholeheartedly. The gifts of the Weatherall
Foundation are intended to help people in need, and I believe that is what we've accomplished.''

She pulled out a list of papers and commented, ''It feels
like I'm reading the will,'' which brought her much appreciative laughter from the crowd. ''We have several large
gifts to announce. First, as Andrew is a gay man and since
I am from San Francisco and have many gay friends, AIDS
was at the top of our list. We are giving ten million dollars
each to Project Angel Food and Project Open Hand, pro-
viders of food to people with AIDS in New York and San
Francisco, respectively.'' Audible gasps from the audience
at the size of the gifts ensued. ''Ten million dollars each
to the AIDS Emergency Fund in San Francisco and the Gay
Men's Health Crisis in New York. One million dollars to
Prevention Point, the needle exchange program. Five million dollars to the legal defense fund for operators of med-
ical marijuana clubs in California.

''Andrew is also extremely interested in the role of the
media in society, and it is with that in mind that we are
granting ten million dollars to FAIR, Fairness and Accuracy
in Reporting, with an extra million to their Kildare Watch
program.''

The list went on, like a progressive's dream lottery:
buckets of money to Amnesty International, Asia Watch,
NORML, NPR, a smattering of think tanks and media
watchdogs. No reporter would leave the press conference
feeling like he didn't have a story.

Binky wound up the list by disappointing the Sugars and

Tigers (and making further headlines in another section of the next day's *Times*) by allocating money for the arts to a smattering of small theaters, avant-garde performers (including several who had been through the Jesse Helms/NEA wringer), back-alley museums, and generally slighting every major arts institution in the city, and then opened the floor for questions.

"Several of these gifts seem to be directed not so much to helping others as to hurting Herbert Kildare," a reporter from the *Times* noted. "What prompts the foundation to give an extra million dollars just to Kildare Watch other than the long-standing emnity between Mr. Kildare and Mr. Weatherall?" she asked Binky.

"Would you like to take this one?" Binky asked Andrew, who had been standing behind her in Al Gore mode, saying nothing but nodding approvingly for the camera at her every utterance.

"This is your show," Weatherall apologized, "but I think I had better field this one."

"I think you had better, too," Binky said to general laughter, retreating from the limelight and feeling that she'd acquitted herself well.

"Herbert Kildare," Weatherall began, lapsing into an oratorical mode that made him such a favorite guest on the talking head shows, "is a media baron. And 'baron' seems to be the right word. It conjures up not just robber barons, but feudal barons, lording it over the serfs. Of course, one might say, well, we are all free to choose and you can choose not to watch KNN or read the *Beast*, and all that is true. But the fact is, Herbert Kildare preys on weak minds, and that threatens the rest of us. We are allowed to choose our elected representatives, but not to choose who is qualified to do the choosing. Kildare preys on the fears of his readers—indeed, he makes them afraid where before they were not, and then tells them who is to blame for their fear. And it is never Herbert Kildare, oh no. It's the homosexuals destroying the family, it's the liberals keeping prayer out of schools, it's the single mothers demeaning fatherhood. Herbert Kildare gets people to fear people who cannot hurt them, and then he uses that power to get them to do what he wants. And of course, what he wants is to take his ability to create this great bloc of frightened sheep he can herd together and manage so ably, and sell that talent to the highest bidder, whether that be a Republican senator from Dixie or an East Asian dictator.

"Herbert Kildare controls a great deal of the news that people see, and he seems to be constitutionally opposed to delivering that news objectively. Why serve up objective news, after all, when one can serve it with a slant that both gets him advertising revenues *and* gathers unto him more sheep to be shorn?"

Andrew Weatherall could be a charming and quotable man, but when it came to the thugs of our day, a Herbert Kildare or Trent Lott or Jiang Zemin or Pat Robertson, he could become apoplectic, and was on the verge of doing so today. He was startled when Binky moved in front of him at the microphone. "The answer to your question is, only someone with as much power as Andrew Weatherall can stand up to Herbert Kildare, and *somebody* has to stand up to Herbert Kildare." A few heads nodded among the media at this.

Andrew smiled and relaxed. "It's like the Academy Awards, I suppose, and Binky has just played my song." Amidst general laughter and applause, they both left the podium.

The involved parties headed to a reception down the hall for the award winners and Weatherall's people. Binky's palms were slightly moist, as she wondered if she'd overstepped the bounds of her position, but she was quickly put at ease by Andrew, who put a glass of champagne in her hand, winked, and said quietly, "Thank you for saving the day." Then he spoke up to the crowd. "Ladies and gentleman, to Binky!"

"To Binky!" they roared, and she flushed with pride as Luke appeared by her side.

"Darling," Doan whispered in Tim's ear, "life doesn't get any better!"

"Fuck!" Andrew Weatherall shouted, hurling a paperweight through the television screen. "That fucking monster, he did this on purpose!"

Binky, Doan, Tim, and Luke sat frozen in their seats.

The day after the press conference, Andrew had invited them over to his house to watch the Commander pitch his first game for the Windy City Wizards. Binky and Doan had excused themselves as quickly as possible from the initial chitchat to investigate the house. With his typical acumen, Weatherall had picked up an old brownstone near the meat-packing district for a song and had it transformed into a showplace. Binky had sighed audibly over the king-size bed and the sheets that had cost about what, until recently, she'd made in a year, while Doan went into practically catatonic pleasure shock in the kitchen, tenderly fingering the copper pots and utensils hanging over the restaurant-style freestanding range.

But that had been before the game. Doan understood little of baseball, but gathered from the announcer that a pitcher was usually taken out of the game after about one hundred pitches, a mark the Commander had hit in the sixth inning. Weatherall had been cheerful at that point, explaining that Bowers just needed a period of adjustment with his new team and that it was no crisis for him to lose his first game, as he was plainly doing. But things had gone from bad to worse as it became apparent that the Wizards' manager was not about to take Bowers out of the lineup any time soon. One hundred ten, 120 pitches, and Weatherall's face began to darken, the alcoholic cheer fueled by Veuve Clicquot and enjoyable company becoming alcoholic rage as the camera closed in on poor Mark, his hat drenched with sweat, trying to keep the expressionless face of the top-notch pitcher but his exhaustion clearly apparent nonetheless. At 130 pitches Andrew had turned practically black with rage; nobody had dared to say a word after that. Doan had known some angry people in his life, but he'd never seen anyone quite as pissed as Andrew Weatherall at this moment.

Finally the game ended, the Wizards hopelessly creamed, with the ever-candid Joe Morgan asking himself, his fellow announcer, and millions of fans what the hell the Wizards' manager had been thinking, letting Bowers pitch such a wretched complete game. "I'll tell you one thing," Morgan noted, "after throwing 140 pitches tonight Mark Bowers is going to be very sore tomorrow, at best, and won't be seen in the lineup for some time.''

"That bastard did it on purpose," Weatherall hissed, pacing around the room angrily. "That goddamn Herbert Kildare did it on purpose. All of it! He leaned on Stein-brenner, God knows what leverage he used but he used it, to get Mark on his team, and he told that manager to leave him in until his arm was . . . toast," he said, breaking down and sobbing. "He did it to get at me, he couldn't get to me so he got at me through Mark. . . ."

Tim found himself impulsively moving to comfort Andrew. "Hey, hey, it's all right. Mark's a pro, he'll put some ice on it and he'll be back in five days."

"No, he won't," Andrew cried. "They broke him, they broke him on purpose, to get to me!"

The phone rang and Luke answered it. "Hi, this is Mark. Is this Luke?"

"Yeah, hey, how are you?"

"I've been better. Trying to avoid the press right now; everybody wants my opinion on what the hell that was all about."

"Andrew has a theory about that."

Bowers chuckled. "I bet he does. Can I talk to him?"

"Sure, hold on. Andrew, it's Mark."

"Thank God." Weatherall took the phone. "Hello? Hey, baby. No, nothing. No, I wasn't. No, really. How are you? Yes, we all saw it . . . yes, I do. I know. No, I won't. I won't!" He sighed. "I promise. I swear, okay?"

He turned to Luke. "Can you have them gas up the plane? I'll need it tonight." He walked out of the room, trailing the conversation behind him. "I'm flying to Chicago tonight. I'm coming to see you. No. No. No, I'm coming, damn it. I need to see you with my own eyes, make sure you're all right . . ." He went into the study and closed the door behind him.

Binky and Doan looked at each other. "What just happened?" Doan asked.

"Looks like Herbert Kildare knows about Andrew and Mark," Tim surmised.

"And is using it to his advantage," Binky added.

Luke sighed. "I'd better pack. I think I should go with him, just in case."

"Just in case he decides to drop by the clubhouse and beat the shit out of the manager?" Tim asked.

"Yeah, something like that." He turned to Binky. "I imagine we'll go straight to Vegas and Comdex after this, but I'll be back by Friday, I hope, so don't cancel those weekend plans."

She hugged him. "I won't. And keep a close eye on him, would you? I don't . . . he's just . . . I don't know."

"Ready to blow a gasket?" Doan suggested.

Binky nodded. "Yeah, I think that sums it up."

Luke had little to worry about in Chicago, at least at first. Weatherall's jet arrived in the early morning and a car sped them to the dreary corporate apartment in which the team had put Mark up. "I wonder if the place is bugged," Andrew mused idly as they rode up the elevator.

Luke kicked himself for not having thought of that. "If we're right about Kildare, I wouldn't be surprised, actually. I should have brought some equipment along to make a sweep. . . ."

Weatherall put a hand on Luke's arm. "Don't worry. If Kildare already knows all, I don't really give a shit if he hears what I have to say about him. And it's not like Mark's going to have the energy for any wall-pounding sex, after all."

Luke laughed. "All the same, maybe it would be best to pick him up and take him to a hotel."

Weatherall shook his head. "He's got to be exhausted and in a lot of pain; the last thing I want him to do is . . . well, anything other than rest. It'll be all right."

Mark opened the door and Andrew greeted him with a fiercely tender embrace, all the more poignant as Bowers was managing to return it just as fiercely with only one arm—the other dangling practically limp at his side. "I'll call you," Weatherall said with a smile, and Luke left them together, having brought several of his people with him from New York to watch the door and the building.

●　●　●

Luke and Andrew were back on the jet the next morning,
on their way to Las Vegas for Comdex, the computer industry trade show. It was a crucially important event on
Weatherall's calendar, not to be missed even if it meant
cutting short his visit with Mark. A good number of the
technologies in which Weatherall had invested would be
premiered at the show, and it was crucial to their success
that he be there to stand beside the inventors and lend his
imprimatur to the product.

A large advance team from Weatherall and Associates
was already in place for the event, with a whole floor of
their hotel sealed off from prying journalistic and compet-
itive eyes. They briefed Andrew on the day's schedule,
looking plainly uncomfortable.

"All right, cough it up," Weatherall demanded. "Something's wrong."

"No, sir, nothing's wrong, but . . . Herbert Kildare is
here today."

"Of course he is," Andrew said, waving their concerns
away with a brush of his hand. "And as much as I'd like
to see him get the same pie in the face, or worse, that our
friend Mr. Gates got a while back, we will be civil when
we see him—at least in front of the cameras." Weatherall
smiled.

The group laughed and relaxed. Luke wondered how
many of them knew about Mark Bowers and consequently
about Herbert Kildare's guerrilla war against their boss. Or
had Weatherall's enmity toward Kildare always been a fearsome thing to behold?

Whatever rage his boss may have felt about the recent
incident, he gave no sign of it on the floor of Comdex. It
was only here that it really hit Luke what Andrew Weatherall meant to the world of high technology; people treated
him like Bill Gates and Warren Buffett rolled into one, a
techie who was also a whiz at investment. Weatherall
signed autographs like a rock star, granting a personal sentence or two to reps from every major media outlet (save
of course KNN; it was one of the jobs of Luke's security
team to make sure that outfit didn't even get close to Andrew), addressing the reporters from the big networks by
their first names on camera, his play to their vanity ensuring

the rest of his sentence would make the evening news no matter what its content. It was becoming clear to Luke that the secret to Weatherall's success was not just in his technical and financial acumen, but in Andrew's persona; like the dollar, people believed in what Andrew promoted because of that intangible aura behind it, the aura of rocklike stability and guarantee.

As Weatherall bantered with Tom Brokaw, an aide itched to whisper in his ear, finally catching his eye and communicating some confidence. Weatherall's face darkened momentarily but he recouped his TV face and made his smiling excuses. Like a flock of birds, his army turned and moved in his wake across the floor of the convention center.

Luke guessed where they were going, and he was right. They found as discreet a position as they could at the back of the huge crowd gathered to hear Herbert Kildare introduce a new product.

"Kildare Digital Radio, or KDR, will quite simply revolutionize the way you listen to music," the dapper Kildare was saying on the platform built to give him visibility amidst the mob. "Now instead of waiting for the song you want to hear on the radio, or even as you're required to do with current digital music technology, *you* can program your own radio station. KDR will allow you to select from practically every recording on disk today, letting you program a station so eclectic you can hear Marilyn Monroe back-to-back with Marilyn Mason."

"Manson," Weatherall muttered darkly. "Marilyn Manson."

"And as KDR is a continuous download through your Internet connection, your service won't log you off."

"As in *Charles Manson*," Weatherall growled. Luke shuddered at the enthusiasm in his boss's voice. Andrew turned his dark visage on his team. "I want to know how the hell he got ahold of our product and I want whoever gave it to him *killed*." And with that he was pushing his way through the crowd to the front, Luke trailing behind him. Luke was bigger and taller than Andrew, but Andrew was faster, and Luke dreaded what would happen if Weatherall got to Kildare alone.

Fortunately, Kildare was just wrapping up his presentation and coming down off the platform when he found himself face-to-face with Weatherall. Luke couldn't see Andrew's face but he could see Kildare's, and there was a moment of genuine surprise there when he saw Andrew before he smoothed it over with a cool, professional smile.

The men were in a Mexican standoff when Luke caught up to them. They did not shake hands. "I have to hand it to you, Kildare, you only steal from the best."

Kildare smiled. "My dear boy, I don't steal. I acquire. If someone has betrayed you, I suggest you direct your rage in that direction."

"Oh, I will. And one more thing." He leaned into Kildare, and this time his enemy couldn't hide his fear. Herbert Kildare was in his sixties, a lifelong desk jockey, while Andrew Weatherall was a thirty-something gay man who, in addition to his devotion to the gym ablutions mandatory among his people, had taken up boxing as an outlet for his temper and had excelled at it through his usual fearsome determination. Luke could see that for a moment Kildare wondered if he had gone too far, if Andrew was going to simply discard the rules of combat and break his neck in front of a thousand witnesses.

Instead, Andrew whispered something into Herbert Kildare's ear that made the other man's face darken with a rage equivalent to Andrew's. Kildare said nothing but gave Andrew the full force of his glare, and unfortunately at that moment a keen-eyed photographer snapped a picture of the two of them, radiating perfect hatred at each other.

And then Weatherall turned his back on Kildare and his army turned with him, an almost exquisitely choreographed slap in the face. There was a sharp intake of breath from the audience, but Kildare had resumed his usual mask of bored amusement.

"What did you say to him?" Luke asked Weatherall on their way to Weatherall and Associates' private party room in the hall.

"I told him that he could do what he liked to me, I know the rules of this game and I can defend myself, but if he harmed my loved ones I would personally break every bone in his body, after seeing that his loved ones experienced equal if not greater hurt than mine had."

"Andrew, I'm just your employee, but until recently I was a cop, okay? If you're going to play hardball with Herbert Kildare I'd advise you to put a cap on the public threats."

Weatherall smiled. "Yes, officer." He put a hand on Luke's shoulder. "I do have a temper, as you've seen. And when I'm pushed too far, well, this is what happens. Hell, if I were to rid the world of a monster like Kildare, there's not a jury of my peers that would convict me."

Luke shuddered. The rich were different, more so now than they had been in this country for a hundred years. But he knew it was once again possible here for a rich man to kill and get away with it, and he imagined Andrew knew it, too. Still, it was another thing for one rich man to kill another. . . . What would happen then? he wondered idly.

"Oh, look!" Andrew said delightedly. "A lucky penny." He bent to pick it up.

"Don't!" Luke said impulsively.

Andrew froze. "Why not?"

"It's facedown. It's not a lucky penny if it's facedown."

Andrew laughed at him. "A penny is money, Luke, and free money is always good luck." He bent down and picked up the penny and pocketed it. "There. Call my accountant and advise him of a change in my net worth." He laughed.

Luke smiled but swallowed hard. Maybe it was just the superstitions his Italian grandmother had drilled into his head, but he wished with all his heart that Andrew hadn't picked up that penny. The incident with the Commander, this little altercation on prime-time TV . . . things were going to get worse before they got better, he sighed, as Andrew put his happy face back on for the guests in the courtesy suite, as if he hadn't a care in the world.

Luke made good on his promise to Binky and was back in the city just in time to leave it again, this time for one of Weatherall's "little hideaways," a cabin in the Berkshires that he'd sworn to Binky was pretty much the most romantic place in the world as fall crept across the East Coast. It was the first real face time they'd had together since starting their new careers, and both of them were ecstatic about the fact that the cabin had no connection with the outside world.

Doan had hammered this point home so often to Tim that around the third time he'd enviously mentioned his best friend's good fortune, Tim had gotten the hint. "I was thinking about taking this weekend off," he mentioned to Doan at breakfast on Friday.

"Can you do that?" Doan asked, unable to repress it. "What will happen if you leave them to their own devices for seventy-two hours?"

"I don't know, but since I was only planning on leaving them for forty-eight hours, I'm willing to risk it. So what should we do?"

Doan had not dared to hope for this; nonetheless he had planned for it anyway, just in case his whining worked. "I don't know, why don't we, say"—he pulled two tickets out of his purse with a smile—"take the train upstate to a little bed and breakfast that will soon appear in the pages of *Moda* and thus never be the same again?"

Tim laughed. "Doan, you little schemer. I think high fashion is just the place for you."

Doan nodded solemnly. "Machiavellian attributes *do* make one's career trajectory easier. I imagine you'll want to work late tonight to make up for taking the weekend off."

"And you'd be working late anyway, what with Jacob's show coming up. How's that collection coming, anyway?"

"Are you asking as my mate, or as press?"

Tim smiled. "Ah, blurry lines. How do you want to answer, as my mate or as maven?"

"Well, both of me are dying to tell you—this collection is going to be *big*. I just think it's time, you know? All those straight boys are just so *ready* for a makeover, they're still all dressing in floppy stuff like it's still the age of Grunge, and they're just not as hung up as they used to be about the gay thing, so I think, I really do, that Jacob is going to make money *and* history."

"Spoken like a flack." Tim grinned. "Better watch yourself or you'll soon start using the word 'genius' when referring to accessories editors," he cracked, making a reference to a classic Fran Lebowitz line that he knew Doan would get.

"You wait and see," Doan huffed. "You *are* going to be at the show, aren't you?"

"Absolutely. At Jacob's studios, right?"

"No," Doan said gleefully. "This show is going to be not only the show of the year but the party of the year!"

"Flack flack flack," Tim chided.

"We're having the whole thing at Splash," Doan said triumphantly, naming the biggest, hottest gay bar in New York City. "Go-go boys, shirtless bartenders, the *works.* Not that there's anybody in the fashion press who hasn't been *there* before, though God knows this means they'll all show, what with the combination of naked flesh, free drinks, cruising opportunities—*all* during the paid work-day!"

Tim roared. "Was that your idea?"

Doan smiled. "Jacob said, 'Let's make it as gay as it can be,' and I said—"

Tim, suddenly and startlingly teary-eyed, hugged him. "I'm so happy for you."

"What do you mean?"

"You said you'd land on your feet, and I'm just so glad that you've not only landed on your feet, you've done a triple somersault in the process and gotten a 10 from the judges."

Doan sighed, hugging him back. "I know. I wondered for a while, actually. It's a tough town, have you noticed? It's like, in San Francisco being weird is not only all right, it's your duty as a citizen to be weird, to keep the theme park entertaining for the tourists. When we were in L.A., being weird was *so wrong,* because it wasn't good box office. And I've figured out that here, being weird is good, just as long as you can sell it. There! Our national character in a nutshell."

Tim smiled. "What about the rest of the country, you know, the part between the coasts?"

Doan blinked in mock ignorance. "What about it?"

"Come on, I'll give you a ride."

"Oh, I'm going downtown and you're going uptown."

"No," Tim said, turning around and bending over, offering his large, solid frame. "A piggyback ride, silly."

Doan clapped with glee and hopped on, his lithe figure no burden to strapping Tim. "The enemy is sighted! Nothing can stop us now!" Doan shouted with glee, waving an imaginary sword. "Charge!"

Tim carried Doan into the elevator and set him down, pressing the button as the two of them giggled like kids. Doan was talking up their weekend destination as he walked out the door, momentarily oblivious to the fact that Tim was no longer at his side. When he realized, he turned back to find an ashen-faced Tim in the lobby, holding some other tenant's copy of the *New York Beast*. Just as he was about to ask what was the matter, he saw the huge headline:

SAY IT AIN'T SO!

Mark "the Commander" Bowers's Secret Gay Life with Outrageous Billionaire!

"Uh-oh," Doan mustered. "Not good." The headline was accompanied by a photo of Andrew Weatherall in his front-row seat at Yankee Stadium, smiling tenderly at a grinning Commander, their fingers touching through the protective mesh.

"Shit," Tim said. "Shit, shit, shit." He turned to Doan. "I don't know if we're going anywhere this weekend."

"I don't think we are," Doan said decisively. "He's your boss, but he's also . . . well, I don't know if you can call him our friend, but he's one of our people, isn't he? And he's going to need some support right about now."

"He's going to need a straitjacket," Tim said darkly, "and Luke isn't around to hold him back. And we've got no way to get hold of them."

"Well . . ." Doan said, looking away.

"What? Doan, do you know something I don't?"

"Actually, I do. . . ." And he spilled the beans. "Binky has her cell phone with her. Luke's not supposed to know about it. But he told her he wanted to do some fishing, and when she realized she was going to be in the boonies with not only no TV, fine, no radio, fine, no microwave, well, she'll manage, but *no phone* while Luke sat around holding some stick over the water . . . well, that was unacceptable.''

Tim nodded. As long as he'd known Doan and Binky, there had been one inseparable link between the duo, that provided by one Baby Bell or another. In fact, their first purchase with the avalanche of money from the Breeze case had been top-of-the-line cell phones, all the better to keep up a constant stream of chat. It crossed his mind for a second to ask Doan if he'd planned on bringing his with them on their own trip, but decided to let sleeping dogs lie. Today at least, their addiction was a lifesaver.

''Call them up and tell them what happened.'' He looked at his watch. ''They're probably not that far north yet; we can get them to turn around. Luke will need to be here to handle security, what with all the press that's going to descend on Andrew's head.'' He put a hand to his own head. ''Oh, God. This is war, you know.''

''With Kildare? Yeah, I guess it is. Well, at least we're on the side of good. And good usually wins . . . doesn't it?''

''Yeah,'' Tim said grimly. ''Usually.''

Luke had glared at Binky when the phone rang, and she had answered it guiltily, but once she handed it to Luke and Tim filled him in, as with Doan's own plan to bring a phone along, it was suddenly water under the bridge. Luke took the first exit and hightailed it back to the city, keeping Binky busy making calls to track down Andrew's current whereabouts. All four of our friends gathered at Andrew's house to . . . well, watch and wait, basically.

It was a most unfortunate combination—a sexually salacious story, in the media capital of the world, on a slow news day. Moreover, as media-savvy Tim couldn't help but note, Kildare's *Beast* and KNN were directing and feeding the frenzy. In addition to the shock-shock horror-horror headline and the accompanying article, the *Beast* had featured a broad selection of Weatherall's ''most outrageously sinful and unpatriotic'' utterings, as well as a broadside from *Beast* columnist and conservative luminary Thom Wont.

Wont was capable of writing exquisitely and rhapsodically about baseball, his favorite sport, and yet the mere topic of homosexuality reduced Wont in print to a state of ranting, vituperative incoherence. "Regardless of his talents, Mark Bowers must leave the game of baseball," Wont commanded imperiously. "Our national pastime is more than a game, it is a moral beacon to youth. Mark Bowers has not only elected to betray the game and America's children by indulging in his chosen immoral lifestyle, he has done so in the company of one of the most wicked men in this nation, a man who has used his wealth and power to swing an ax at the foundations of American society, indeed, of civilization itself." And so on.

Meanwhile, KNN cleverly rationed out its insider information in a series of "this just in" bulletins that kept the other networks, ever obsessed with beating the competition by even a few minutes with even the most trivial of details ("This just in: NBC has learned where Monica Lewinsky has her hair done"), scrambling to dig up dirt of their own. Andrew Weatherall was seen to smile just once this day, when a KNN reporter (formerly with *Hard Copy* and thus used to worming in where he wasn't welcome) sneaked into a Yankees batting practice session. Now, Mark Bowers hadn't gotten his nickname from his fellow Yankees for no reason; the respect he had earned was not to be lost because he was out kissing men, especially not on a team where more than one member had been arrested for far worse crimes. And so it was that when the Commander's former catcher was confronted with a KNN microphone and asked on live TV "how it made him feel" to know that his former locker room companion might have been checking out his package, he proceeded to punch the hack "journalist" in the nose, earning himself a three-game suspension, a five-thousand-dollar fine, and an offer of unlimited free drinks from most of the gay bars in town.

"I need a flack," Andrew, sprawled on his couch in a polo shirt and jeans, said to the foursome. "I used to love the media, you know? If they wanted me, I loved to go out there and stand in front of those cameras and give 'em what they came for—entertainment! Sound bites! Charm on a stick!" He sighed. "I don't want to go out there now," he said, referring to an army of press encamped outside his house, "a media circus almost as large as that at the Jackie O death watch," according to NY1.

"I could read a statement for you," Binky offered.

Andrew smiled. "Thanks. You'd do it very well, too. But Mark called me and told me to say nothing. The ultimate sacrifice for me, you know." They all laughed, relaxing a bit at seeing him taking it so well. "He's scheduled to pitch Sunday, can you believe it? Five days' rest, as if his last outing had been perfectly normal. And he says he's fine. And I can't go see him. It's enough of a carnival on his end, too, without me showing up to make it worse."

"What will happen to him?" Tim asked. "They can't just fire him, can they? Just for being gay?"

"I don't know." Andrew sighed. "I don't know what they can do. No pro athlete has ever come out—well, he didn't *come out* but you know what I mean—while he was still playing the game. Who knows what will happen. . . . But he's not quitting." Andrew smiled tenderly at the thought. "He's not quitting. They can drive him out, but he's not quitting." He stood up. "And neither am I. It's a weekday, isn't it?"

"Yes, sir," Luke said, smiling.

"Then it's time to go to work."

"I've got a car in the back . . ." Luke began but Weatherall raised a hand.

"No, we will go out the front door, and smile and wave at the cameras." His face darkened for the first time that day. "Herbert Kildare will not have the added glee of forcing me to scuttle out of my own house like an indicted criminal."

And so out the front door they went, Andrew leading the way. "Andrew! Andrew! Is Mark going to leave baseball? How can he go on being a role model to children? How long have you and Mark been gay lovers?"

Weatherall stopped, his promise to Mark seemingly about to be broken. "Why is it," he mused calmly to a suddenly hushed crowd, "that the papers always seem to need to add the word *gay* when two men are involved; isn't that an oxymoron? You know Mark Bowers is sleeping with a man, so why isn't it his lover, why is it his 'gay lover'? Makes it sound so seedy, doesn't it . . . but then, I suppose that's the effect you're after." And he kept walking.

"Andrew, one question," a woman reporter from CNN pleaded, practically blocking his way.

"Sorry," he told her with a smile, "Mr. Bowers is my Commander, too, and he has me under a gag order."

Luke was about to pick her up bodily and place her out of the way when she persisted. "Andrew, remember the Collins deal—you owe me one big favor and I'm calling it in."

He stopped, clearly pained. "All right, Cynthia. Ask me, and we're even."

"Mark Bowers was traded from the winning Yankees to the losing Wizards, owned by Herbert Kildare. He was left in for 140 pitches earlier this week, something our sports reporters told me is something no manager would do to a pitcher unless he was under inescapable orders. And now Kildare's media empire is tearing at you and Mark tooth and nail. Is Herbert Kildare using Mark Bowers to get at you?"

The nearby reporters were hushed—nay, stunned. More out of embarrassment than anything else; it was one of those questions that every reporter wants to ask in a situation like this—one where the answer was inescapably contained in the question. It became immediately clear to everyone that this was exactly what was happening and suddenly Andrew Weatherall and Mark Bowers were the victims and not the criminals.

Andrew knew it, too; he smiled at the reporter. The truth was too obvious for spin, and Andrew was no fan of spin in any case. "Now I owe you two, Cynthia. Yes, that is exactly what is going on. In the past month, Herbert Kildare has stolen a valuable new technology from my company, he has attempted to subvert my employees and even seduce several of my key people into his organization, and now he is attempting to destroy my partner's career. In short, he is fighting dirty." Weatherall deliberately turned to the KNN camera. "I am not afraid. And I will fight back. You will not break me, and you will not break Mark Bowers. And you will lose." He turned back to the rest of the mob. "I wish you all good hunting today; as for myself I am off to work.'' And in a flash he was in his car and gone, leaving behind a shocked but satisfied press corps, almost none of whom would even look at their comrades from KNN.

Doan had not wanted to gather at Andrew's house on Sunday for another baseball game. ''I've seen enough Waterford paperweights tossed through widescreen TVs this week,'' he pleaded to Tim. Binky had pleaded similar stress at the thought, and so Tim and Luke made the trip to Andrew's house for the ESPN Game of the Week alone.

Which, all told, turned out quite well. Without Binky and Doan, ''the guys'' loosened up considerably, enjoying beers and greasy chips rather than the champagne and little toastie thingies Binky and Doan favored, nay, insisted on. Shoes were removed, belching was allowed, and hollering was encouraged. All three were long-standing ball fans and no sidebars were required with the mates to explain infield fly rules or remind anybody that it was *four* balls and *three* strikes.

The Commander was pitching well—very well, in fact. Years in the majors taught every ball player to ignore the fans and concentrate on the game, though of course there was no shutting out a truly unified hatred or love from such a massive beast. All three of them had dreaded the crowd's reaction to the first publicly gay ball player in America, but people have a way of surprising you and tonight was no exception—yes, there were boos when Mark took the mound, but cheers as well.

''He's up to bat in the bottom of the third, isn't he?'' Luke asked. It was an interleague game, one of the additions baseball had made recently to spice up play, and when AL teams played in NL parks, NL rules prevailed—that is, no designated hitter, and the pitcher had to hit for himself, which made it the perfect game in which to play a pitcher who had worked so ruthlessly on improving his hitting.

Andrew nodded. ''First up. All that time people gave him shit about batting practice when he was an AL pitcher, and here it is about to pay off.''

''Can he hit?'' Tim asked.

Andrew looked at him with mock indignation. ''Can he hit! Well, he's no Mark McGwire, but he's not one of those 'why bother' pitchers who get up there and give it a girly swing, mustn't tire one's arm, two more innings to pitch before one's blessed relief comes in. No, he can get on base, at least.''

They were silent with a happy tension as the announcement rang out. ''Now batting, the pitcher, number thirty-two, Mark . . . Bowers.''

Andrew smiled at the cheers of the crowd. ''One minute you're a Christian, the next you're a lion. Go figure. . . .''

But Luke froze when the big-screen TV showed a close-up of the opposing pitcher's face, set into a display of raw hatred. This guy hates fags, Luke thought with dread. Sure enough, his first pitch went whizzing straight for Mark's head; Mark reflexively bent back and almost fell over. A chorus of boos from the crowd indicated that nobody thought it had been an accident. The umpire warned the pitcher and signaled for the game to go on.

The camera cut to Bowers's teammates standing in the dugout, having leapt to their feet. Mark had gotten a warm reception on his arrival, his reputation preceding him, but since the news about him and Andrew had broken, the clubhouse had been a chilly place. Still, for all their prejudices, these men were watching a member of their team whose forehead had nearly gotten a 93 mph dent.

Mark was cool; he squared up, tapped the plate with his bat to show the pitcher where it was (to a handful of appreciative chuckles), and steeled himself. The opposing pitcher wound up, and threw. . . . Mark had time only to turn and take the ball in the back rather than somewhere it would do more damage.

There was a pause—a moment that people who were there would remember always. A hesitation, and everybody watching, there and on television, held their breath. A second, just long enough for a gasp of shock and for someone to make a decision. Mark turned to his dugout, and just *looked*—not asking, not hoping, just checking to see if he was on his own . . . and then he set his shoulders down and charged the mound.

And as soon as he did, his teammates were out of there, up the steps, onto the field and racing for the mound. Guilty and ashamed, the visiting team stood there for a second before instinct took over and they, too, headed into the fray.

Luke and Tim turned to see Andrew's reaction, to see how angry he would be at this latest attack that Mark had taken, taken because of him. But he was smiling—and crying, tears of joy and pain. The other men understood; Mark had taken the ball but the unwritten rules of the game required him to beat the shit out of the man who'd intentionally hit him, no matter why, or lose face. And there had been that one moment, when it looked like he might have to charge that mound all by himself, but he was going to do it anyway, if he had to. And in the end, he hadn't—his team had come through for him.

None of them said anything as the fight escalated, as the fans jumped onto the field and the whole place became the ancient Coliseum that Andrew had alluded to only moments before. "I'm so proud of him," Andrew Weatherall whispered. "I would do anything for him, you know. Anything."

Luke handed him another beer. "Yeah. I know." *That's what I'm afraid of,* he thought.

Doan had thought Jacob Mannheim's show would be a hoot, an inside joke for the fashion mavens; he was totally unprepared when the event threatened to meet his own hype and become just what he said it would be—the event of the year.

Splash was the perfect venue for a collection that was unabashedly designed to be the gayest men's line ever. It was less a bar than a gay theme park, the main attractions of which were the incredibly hunky men who danced on the tile floor above eye level and did *Flashdance*-inspired numbers under the working shower heads (thus the name of the place), and the incredibly hunky bartenders, who rarely if ever wore shirts and were notoriously flirty with just about everybody. Many were the Chelsea bars that Splash had sunk in its juggernaut. And most amazingly for an of-the-moment town like New York, the bar had managed to remain *the* place to go for years.

Nineteenth Street had to be closed off to accommodate the crowds of onlookers and attendees. If the degree of successful and attempted gate-crashing was any indication of an event's success, Jacob's show broke all records, with approximately 177 percent more people attending than had been invited.

The models used the bars proper as catwalks, and Doan had seen to it that the boys with the best bone structure were strategically placed on the dramatically lit go-go platforms, where they gyrated madly in Mannheim's Lycra zip-front bike shirts with nipple rings sewn in, grinding in thigh-hugging knee-length pants ("Capri pants for boys," one critic who was too fat to wear them sniffed later) before stripping to Mannheim's revealing underwear collection, notable for the fact that the models were not tucked for TV, a fact that caused great consternation among the producers from Fashion TV and CNN's *Style with Elsa Klensch*, but which most everybody else was pretty happy about. The models were about half professionals from the agencies and half studs whom Doan had had the pleasure of recruiting from Chelsea Gym and the escort pages of *HX*.

The crowd was mad for the whole thing; there were a few sourpusses in imposing black eyeglasses (that telegraphed their "seriousness") who sat on barstools the whole time making notes, but pretty much everyone else got into the spirit and got drunk on the free booze and gyrated with the models, who were liquored up and sent out onto the dance floor after their part in the show was over to, er, socialize with the crowd. It was one of those events that would become a milestone on people's calendars—a party where you were either there and you were somebody, or you weren't . . . and you weren't.

Jacob found Doan in the crowd and hugged him. "Darling, this is sensational! Oh, my God, you have *saved my bacon*! Look at these queens, they're eating it up! It was brilliant of you to send the boys out to mingle, everybody gets a close-up look at the collection, or can pretend that's what they're looking at. . . ."

"I've gotten three complaints already from some boys from Elite who've had their material fingered a little too lovingly!" Doan gloated.

Jacob was pulled off to the side by Anna Wintour for a quote and Doan was left to survey the bacchanal with satisfaction. A pair of strong arms encircled him from behind;

without turning he knew they belonged to Tim. "Your fifteen minutes are here," Tim whispered.

Doan turned to him and smiled. "And now that it's here, you know what? I'd rather have fifteen minutes alone with *you*."

Tim laughed. "This is a great bash, you know that? If fashion doesn't work out for you, you can make an excellent living throwing parties."

"Talking on the phone all day, ordering cases of champagne and buckets of flowers and several schools of sturgeon's worth of caviar . . . sounds like a dream," Doan sighed.

"Is Binky here?"

"Oh, yes, somewhere. She and Andrew are commiserating over absent spouses; Mark's in Chicago and Luke's working overtime trying to figure out how Kildare got ahold of that digital radio thingie."

"I wanted to thank you for inviting everyone from *EH*. You didn't have to do that, you know, but it's been a great outing for all of us. We've been putting in some major hours what with the revamp and redesign."

"I am well aware of that, stranger," Doan said, grinning. "I figured inviting everyone else was the only way to get you here—if you'd told them they couldn't go you would have had a mutiny on your hands."

"Hey, I would've quit if I'd had to, if that's what it took to get here and see your big production number."

"I know," Doan said, kissing Tim tenderly.

"But as a matter of fact, I do have to get back—"

"I thought so! You didn't even have a cocktail, did you?"

"Well . . ."

"Goddamn it, Tim O'Neill," Doan said, pulling Tim's two-hundred-plus pounds along with him with more determination than muscle, "you march right over here with me and drink a toast before you go anywhere!"

Tim rolled his eyes but obeyed. "To Doan McCandler, party animal."

"To us, to Andrew Weatherall, to Jacob Mannheim, to New York City!" They drank up and Tim sheepishly refused a refill. "Okay, okay, back to work with you." Doan kissed him goodbye and went in search of Binky and Andrew.

He found them flirting shamelessly with one of the bartenders. "Maybe we can work out a timeshare deal," Binky was saying to Andrew.

Doan grabbed her by the ear and left the field clear for Andrew. "Hey!" she protested.

"I've spent enough time in this life getting you out of man trouble, missy, I don't have any more to waste."

"Doan, he's gay, nothing's going to happen."

"You underestimate your own effect on the male of the species. Luke couldn't make it?"

"No, he's working with Kevin Stocker, trying to find any security breach in the computers they might have missed at the time. He's missing a great party."

Doan flushed with pleasure. "Yes, it is. Jacob's ecstatic; he's seen at least half a dozen people from Randall Reid's studio, presumably sent here to spy and report back, but two have disappeared with one of the models, one's drunk off her ass, and he's hired the other three! Complete and total victory!"

Binky put an arm around Doan's shoulder and watched the carnival. "You know, Doan, this is exactly what we dreamed of all those dreary, underfunded years. And you know what? It's just as fabulous as we hoped it would be."

Doan nodded. "We've really got it all, haven't we?"

"Don't say that around Luke. He's superstitious, you know. He thinks things are too good—that something horrible is bound to happen."

Doan dismissed that lightly. "He's just spent too many years as a cop, digging up dead bodies and watching people get away with murder." He nodded authoritatively. "Everything is going to be just fine from now on; I'm certain of it."

Tim was a little tipsy when he got back to the deserted offices of *EH*. He probably wasn't going to get much work done after drinking, he realized, but he could collect some papers and take them home for later. He tossed some files into his backpack but couldn't find his strategy file, the most important of all as it contained the plans he'd laid out for the magazine at his first all-staff meeting.

He heard buttons being punched on the fax machine down the hall and decided to see who hadn't made it to the party. When he came around the corner, he froze—there at the fax machine, just putting the strategy file's contents back into its folder, was David, the shoe editor.

Tim couldn't say why he didn't confront his nemesis (for nemesis David had surely been, ever since that first day), but he backed up, making sure David didn't see him, and ducked into the kitchen. He watched David go down the hall, put the file back on Tim's desk, and leave the office.

He picked up a phone and dialed Luke's cell number. "Hey, I have a request for you. It's business related, I think. It's a little irregular . . . maybe even illegal."

On the other end, Luke tensed up and Kevin felt it. "What happened?" Luke asked.

"I need you to trace a number for me. Someone I don't trust faxed some key documents to . . . I don't know who." He punched redial on the fax machine and read the number off to Luke. "Can you do that?"

Luke smiled and looked at the expectant Kevin. "I think I know someone who can help you."

A few minutes and one illegal entry into the NYNEX computer system later, Luke called Tim back. "Bad news. That number is a fax machine at the *New York Beast*."

Tim colored. "Damn it. Damn it!"

"What's up?" Luke asked.

"Andrew's not going to like this, buddy. But it looks like Herbert Kildare has gotten another claw in Andrew's corporate body."

Luke made the call to Andrew. He got him in the back of his car, heading home from Mannheim's show. To his surprise, Weatherall was blithe about the whole thing.

"So now he's going to dynamite the publishing empire I snatched from under his nose, is he? Ah, Herbert, Herbert. Don't worry, Luke. I have it all figured out. A secret weapon to end the war." He laughed. "You just go on home to Binky. I'm going to Mrs. Keith's house for dinner tonight, no security detail please. Nighty-night!"

So Luke did what he was told. But somehow he wasn't surprised when the phone rang late that night.

"Mr. Faraglione, we've had an incident here at the offices. There's been a murder. Or at least it looks like a murder. A dead body has been found in Ms. Van de Kamp's office."

"One of our employees?"

"Uh . . . no, sir. Actually, it's . . . well, sir, it's Herbert Kildare."

five

~~~~~~~

Many is the American citizen who thinks that the only legacy of the O. J. Simpson trial is a bitter taste in the mouth of anyone who has ever endured the legal process without the best lawyers millions of dollars can buy. But thanks to Mr. Simpson's Bronco ride, when he took his passport and ten thousand dollars cash on his visit to his wife's grave, it has become a little more difficult for celebrity murder suspects to flee the country. Andrew Weatherall knew he had enemies other than Herbert Kildare, but he was not aware of the vast extent of their power until, a mere eight hours after Kildare's body was discovered at Weatherall and Associates, his assets were frozen and the same officers who came to arrest him also brought a court order demanding his passport.

"I'm broke!" he said disbelievingly to our foursome, gathered in his office at the end of a very long day. "I cannot get *any money* out of the bank. My ATM card doesn't even work, and my accounting department is under orders not to give me any petty cash. Unbelievable!"

Mark was there as well, and put an arm around Andrew's shoulder. "Well, they haven't frozen my assets yet. Guess

I'll be feeding and clothing you for a while," he said in an attempt at levity.

Andrew smiled weakly and squeezed Mark's hand. "This is the most awful day of my life."

Nobody present would disagree with that; in fact, it was perhaps the worst day of their lives as well. Luke had raced to the offices when he'd gotten the call, having first chewed out his subordinate for not calling the police before calling him. He'd found himself for the first time in the uncomfortable position of being the one answering police questions rather than asking them, and while he'd thought that his previous life as an SFPD detective would have gotten him at least a little professional courtesy, he'd been sadly mistaken. The NYPD detectives considered him nothing more than a rent-a-cop now; Binky had soothed his ego by reminding him that he was making about ten times what they would ever make (legally, anyway) and that was why they'd been so hard on him.

It had been an ugly scene of crime, too. No poison for Herbert Kildare; the murder weapon had been a bullet to the back of the head, and a gun of the same caliber was found on the spot. Binky's office would be uninhabitable for some time due to the copious amount of blood spilled, from which it was evident to Luke that Kildare had been killed on the premises. The cops had asked for the surveillance tapes, and at that moment Luke had remembered, and volunteered, that there was no tape of Binky's office.

"But you have tape on the rest of the building," Detective Matthieson pressed.

"Yes, of course."

"We'll want to see all that for the night."

"Of course." With a sick feeling, he thought about the fact that Kevin had removed Binky's office from video surveillance at his request. So whoever had shot Kildare had known that there would be no tape there, and how did they know that unless . . . He would have to have a talk with young Kevin as soon as possible, but for now he wasn't going to share that with the police. It was all too confusing—a shot to the back of the head suggested an execution, which threw guilt on Andrew, who could certainly afford to order a hit. And yet who would be fool enough to kill a rival in one's own offices? And yet, couldn't doing it right here be *so foolish* that it could actually throw suspicion *off* the prime suspect? And yet, who else would know they could shoot someone in this office, and this office only, and get away with it? Seasoned detective or not, it was making Luke's head spin.

Binky had not had a good day, either. Her eagerly awaited lunch with Mrs. HMB Jr. had to be canceled, both because she'd spent an enormous amount of time with the police (it being her office, after all, in which Kildare had been found) and because she wanted to do it before enduring the humiliation of having Mrs. HMB Jr. cancel on her, what with the dark shadow of crime now cast over Weatherall and his good works. Nobody had returned Weatherall's money, thank God, at least not yet, and all of the checks had been promptly deposited by the cash-needy organizations who'd received them, so there wouldn't be the added embarrassment of bouncing checks—a possibility, thanks to Weatherall's insistence on simply writing them as he would off a special personal account rather than setting up an official "foundation."

Tim had his own Weatherall-level apoplectic explosion that morning upon picking up the *New York Beast* and discovering that whatever the evil shoe editor had sent them was not the first but the last communique—the *Beast* had run its own story about how to win on *Jeopardy!*, this one by a mere three-time winner and nowhere near as informative, or amusing, as the one *Edgy Hipster* had planned. Also on the front page of the *Beast*'s style section had been an article on Ithaca, New York, the newest hot college town for music trendies—practically the same article that Tim had been editing for *EH*. God only knew what the next issue would bring but he was sure it would contain still more scoops of the magazine, which with its lag time couldn't possibly compete with the daily paper. He'd even been denied the satisfaction of firing David, who'd "resigned" in a fax sent to the mag in the middle of last night.

Doan was perhaps the most fortunate of them all, as his livelihood did not depend on the continuing solvency and freedom of Andrew Weatherall, but it had screwed up his day, too—a reporter who'd showed up at Mannheim's stu-

dio to do a lovefest puff piece on him for *Time Out* was
suddenly full of questions about his friends and associates
and their relations with Andrew Weatherall. He was eter-
nally grateful to Jacob for rescuing him by informing him,
within the reporter's earshot, that Naomi was here for her
fitting and would they like to come along?

"By the way, if anyone cares, I didn't kill Herbert Kildare," Andrew added. "And under the circumstances I
wouldn't wish him dead—he seems to be even more grief
to me dead than alive."

"None of us believe you did it," Mark said assertively
and protectively, looking around the room to make sure
everyone was on the right side.

Weatherall got up. It was an appalling sight to the people
who'd worked with him; he seemed like a beaten man. "I
am going home—out the back door this time." He smiled.
"I just can't deal with press, and my lawyers say it's gotta
be 'no comment' all the way home. The bar's open," he
said, indicating his glittering and well-stocked liquor cabi-
net. "Enjoy it before they freeze that, too." And he and
Mark were gone.

Luke got up. "I could use that drink, frankly. Anyone
else?"

Three hands were raised. "I'll make the martinis," Doan
volunteered.

"He looks terrible," Binky said.

Luke took two beers and handed one to Tim. "Andrew
has made a lot of enemies, by being outspoken and, frankly,
just by being rich and gay. Now is everybody's opportunity
to kick him while he's down, and nobody's waiting their
turn."

Doan looked at Tim, who'd clued him in on the events
at *EH*. "What?" Tim asked. "Doan . . ." he said warningly. "I know that look."

Doan turned to Binky. "You know what I think?"

Binky sighed. "I sure do."

Luke raised a hand. "Now wait a minute. You two are
going to go putting your nose where it doesn't belong and
you're going to get it cut off. This isn't the San Francisco
art world, and it isn't Hollywood—we are talking about a
dead billionaire and another billionaire who might fry for

it. And if Andrew *didn't* murder Kildare, you're liable to find that whoever did is more powerful than the two of them combined.''

"What do you mean, if Andrew didn't kill Kildare?" Doan asked. "You don't mean to tell us that you think that he did?''

Luke hesitated. "Andrew is . . . volatile. He has a temper, we've all seen that. He believes in what he believes so passionately that . . .''

"That he'd kill for it?" Tim said. "But why would he? He doesn't have to kill anybody, Luke, he's got billions of dollars—he can destroy anyone he wants, yes, even Herbert Kildare if that was the project he put his mind to.''

Binky took a martini from Doan and slugged it back. "Oh, God, that's good. Guys, I know what this is about. Luke was a cop for a long time. So by nature, he's . . .''

"Suspicious." Luke smiled at her.

She nodded. "Suspicious. Which is exactly what we need now that we're back in the detecting business.''

"Oh no," Luke groaned. "Don't do this, Binks.''

Doan stood up. "Yes, back in the detective business. Luke, you said it yourself—Andrew has enemies, lots of them, besides Kildare. The kind of enemies who could see him if not tried and convicted and jailed, at least ruined. The kind of enemies who can lean on the police so that they don't look too hard in other directions. So if anybody's going to solve this case, it's going to be . . .'' He raised his glass.

Binky raised hers, having promptly refilled it from the pitcher. "Us.''

Glasses raised but not sipped, they looked at their partners. Tim shrugged and raised his bottle. "Us.''

Luke had been in this situation before. It was no use. He raised his bottle. "Us," he sighed.

Binky was amazed at the alacrity with which Will Powers clasped her to his bosom—figuratively, that is; he had never shown a whit of sexual interest in her. All she'd had to do was call and within minutes Powers was offering her a job.

"Of course you don't want to be footloose in New York City, you need employment. Now that things are over with

Weatherall, it's time to move on, no shame in that.''

"But now I'm not exactly the prize I was for you—"
Binky started.

"No," Powers admitted, "you're not. Nonetheless, by
dint of your stint with Weatherall and your appearance on
the cover of *New York*, you are officially a somebody in
this town, and a great asset to me.''

Whatever else Binky thought about Powers, she had to
admire his ruthless honesty. Yes, he was venal, but you
would always know where you stood with him.

The next day, a car whisked her to Powers's offices. She
was at first disturbed to discover that they occupied a floor
in Kildare Worldwide's monolothic black-glass headquarters, but she cheered up when she realized that this would
provide her with easier access to Kildare's offices (if need
be, she qualified), and also that she wouldn't be the only
spy in the house, as Tim would be upstairs at KNN.

She hadn't gotten what she'd expected, a typical office
setup. Instead, Will Powers Seminars was more like a
direct-marketing boiler room—well, it *was* a boiler room.
"It's deserted now," Will said, waving his hand across a
field of empty desks separated by soundproofed Plexiglas
dividers. "Late at night and early weekend mornings, this
place is jumping.''

"That's when operators are standing by when the infomercials run.''

Will's marketing background overcame his honesty; he
made a face and said, "We call them informational pro-
gramming here. Now let me show you the jewel in the
crown.''

The next room was also a boiler room, only half the size
and packed with men in white shirts and red ties, all talking
into their telephone headsets and clacking busily on their
computers. "This is one of the services my clients can subscribe to. We try to teach them to rationalize anything
themselves, but sometimes they need a little help.'' He put
a hand on the shoulder of one operator. "This is Jake, one
of our finest operatives.''

Jake turned around and shook Binky's hand. He was of
the same genus as Powers—a young shark with conven-
tional good looks and a Wall Street haircut, but his eyes

set him apart: dark, deep-set, glittering eyes that seemed to find enormous amusement in his situation. "Good morning, Miss Van de Kamp. Would you like to listen in on a few of our client consultations?"

Will encouragingly handed her a second headset, and she put it on as Jake hit the button to accept an incoming call. "Good morning, 'You Can Rationalize Anything.' May I have your subscriber number please?"

"Oh, one two seven nine eight five."

"One moment." Clackety-clack. "Mr. Venal?"

"Yes."

"How can I help you today?"

"Well, I have this problem . . ." the caller began hesitantly.

"Of course you do, Mr. Venal," Jake said in a soothing tone. "That's what we're here for."

"Yes. Well. Here's the deal. I work for a large tobacco company, in fact I'm a senior executive. I didn't want to work in tobacco—"

Jake cut him off. "Congratulations, sir. Don't apologize for your success."

"Yes. Yes. Well, it's just that my children are in college now, and they're not speaking to me because of my job. And I'm finding it harder and harder to face the media and defend my company because I know everything I say is going to get back to my kids."

"Mr. Venal, don't you know what a hero you are?"

"What?"

"Haven't you been paying attention to what your fellow tobacco executives have been saying? Mr. Venal, you and your fellow executives are the champions of *working families.*"

"Oh, but that's just—"

"But? But! Sir, who grows tobacco? Small family farmers! Who smokes tobacco? Poor people! Who's going to be hit if tobacco consumption decreases and tobacco taxes rise? *Working families!*"

"That's just PR bullshit," Venal said testily.

"Is it?" Jake asked incredulously. "I don't think so. I think it's true. I smoke, you know, and I *applaud* your stance. Between you and me, I don't make a lot of money here," he whispered, winking at Will and Binky. "But I do it because I love it. And it's a privilege to help someone like you, sir. You've just *got* to believe what I say is true!"

"Oh, come off it."

"Sir, you ought to be able to look your kids in the eyes and tell them, 'I'm the champion of working families!' And they will respect that."

There was a pause on the other end of the line. "You're going to have to do better than that. If you really think you can feed me the same bullshit I'm feeding you and all the other suckers, this service isn't worth a plugged nickel." And the line went dead.

The call ended and Jake turned to them, smiling nervously. "Well, that was an unusual call. Not too many tobacco executives on our client roster, fortunately. They're definitely a tough sell."

Then again, maybe you *can't* rationalize everything, Binky thought, but she bit her tongue—she was undercover to learn, not to preach.

Powers put a consoling hand on Jake's shoulder. "Even we have a limit on what we can do. Some behaviors are just beyond the pale: serial murderers, wife beaters, tobacco executives. . . ." He smiled and they all laughed appreciatively, Jake most of all.

Binky and Will adjourned to Powers's office; he offered her a drink and she accepted gratefully. "So what will I be doing for you?"

"Endorsements, of course."

Binky's face fell. Yes, she was undercover here, but even so it was a blow to her ego to think she'd only be a spokesmodel. "Is that all?"

"Well, I saw you at Weatherall's press conference and you acquitted yourself marvelously there." He smiled, and Binky flushed with embarrassed pride. "I can see a role for you in our PR department, maybe even helping me put on the seminars."

Binky nodded, satisfied that she would have a more prestigious role than mere talking head. Then, her ego satisfied, she remembered why she was actually here. "I know it doesn't matter much now that he's dead, but I'm curious. Just how did you end up in business with Herbert Kildare?"

Powers nodded; the mention of the dead man didn't faze him, Binky noted, but that could be because he'd had nothing to do with the murder or then again because the murder had solved any problems he might have had with Kildare.

"I got my start running my program in a few small TV markets, mostly in Texas. Mr. Kildare was on a business trip to Houston and was up late in his hotel one night and saw my show. The next day, I had the cash to broadcast the seminars nationwide."

"Wow. And what did he get in return?"

Powers regarded her coolly. "A stake in the company, of course."

Binky wouldn't press it further today. "Well," she said, getting up, "it's good to be on board."

Powers shook her hand. "You won't regret it." He smiled. "You'll find life a lot easier now that you're on the right side of the law."

Turn to the dark side, Luke flashed through Binky's mind but she smiled sweetly and said, "It's good to be here."

Powers nodded, not questioning the truth of that. "New York is a hard town, as I'm sure you're finding out. When someone takes a fall, as Mr. Weatherall has, the knives come out and nobody around them is safe." Binky shuddered but said nothing. "Self-preservation is the most admired trait here, Binky. Don't feel like you're doing anything wrong by saving your own newly brilliant career."

She nodded. "Better him than us, right?"

Powers beamed at her, a frighteningly malicious grin. "Absolutely."

Tim's face had practically fallen off when Andrew had suggested suspending publication of *Edgy Hipster*. But he knew there was no other way around it; before his death Kildare had seen to it that the next three issues were unpublishable, thanks to the leaks by David the shoe editor. How on earth could a Weatherall publication print stories that had already appeared in Kildare's *Daily Beast*? Not for the first time in his life, Tim cursed the slowly grinding wheels of magazine publishing. "Next time, I'm going to work for a daily paper," he grumbled to Doan over dinner out, where the two of them consoled themselves with several bottles of wine.

"Actually, I have a better idea," Doan replied, having discussed this with Binky.

"Uh-oh." Tim dropped into a Ricky Ricardo accent. "Oh, Lucy, you and your crazy ideas!"

"It's not crazy!" Doan said defensively. "Binky tells me that you met Kildare and Peter Cures that day, and they practically offered you a job."

"Kildare offered me the job; and he's dead. Peter Cures is as likely to hire me as . . . well, as the *New York Times* is to hire Matt Drudge."

"I don't know, seeing how Will Powers scooped up Binky it looks like it's a seller's market for anybody who wants to jump Weatherall's ship for the other side."

"And just what would I do there?" Tim asked. "Oh, don't tell me. Spy, right?"

"Of course! And what else are you going to do with yourself now that the magazine is at least temporarily dead?"

Tim rolled his eyes. "And what do you expect me to find?"

"Think about it," Doan pressed. "Binky says Kildare treated Cures like a lapdog that day. Right?"

"It was pathetic."

"And that Kildare had plans to farm Cures out and liberalize KNN."

"Well, eventually. . . . He said that in time it would be the pragmatic thing to do. . . ." Tim suddenly realized where Doan was going and also realized to his horror that what Doan was suggesting was making sense.

"So you follow politics, darling, far more than I do—is Peter Cures a pragmatist or an ideologue?"

"Because if he's a pragmatist," Tim said, thinking aloud, "the last thing he'd do would be to bite the hand that feeds him, since Kildare's heirs might want their own lapdog in his place if Kildare died. But if he's an ideologue, he might have offed Kildare to keep KNN as the voice of the right, even if it cost him his own job."

"Exactly."

Tim sighed. "And I guess I'll have to join KNN to find out which is the truth."

And as Doan had predicted, Tim's call to Cures was put right through and he was given an appointment the next day. Even as Binky was watching a Powers doppelganger try to convince a tobacco executive that he was the agent of goodness and light, Tim was being ushered into Peter Cures's office several floors above.

Peter Cures was a different person now; at least, he was not the dark and sullen character he'd been when Tim had first seen him, his light hidden under Herbert Kildare's bushel. His pudgy, florid complexion no longer made Tim think of a bitter alcoholic drinking away his social security check in an SRO with a brick-wall view; now it was the jolly glow of the well-fed and malevolent, the sort of man never seen in public in anything but a suit or golf attire, the sort of man whose grin of satisfaction is that of the cat who knows he can eat the canary on a daily basis and will never get whacked with the broom for his crime.

"Come in, Mr. O'Neill. I see you've reconsidered my offer. Excellent. Drink?"

It had been Kildare's offer, Tim well recalled, but no matter. "Just water, thanks." It was eleven o'clock; Cures poured himself a healthy scotch straight up and cracked open a Calistoga for Tim.

"Well, we're all very excited to have you on board." He assumed a Clintonian mask of official sadness and regret. "Terrible about Weatherall suspending publication of *EH*. Not my cup of tea, of course, but I believe my children read it."

"Yes, I'd hoped to make a go of it, but . . . well, no point my sitting around doing nothing for three months waiting to resume publication. And Mr. Weatherall was aware of that, he was very gracious about letting me out of my contract." More than gracious, Tim well knew; while the recent events had taken the edge off Andrew's usual chipper demeanor, the news that Tim would be leaving Imminent Publications to go undercover at KNN had provoked the first complete and total glee Weatherall had demonstrated since the murder.

"Absolutely, absolutely."

"But I'm wondering how the death of Mr. Kildare is affecting long-range plans here. I mean, his family owns most of the stock, right?"

Cures darkened at the thought. "Yes, young Mr. Kildare is dealing with the funeral arrangements and all that, the will to be read, et cetera, and then he will be turning his attentions to the holdings and . . . well . . ." He sighed self-importantly. "Well, I can't really reveal more than that."

If you even know, Tim thought. "Well, let me put it to you this way. I don't want to get under contract in another job where I suddenly find myself vice president in charge of nothing, pulling a paycheck with an office and a secretary and nothing to do because the new regime has decided to pull the plug." He leaned forward, a confidential smile in place. "If I could just have your assurance that this was a job you wanted me to do, and that *you* weren't going anywhere, I would feel more secure about taking the position."

Like any good reporter, Tim was a good actor as well. The interviewer has to master the art of looking interested when bored, looking sympathetic when full of contempt, coaxing intimacies out of someone who thinks they've found a new friend when in fact they have just clasped an adder to their bosom. And he had refined his acting skills as an editor, receiving utter pieces of crap a day after deadline with no time to rewrite it himself, his only option to call the writer and bill and coo and add, "but I need just a few minor changes. . . ."

To Cures he projected all the reportorial sympathy he had in him, and Cures swallowed the bait. The man smiled, willing to participate in the illicit intimacy at the expense of their mutual employer. "Well, I can tell you that I'm not going anywhere. And I know the new regime is as interested as the old one in soft content. Everyone wants to put out the next *Entertainment Tonight*," he said, naming the highly lucrative nightly infotainment show syndicated around the country.

"So the plans to liberalize KNN were those of Mr. Kildare, Senior, only?"

Cures hesitated, remembering that Tim was, after all, a

gay man, and thus not entirely "one of us."

But Tim smiled winningly. "I'm just curious. I don't really care what goes on in the hard news side, as long as it doesn't affect me."

"Oh no, it won't." Cures smiled in return. "As long as what goes on over on your side doesn't, well, conflict with our side too much. If you know what I mean."

Tim leaned back. "Oh, sure. No one-hour specials on the kind of people that the hard news viewer base doesn't want to see, right? No chocolate-covered performance artists or bullwhips stuck in interesting places."

Cures laughed. "Mr. O'Neill, you have it exactly right." He got up and extended a hand. "Welcome to KNN."

Tim got up and gave Cures a warm handshake. "Mr. Cures, what I'm going to do here is going to be a pleasure."

After the dust had settled around Weatherall's offices and the police had finished questioning their suspects, Luke was ready to do some questioning of his own. He hated to admit it, but his goal was not that of his three friends—they were out to prove Weatherall innocent, whereas he, cop to the bone, was out to find the guilty party, whomever that might be. And the first place for a cop to start was with the suspect. He knew Andrew had spent the night with Mrs. Keith, or claimed to. He couldn't start with Andrew, whose volatility he had already come to know (which truth be told was part of why he wasn't entirely sure his boss was innocent), but he could hear for himself the story Mrs. Keith had told the investigators.

"I'm just trying to make sure we have all the information the police have," he'd said to her at the start of their meeting, wanting to put her at ease.

"Of course." Mrs. Keith nodded, smiling serenely. She was an imposing woman, Luke thought. He didn't know if it was a racist thought but in his experience there was something about certain large black women that brooked no quarrel—he thought of Jessye Norman or Toni Morrison. Mrs. Keith was of their dimensions, physically and spiritually.

"Mr. Weatherall came over for dinner at approximately eight o'clock P.M. the night of the murder," she said smoothly, having already arranged this chronology for presentation to the police, as any efficient secretary would do. "I served what you might be surprised to find is his favorite dish, a simple roast chicken with potatoes and carrots. And stuffing," she added meticulously. She smiled. "Mr. Weatherall enjoys his carbos. We had several bottles of wine with dinner and several liqueurs afterward."

"And the rest of your family was absent?"

"My husband was away on business and my son attends boarding school. Mr. Weatherall and I were alone." Her eyes twinkled. "And as I'm sure you know, he's not about to try any hanky-panky with his secretary, at least not a female one."

Luke smiled. "And he stayed the night at your house?"

"Yes, it's not the first time. We have a guest bedroom and he was quite comfortable and quite tired at the end of our evening and in no mood to put his shoes back on and get in a car and go home."

"How often would you say he spends the night there?"

"Well, he used to quite often, especially at the holidays. He has no living family, so we . . . well, I sort of mother him. He would always spend Christmas and Thanksgiving with us, but since he met Mark they've often visited us on the holidays but spent the night . . . elsewhere," she finished discreetly. "So he hasn't spent as many evenings with me or my family as he used to."

"It's rather unusual, isn't it? For a boss to be so close to his assistant?"

Mrs. Keith nodded. "In my experience, yes. Not that I have that much outside of working for Mr. Weatherall."

"Oh?"

She raised her eyebrows. "Oh, you don't know the story?"

"*The* story?" Luke said, emphasizing the article.

"Of how I started with him." She smiled. "It was a few years ago. He was working out of a little office in Brooklyn, all he could afford, at the time—*and* it had windows that opened." She winked, and Luke laughed along with her.

"I was a welfare mother at the time—a single mother, just my son and I. My current husband isn't the boy's natural father," she explained. "Well, as you remember there was a great push to get the welfare mothers off welfare, very good politics at the time," she said, not without a hint of bitterness. "The state was offering incentives to employers to take on a few welfare queens, and I had the good fortune—as it turned out—of being placed by my case worker with a temp agency. Ostensibly I was to be sent out to do drudge work, the sort of thing even the uneducated can do: make copies, answer one-line phones, keep the coffee brewing. But this agency was not the least bit interested in actually putting me to work, only in collecting the stipend for having me on the books and thus off welfare. So there I was, not getting welfare and not getting work. The agency had an impressive list of large clients, none of whom it wanted to alienate by sending them an ignorant darkie. But since they had to send the likes of me *somewhere* to keep me on the books and collect the state money, they would send us to the one-shot clients, the little guys who called for the first time and probably wouldn't call again for a long time to come, the kind of clients the agency wouldn't have bothered with otherwise.

"Andrew was one such client. He just needed someone to open the mail, take messages, very basic stuff. As you know, he used to be a secretary himself and he was quite a whiz with a computer; it would have taken him more time to dictate a letter than to type it. Near the end of the first day, I was out of work and asked him if he had something for me to do. He looked at me strangely—assessing me, I realized later—and he asked me what I knew about finance. I said I knew how to cash a check and he laughed. He asked me to read a prospectus and tell me what I thought. Well, I was quite startled but I read it. I wasn't dumb or illiterate," she said defensively, "just poor and uneducated. But I read the paper and watched the evening news and I knew a thing or two about this industry.

"I read it and I told him what I thought—that it was a bunch of bullshit. He laughed and asked me why I thought that. Well, what it was, was the prospectus for *Wired* magazine's IPO—initial public offering," she explained, and Luke nodded. "I said, there is not a magazine in the world, except maybe *TV Guide*, that is worth this kind of money. It looked to me like a handful of techno-savvy people who'd made the mistake of ending up writing about the computer industry instead of working in it were trying to cash in on the tech stock IPO boom, and that they were hoping there were enough gullible people out there willing to buy damn well anything with the words *technology* or *Internet* on it, no matter what it was really worth.

"Well, he just about busted a gut laughing, and told me that was exactly what was happening. He asked me if I wanted a permanent job, right then and there. 'I don't have any computer skills,' I protested, 'I don't know how to type, I probably can't even lick a stamp right.' But he said, 'Any fool can learn how to type; I need someone with a bullshit detector, and that, my dear, you have got in spades.' " She leaned back and smiled. "I have been with him ever since."

"And you've done well working for him?"

"I will never starve," she said. "My son will never starve. His children will never starve. There will always be a roof over their heads and money in the bank. Andrew pays salary and bonuses, and my salary is nothing compared to the bonuses. You'll see, when all this is over and things get back to normal around here."

"If they get back to normal."

Mrs. Keith frowned. "What do you mean?"

"If Mr. Weatherall is innocent—is found innocent," he corrected himself but too late. Mrs. Keith got up.

"He is. I have told you he is. He doesn't need to kill anybody, or have anybody killed. But he's made a lot of enemies, powerful people who would love to see him fall. People who hate to see welfare mothers and gay men and teenage hackers, and all the kind of people he's helped, become rich and powerful enough to defend themselves. You go look at their agendas, Mr. Faraglione. That's where you'll find your killer. Good day."

Luke sat alone in his office after she left. Two thoughts warred in his head—first, that she was right, Weatherall had enemies. But second, that it was obvious she had a stake in this bigger than just the money. She believed in Andrew Weatherall and his causes and his mission—and true believers would do anything for their cause. Mrs. Keith wouldn't kill anyone, he would swear to that, but would she lie to protect the man who had turned her life around? He couldn't answer that one, not yet.

six

~~~~~~~~

It was a glum Kevin Stocker who let Luke into his apartment the next day. The place was a mess, a typical teenager's first apartment . . . that is, if a typical teenager was pulling down millions a year and had a SoHo loft. The space was vast and yet Kevin had managed to fill it with clutter—wires were taped down haphazardly across the floor, more wires hung from the ceiling, all connecting an array of computers and other digital equipment whose purpose Luke could only guess at. Papers and manuals and circuit boards were scattered across the floor. There were several nice pieces of furniture, a large comfy couch in front of the giant-screen TV, and some matching chair-and-a-halfs, all of which had some kind of food or liquid stain on them.

The young man hadn't gone back to work since the day after the murder, and while initially Luke had been unable to resist suspecting some guilt or shame over his complicity in the crime as the reason, Kevin soon set him straight. "They worked me over," he complained. "They hauled me down to the station and grilled me for hours. After all, I've got a criminal record, right?" he snarled. "Then it was the same damn questions over and over again: 'Why did you turn off the surveillance in that one office? Who else knew it was off in there?' Then they let me stew without a cigarette or a glass of water. Then they come back: 'There's nothing on the other tapes showing someone coming or going through the rest of the building, so how did the killer and the victim get in there?' So they start insinuating that I must have sabotaged the rest of the surveillance system.'' This filled in a hole in Luke's picture of events; the police had asked him to provide plans of the building; presumably they had been looking for other routes of access to Binky's office.

"So I say, well, the floors are practically hollow, they have to be to accommodate all the lines for the Bloomberg terminals and the phone lines and the LAN and everything else we've got wired in there, someone could have crawled through there and lifted a panel in the floor; there would be plenty of room.'' He smiled bitterly. "*That* pissed them off because it was something they should have thought of themselves, and they knew it and I knew it. Fucking cops are so stupid,'' he said with the arrogance of genius before realizing who he was talking to. "Not you. But then you're not a cop anymore, which is a sign you were too smart.''

Luke let this slide. "I hadn't thought of that, either. But you know, thanks to Andrew's predilection for fresh air, all the windows open, too. Someone could have gotten through that way—a little more complicated, hauling someone down from the roof on a rope, but . . .'' He was lost in thought for a moment. "But for that to happen, Kildare would have to have been knocked out; if he'd been struggling while they moved him in there it would have attracted too much attention outside.''

Kevin smiled. "Well, there's only one way to find out, and that's to look at the autopsy.''

Luke frowned. "Considering that the police are already watching you, I don't think now is the time for you to break into the coroner's computer system.''

"Why not? If it helps catch the killer—''

"No. That's an order,'' he said with all the parental authority he could muster. Kevin held his gaze defiantly for a moment but Luke was an imposing man, tall and muscular and stern when need be, and Kevin soon dropped his eyes and shuffled a bit. Then it was good-cop time: "Kevin, I'm going to need your help and you can't help me if they trace your hack and toss you in a jail cell." He didn't add that he still hadn't put it beyond Kevin to create an exquisitely devious digital trail to throw the scent off Andrew Weatherall, be their boss guilty or not.

"Okay. But just remember it can be done. Easily."

"I'm sure it's easy for you. Right now I need you to check some things out. If the killer and the victim really did come through the floor, there might be some sign of disturbance—some wires loosened or even pulled out, like brush being cleared with a machete. I need you to get in there and see how it looks."

"But the police still have that 'do not cross' tape all over the office door."

Luke smiled; it was his turn to be devious. "But there are also access panels to that crawl space in the office below Binky's right? And there's no tape on that office, is there?"

Kevin laughed, his eyes sparkling and his mood lifted. "My man, you may look like a straight arrow, but you have the soul of a hacker."

"No, kid, it's the soul of a cop—a good cop. Don't forget there are some here and there, you know."

"I'll take your word for it." He pulled a baseball cap down over his eyes and pointed dramatically out the window, like the irrepressible kid he was. "To the scene of the crime!"

While Doan was thrilled in the abstract about returning to the world of detecting, after the initial excitement had passed he realized that there was no undercover or investigatory role for him to play, a realization that had taken quite a lot of wind out of his sails. Tim was dining with the devil at KNN, Binky was at Will Powers Seminars, and Luke was, well, everywhere. Still, it was hard for Doan to be too depressed for too long under any circumstances, and Jacob's show at Splash had been an unmitigated triumph. Orders for the collection were pouring in, and the financial solvency of the studio was guaranteed for years to come.

The same morning that found Luke at Kevin's apartment found Doan at his desk munching on a strawberry tart (or two) and turning the pages of *Moda* with sticky fingers. He'd had to confess to Tim that he'd felt some anxiety about his new job at the beginning—certainly at first there had been the challenge of clearing out the deadwood from around Jacob, but always in the back of his mind had been the nagging fear that after that, he would have nothing left to contribute. "The Chelsea Collection," as it had been tagged in the press, a tag which Jacob had wisely sewn into the clothes, had proven to Doan that he could indeed handle a real job with real responsibilities—at least, as long as those responsibilities consisted of eating pastry, reading fashion magazines, and dreaming up wild schemes, which was exactly what this job required. Had this happened back in San Francisco, Doan would have done the San Francisco thing, which was to do one great thing and rest on one's laurels for all time. In New York, this was not acceptable: "What are you going to do next?" was the question he was constantly being asked by the fashion press. He had no idea, but he knew that it would come to him in the fullness of time—and he was still enough of a San Franciscan to know that the profits from the Chelsea Collection were going to be impressive enough to pay his salary without a peep from Jacob or his accountants for some time, whether he dreamed up something else or not.

If anything, Jacob had been *too* New York when Doan had come on board, too obsessed with topping himself; in that respect alone Doan had been good for him. Now Jacob also started his morning with a fluffy pastry and some fluffier reading material, rather than with a double espresso and a shot of panic. When he got up in time, he would even join Doan for a "working breakfast" and they would pore over the trades together and have a bull session, or at least a good laugh.

But this morning Jacob was 100 percent New Yorker as he burst into Doan's office, startling him into dropping a blob of custard onto the magazine. "Oh, my god, you are not going to believe this!" Jacob practically squealed.

"You just made me make a mess on Karl Lagerfeld's face," Doan complained.

"Oh, that old thing." Jacob waved an imaginary fan and lapsed into a cruelly accurate accent. " 'I like to keel zee little animals so zee vimmin can vear zee fur.' I was asked by a dear client to keep a couture fitting slot open this afternoon, but she asked me not to ask her who it was for. Well, that was painful, let me tell you, but she's bought a ton of stuff and I was dying to know who was so famous that they needed to keep their appointment a secret till the last minute.''

"Someone who doesn't want the press staking the place out and snapping her pic, I'd guess.''

"You got it.'' He jumped up and down with childish glee. "And guess who it is!''

"Madonna.''

"No, better.''

"Better? Hmm . . .''

Jacob couldn't wait. "Mrs. Henry M. Boston, Junior!''

"Oh, my god!'' Doan shouted, the remaining custard in his tart ruining a Lagerfeld fur. "Oh, my god!'' It took a lot to impress Doan; the advent of Madonna would have made a good story but wouldn't have incited the hysteria that a visit from Mrs. HMB Jr. was bound to create. He asked the same question that everyone would ask Jacob that day: "Is *He* coming with her?''

"No, but *He* might pick her up when she's done. And it gets better—she wants to meet *you.*''

Doan felt light-headed. "Me?''

"Yes, doll, you're the flavor of the month after that show, you know. And word got out about our little visit to Randall Reid; the whole town knows you not only told him off but stole a plate of sandwiches!''

"Uh-oh.''

"Oh, no, hon, that's *good.* Believe me, we're not the only ones who've had to sit there and watch him eat without even a bowl of gruel being tossed our way. And *she* especially appreciated the story, because guess who she used to work for?''

"That's right!'' Doan shouted, a light dawning in his head. When her engagement to Mr. HMB Jr. had made her as much of a household word as her fiancé, every reporter in America had repeated the line attributed to her during her tenure at Reid's studio: "Randall's on her broom again.'' It had been too delicious—the notoriously closeted

Reid outed in every magazine in the nation by the one person who was now so powerful that Reid would still have to kiss her ass!

"We've got to get ready!" Doan said in a panic. "We've got to get lunch ordered, we've got to get this place cleaned up . . ."

"Already taken care of, doll. You and I and Mrs. HMB Jr. will be having a light lunch after her fitting."

"I'm so nervous! I've never been nervous about meeting someone in my life!"

"Don't sweat it; from what I hear from my client, she's a perfect angel."

In our last episode, Doan was exposed to degrees of Hollywood star power that would have rendered most mortals speechless. And while he'd had to admit that actor/director/lesbian Charlotte Kane had cut a pretty impressive figure, still even she, with all her Academy Awards, did not have the hold over the national imagination that Mrs. HMB Jr. had acquired practically overnight.

Henry M. Boston, Jr., was one of America's rarest possessions—a scion of the upper classes but with sardonic, Heathcliffy features rather than the bland, anemic, droopy-lidded, Hugh Grant face of most of his peers; who had more money than most anyone yet who had dedicated his life to good works, turning his back on the family business of politics; who had dated supermodels and movie stars yet who still had a polite smile on the street for gawping secretaries and fluttering matrons, rendered speechless at the sight of his magnificent charismatic self in person. He had seemed to be on the list of permanent bachelors by the time Lisa Crane came along. He'd been intrigued by the well-born girl with the impish sense of humor, who was killing time working as a photographer's assistant at Randall Reid's studio while she waited for something to come along to hold her attention on a permanent basis. He'd asked her out and had been startled when she turned him down; he wasn't an arrogant man but he'd certainly come to take it for granted that he'd always succeed when it came to women. She'd finally gone out with him; and she'd teased him and needled him and generally treated him like, well, a guy, rather than *Henry M. Boston, Jr.,* apple of every eye. They were engaged nine months later.

Most atypically, Jacob had managed to keep from spilling the beans to anybody but Doan, so while the studio was abuzz with rumor about the mystery visitor for whom so many preparations were being made, nobody knew who it actually was (Madonna was still most people's bet). When Lisa Crane Boston arrived, there wasn't a soul who won the pool, though nobody was sorry to lose—this would be their cocktail chat fodder for weeks to come, a far more important currency in New York even than cash.

"Sorry I'm late," she said on her arrival, although she was only fifteen minutes late, which computed to at least fifteen minutes early on star time. She really was an It Girl, Doan thought—star power written all over her. Tall, brunette, and willowy but without the cool reserve of most women of her physique and bone structure, her sparkling green eyes showed her impish amusement at the whole idea that she was a planetary celebrity just because she'd married the most eligible bachelor on earth.

Her fittings took hardly any time at all; Jacob's practiced eye could look at a few photos of a woman and know her measurements, and he had driven his worker bees into a frenzy all morning in order to have half a dozen pieces ready for her. She wasn't fussy, either; she stood patiently while Jacob marked the few nips and tucks that would be required to perfect the fit. Then it was time for lunch.

Doan had done his homework for this day without ever knowing it was coming. He well knew from articles in *Pendennis* and *Manhattan* that Mrs. Boston, for all her sveltitude, was despised by women around the world for not only having snagged the sexiest man alive but for her ability to wolf huge quantities of food without gaining an inch (a calorie-burning talent, Jacob knew from a friend of his who was a trainer at Crunch, which was as due to her daily tithe of time to the Stairmaster as it was to genetics). No little Randall Reid-ish cucumber sandwiches and gazpacho today; Mrs. B was served healthy portions of French onion soup and slices of tri-tip roast with sour cream and horseradish, followed up by a chocolate sorbet and little butter cookies—all elegant yet indisputably satisfying.

"Jacob, this has been wonderful," Mrs. Boston said with a sigh. "It's like you read my body *and* my mind before I ever came in."

"Well," Jacob said, flushing with pride, "we aim to please. And of course Doan here helped me out immeasurably. He was the one who planned the menu."

"Thank you," she said, turning her wattage onto Doan. "I can't tell you how many people try to starve me!"

"Oh, no problem," Doan said, also flattered into inanity. "Wouldn't want you having to stop at Burger King on the way home."

She laughed and leaned forward to whisper confidentially. "Actually, it's usually McDonald's." They all laughed and Doan and Jacob finally relaxed. "I also hear you're the man who stole Randall Reid's lunch."

Doan laughed. "Well, I was starting to feel like Oliver Twist, sitting there watching him eat."

She nodded. "That's Randall for you. Though I guess I shouldn't dish him. . . ."

"Oh, do!" Doan pleaded.

"Okay!" she said delightedly. "I tell you, when I heard the story about you guys' visit, I nearly fell off the chair. That man is a beast."

"Really?"

"Oh, yes. And you know who he's worst to? His gay male employees. You don't even *mention* you just went to Splash or Fire Island when you're around Randall—he can give you a look that freezes your blood."

"As long as everyone else is in denial, he can be, too, right?" Jacob said bitterly.

"You got it. He just wants to pretend there's no such thing as homosexuality, except of course when it's time to sell underwear to gay boys."

"But he's got all those gay friends," Doan said. "Alex Lebedev, Harry Schiller . . ."

"*Closeted* gay friends. Well, not Lebedev anymore, because he was outed. Did you know there was a major magazine piece done on Randall that exhaustively documented his gay past, that actually got killed just before publication because the old witch got Lebedev to throw his billions around and have it suppressed?"

"No!" Doan said. "I want to read it!"

"Although," she said thoughtfully, "that might not have been the only thing in it he hated."

"Oh?"

"Well, there was a whole lot in there about his financial relationship with Herbert Kildare," she added.

Doan blinked. "Kildare?"

"Oh, yeah," she said casually, eating another cookie. "You know he got married to please the money men, right? Well, Kildare was one of those money men. Though Reid didn't know it at the time. Kildare used front men to invest in Reid's operation and only later did Randall find out he was in Kildare's pocket. And as you might imagine, Randall's a control queen, and his new master was not about to let any subsidiary entity have control of its own destiny. So Randall's been *very* unhappy these last couple of years with the constant interference from New Zealand."

Lights started going off in Doan's head. "I didn't know that."

"Not many people know it outside Randall's headquarters—it's not something he'd want to be public knowledge." She smiled at Doan. "But I understand you have some friends who work for Andrew Weatherall, a man whom I will tell you in confidence Henry and I admire very much. We would hate to see him go to jail if he wasn't the killer."

Doan swallowed. This was no time to kill the goose who laid the golden egg, but he had to ask one more question. "Do you think Randall Reid is capable of murder?"

Lisa Crane Boston had obviously already spent some time thinking about this. "I think Randall Reid is capable of deception and dissimulation on a massive scale. Think about it—here's a gay man who's given up any chance of having a loving relationship with another man . . . hell, who can't even have sex with anybody but hustlers because he can't be seen in a gay bar. I mean, God knows Todd Oldham and Kevyn Aucoin and Isaac Mizrahi and"—she smiled—"Jacob Mannheim have been out of the closet all their lives and made plenty of money, but that wasn't good enough for Randall. He wanted into Upper East Side society, he wanted access to mainstream America, he wanted to rule over an international empire. Think of everything he gave up for that power, think of the elegant world he wanted to live in, only to find that he had to take orders from a man who publishes titty papers! A man whose very name means vulgarity! Well, believe me, if you were Randall Reid, that humiliation would eat at you every day.''

She put her napkin down and looked past them with a smile. ''Hello, dear.''

Jacob and Doan turned around to see Henry M. Boston, Jr., in the doorway, smiling adoringly at his wife. ''Those cookies are going to catch up with you someday,'' said The Sexiest Man Alive.

''We'll find a way to burn them off,'' she responded, grinning at him. ''Hank, this is Jacob Mannheim, my new designer in residence.''

''Pleased to meet you,'' he said, shaking Jacob's hand; Jacob responded only with a small whimper.

''And this is Doan McCandler.''

Hank took Doan's hand and shook it with a wink. ''How *were* those cucumber sandwiches?''

Doan laughed and looked at Mrs. Boston. ''They tasted terrible, actually, but as time goes by I'm finding myself happier every day that I ate them.''

Mrs. Boston whispered to Doan as they left, ''Rhianna is the weak link. She's got *her* secrets, too. Get to her and you get to the whole story—even the parts I don't know.''

Then they were gone, Hank Boston trailing some rare form of pheromone behind him that left every straight woman and gay man (in short, the entire staff of Jacob's studio) clutching for some steady object for support.

''She is something else,'' Jacob marveled.

''More than I imagined,'' Doan said, his mind already racing over other territories. ''Doll, I need the afternoon off, okay? I've got to see some people.''

Tim's stint at KNN was not really so bad; he'd decided to look at it as an assignment in itself, a research project he should approach with a reporter's objectivity. The news network's coverage certainly skewed to the right, giving more sound bite time to, say, Brent Bozell or Ralph Reid than to . . . well, Tim had to think hard to come up with some liberal who was as high-profile as these conservatives, and was coming up short. No wonder we're on the ropes, he thought grimly. But the anchorpeople and top reporters had been recruited from the "liberal" news networks, where they'd learned the basics of journalism, and they still, as a general rule, applied them fairly. He reflected that most of these reporters had probably been about as liberal as anybody else in college, but that, over time, their grossly inflated salaries had the effect money usually had on people—it had made them more conservative as they had become the people with something to lose to "big government" rather than the young, idealistic, and of course poor reporters they'd started out as.

The entertainment reporters he'd been hired to organize into a viable "soft content" unit were young, arrogant, overpaid, and oblivious to the politics of the other side of the network. They were far more concerned with making sure they were wearing the grooviest glasses (which, it seemed to Tim, were inevitably also the ugliest), going to the right clubs, up-to-the-minute on the names and styles, both musical and sartorial, of the right bands . . . Tim thought of Cory Kissell at *Pendennis*, the venal character they'd met in their last adventure, a gay man who had no qualms about covering up the secret lives of closeted gay movie stars. These kids, it depressed him to realize, were like a little army of Corys, never thinking of themselves as "selling out" by making a good living regurgitating studio PR pabulum because to them, selling out was not the thing to be avoided but the goal.

But he knew KNN was no place to start changing the world. He kept a low profile, did his job, and kept his eyes open. Tonight he was staying late because *Nightfiring Crossline*, KNN's late-evening debate show, was to feature what could only be an altercation between Mark "the Commander" Bowers and Thom Wont on the subject of "homosexuality in pro sports." The moderator was the popular old warhorse Kenneth Laramie, who over a thirty-year career as a host of such shows had survived three networks, four heart attacks, and five marriages. He was a picture in contrasts—he was a noted supporter of Amnesty International but was a good friend of Henry Kissinger; he would have a movie star on and kiss his ass unremittingly for the hour, but the next night he would ruthlessly grill a politician until he'd torn him a new cavity. Political views had not lured him to KNN but rather the promise of a paycheck greater than any other news organization could offer—in short, enough to pay all his alimony and still live comfortably.

Tim had a word with Bowers to try and put him at ease before the show. Everyone was saying hello to Wont, a regular on the network's Sunday talking heads show, and of course Andrew Weatherall, the person best suited to give aid and comfort to Mark, was hardly able to set foot in the studios of KNN.

"You going to be okay?" Tim asked.

Bowers nodded. "Andrew talked me through some points to use in my defense, told me to treat Wont like he's a pitcher and I'm a batter." He smiled wryly. "And if he hits me with a ball, don't charge the mound."

Tim looked over at Wont, a man he despised. Perpetually apoplectic about the inability of the underclass to pull themselves up "by their bootstraps," he had been born into a comfy middle-class family and gone to Yale, and knew absolutely nothing about either the financial or emotional hardships of poverty. Constantly denouncing Americans for their sybaritic appetites for drugs and sex, Wont had probably never felt a spark of genuine overpowering lust for anything in his life save a baseball card or a bottle of wine for his impressive collection. He had a long, narrow face with pinched little eyes and iron-gray hair parted razor-sharp along the side and starched down so ruthlessly that not a strand flew loose. To Tim's mind, *anal retentive* was a phrase coined for Thom Wont.

And tonight Wont would be letting fly on his favorite subjects, baseball and homosexuality. He and Mark were seated on a raised platform on either side of Kenneth Laramie in black swivel chairs against a black background, with a tiny black table in front of them that could accommodate no more than a few glasses of water and a copy of a guest's latest book. Tim had to wonder about the advisability of putting the short skinny Wont within lunging distance of the six-foot-three, 240-pound Bowers.

"Good evening, I'm Kenneth Laramie. Tonight's subject: homosexuality and professional sports—can they co-exist? My guests are Thom Wont, columnist for the *New York Beast* and author of such books as *Rhapsody on a Theme by DiMaggio* and *Visigoths in the Lincoln Bedroom*, and Mark Bowers, pitcher for the Windy City Wizards and the gay lover of accused murderer Andrew Weatherall."

Tim rolled his eyes. This was going to be some night. He watched Mark shake his head in disgust on the monitor as Laramie set him up and was glad to see that the look had gone out over the live feed.

"Thom, you've been an outspoken critic of homosexuality, tell us what makes it even worse when it occurs in professional sports."

"Well, first of all, it's illegal. Or more to the point, sodomy is illegal."

"In fewer and fewer states every day," Mark pointed out.

Wont pretended he hadn't been interrupted. "If we are to throw a baseball player of the caliber of Pete Rose out of the game for gambling, well, how can we explain to our children that we are allowing a player to stay in the game who has done something our civilization considers ten times worse?"

"It's ten times worse that I do something in my private life that makes you squirm than if I were to bet on professional sports and raise the specter that I was throwing games?"

"Moreover, players of the great American pastime of baseball are not movie stars," Wont said scornfully. "Part of their job is to set a moral example for our youth, and homosexuality is not an example we wish our youth to follow."

"Your youth are born gay or straight," Bowers said impatiently. "The only thing seeing a gay ball player is going to do is make a gay kid a little less likely to kill himself from the stress of living in the world you run."

"If a child is born with criminal propensities it is not for us to encourage them; it is for us to lead him in another direction. As Justice Scalia has pointed out so ably, Western civilization has viewed homosexuality as immoral behavior which threatens the family and the society, and that legislation against it prevents a piecemeal deterioration of the sexual morality favored by a majority—''

''Western civilization was built by the Greeks and Romans, who didn't give a damn who you slept with.''

''*Christian* civilization,'' Wont amended, ''is under attack from the homosexual agenda, which seeks to destroy the family—''

''How does my happiness threaten your family? Can you answer that?''

''Because if we open the door to sexual liberality, we may as well give rights to polygamists as to homosexuals, and watch the traditional family fly out the window.''

''Are you telling me that if polygamy and homosexuality were legal, nobody would want a monogamous relationship anymore? Are you telling me that the only reason people are in monogamous heterosexual relationships is because it's illegal to do otherwise?''

''No, of course not. . . .''

''Then *why does homosexuality threaten 'the family'?*'' Bowers pressed. ''And why do you say '*the* family'—is there only one allowable kind of family? What about single people who adopt, what about grandparents who take on foster children—do they threaten *the* family? And why is it we never hear about the black 'agenda,' or the Asian 'agenda,' but when gay people are after rights it's got to be described some kind of conspiracy dreamed up by some secret nameless cabal?''

Wont was clearly uncomfortable, not only with having been boxed into a corner but from having been put there by, well, a baseball player. Wont was used to interacting with ball players, but of the, well, traditional variety— the foot-scuffin', 'tweren't nothin', it-was-a-team-effort modesty the game—or, more to the point, the game's chroniclers—demanded of them; Bowers's quick and confrontational ways were putting him off his own game.

''Our religious and moral institutions are built around the discouragement of homosexuality,'' he pressed on, ''and natural law itself tells us homosexuality is unnatural. Dis-

couraging or punishing homosexual behavior is a legitimate
and traditional social goal.''

''Your religious institutions were used against black people in the South to prove they deserved to be slaves. Preach-
ers used to say black skin was the 'mark of Cain' and that
black people were therefore sinful beings deserving of punishment. And 'natural law,' whatever that really is, used to
say that black people's skulls were smaller and so they were
dumber and so it was okay to use them like mules. Face it,
your kind of politics needs a scapegoat to go on, and gay
people are the last scapegoat left.''

''I am sure there are many black people out there in-
censed to hear you compare their trials and struggles with
yours.''

''I'm not comparing my trials and struggles with theirs,
I'm comparing the methods you use to get people to fear
and hate us with the methods you used to use to get people
to fear and hate *them*. And they're the same methods!''

''There is a good deal of difference between racial bigotry and moral opposition to sin!'' Wont said, losing his
cool at last.

''You could care less about sin,'' Bowers said, surprised
to find himself the cool one. ''You just need someone to
hate, you need to whip up voters into fearing and hating
somebody in order to motivate them to vote your side, and
gay people are an easy target—we don't have kids, so we
have more money to spend on ourselves, so you can make
them jealous of that. We have lots and lots of sex, and you
know most straight married suburbanites' sex lives dry up
and blow away by the time they're in their midthirties, so
there's some more jealousy you can prey on. You've
thrown us out of the churches, so we don't have to worry
about hell and guilt every time we have fun, and that makes
you even madder because that's even less control you have
over us. Finally, nature has ordained that we'll always be
a minority, so we'll always be the easiest target in the
world.''

''You sleep with a murderer!'' Wont exploded, pointing
a prophet's finger at Bowers. ''Your words are his words,
and his words are the devil's own!''

''Oh, brother,'' Bowers drawled as Wont leapt out of his

chair and attacked him. Pandemonium ensued but Bowers kept his cool, secure in his victory. In front of KNN's fledgling viewer pool, but in a scene to be rebroadcast on the other networks ad nauseam the next day, Bowers simply reached out, picked Wont up, threw him over one massive shoulder like a sack of potatoes, and carried him off the stage, dumping him on a couch in the green room and making for the stairs.

Tim caught up with him quickly. "How the hell do I get out of here?" Bowers asked him.

"This way. You did good, my man."

Bowers grinned. "I wish I'd been there to see the look on Andrew's face when I did that."

Out on the street, Bowers and Tim had a good laugh rehashing the interview. "He was right, you know," Bowers admitted. "Not about the devil part, but about me being there as Andrew's doppelgänger. He had the research department look up all Wont's proclamations about homosexuality, and we came up with point-for-point answers. I need a beer," Bowers said, unselfconsciously adjusting his package and suddenly looking to Tim like any other ball player.

"Beer would be good right now," Tim agreed, and they found a dark hotel bar where they could drink in peace. "I wish things hadn't gone like that, though," Tim said at the table. "I wanted to hear your plans for the future."

"You mean in ball?" He sighed. "I don't know. Kildare's son is a ball fan, and he's no fan of mine because of Andrew and all, but he feels bad about my being used that way to get at Andrew," he said, referring to his notorious 140-pitch night. "So the Wizards are going to let me out of my contract. I don't know if I want to sign with another team or go into broadcasting or try coaching at some college, or what. I don't even know if anybody would have me. I think everything's just kind of up in the air until Andrew's cleared of the murder charges." He sighed. "I wish I'd been with Andrew that night, though I don't know how much of an alibi I'd've been."

"Where were you?"

"Across town, at my place, asleep. Alone. I'd gone to the gym around eight that night and then come home, watched some ESPN, and then I went to bed.'' He looked at Tim. ''Am I a suspect or something?''

Tim laughed. ''Well, not on *my* list.'' He thought of what Luke would make of it; he would have to tell his friend, even though he knew the ex-detective would feel bound to check out Bowers's alibi if only for his own peace of mind. ''I don't see you as the murdering kind.''

Bowers shook his head. ''I'm not. I really had no idea what Kildare was doing to Andrew. I mean, I figured out pretty fast that night on the mound that I was being used, but I didn't know about the stolen digital radio idea, and I didn't know what happened at that magazine you ran, what's it called? *Groovy Slacker*?''

''*Edgy Hipster*,'' Tim supplied, laughing. ''I think it's dead, may it rest in peace. You can't put a magazine on hiatus like that and not lose your advertisers.''

''Bummer. So you don't know what *you're* going to do next, either, do you?'' Bowers asked with a twinkle in his eye. ''I mean, I know you're undercover at KNN, and that's not exactly your kind of place, is it?''

''Not exactly. I guess I'm in the same boat you're in— waiting for Andrew to get off the hook.''

''There are a lot of people who've hitched themselves to Andrew's star.''

Tim sighed. ''That's the problem. All the more people who might do something irrational to make sure that star doesn't flame out.''

If there was any recent event that angered Thom Wont and his ilk at the *Beast* more than Mark Bowers's continued participation in major league baseball, it was the fact that the Weatherall Fund had not dried up and blown away with the revelation that Andrew Weatherall may have murdered his fiercest rival. ''I know he mighta killed the guy,'' one small investor told CNN outside a Schwab storefront, ''but he's made me rich, and unless he goes to jail, he's going to make me richer.''

There had been a shaky moment there, when the fund had wavered after the police had named Andrew as the prime suspect and a run on the proverbial bank had been in the offing, but Andrew had used his acumen to calm the waters. "Your money is not invested in me. I have invested it for you in companies which will continue to grow and thrive even were I to be found guilty and get the chair. The only person who is going to be ruined in all of this is me, because lawyers have figured out a mathematical law that enables them to bill their clients in a life-or-death trial like this for the exact amount of their net worth." Gallows humor it may well have been, but it reminded people where their money really was, and the fund rolled on. Weatherall may have killed someone, but he not only hadn't screwed them but was continuing to make them rich, and there it was.

Luke had finally managed to get some time alone with Andrew, which was no mean feat. He'd continued to come in to work to run the fund—"If Clinton could run the country with Ken Starr on his back," Andrew said, "I can manage to run my business with a few cops on mine." But the bulk of his time that was not taken up with the business was taken up with defense lawyers, even though he hadn't been officially charged with anything yet. "They'll charge me," he said darkly. "There are a lot of people eager to see me take a fall."

So Luke had five minutes with Andrew between appointments. "Have you got any leads? Any other suspects?"

"Quite a few," Luke said. "That's the problem. Unfortunately, a couple of them may have had reason to murder Kildare as a favor to you."

"I see. And how about the others?"

"I don't want to point my finger at anyone just yet," Luke said.

Andrew frowned. "Luke, you are *my* head of security, and I am hoping that if I am officially accused of murder that you will be able to help me throw some light on who actually did it. Unless, that is, you think I did it."

"No, I don't *think* you did it, but I . . . I can't rule anyone out."

"Ah. Still a cop at heart, eh?"

"I'm hoping that my still being a cop at heart is going to be exactly what you need," Luke said, looking him in the eye.

Andrew blushed. "You're right. What can I do to help you?"

"I would like to rule you out, but I have a nagging question. That day at Comdex, you said you had a secret weapon that would remove Kildare as a threat to you and your operations."

"Oh, that. Oh! You think I meant that I was hiring a hit man!" Andrew laughed. "No, nothing so dramatic. You see—"

He was cut off as Mrs. Keith opened the door, looking horrified. "Andrew . . ."

She was pushed out of the way by several dreary-looking men in trenchcoats whom Luke recognized as the detectives assigned to the case.

"Andrew Weatherall, I have a warrant for your arrest for the murder of Herbert Kildare." And with that, a uniformed officer moved to handcuff Andrew, who did not resist, but who only rolled his eyes and smiled knowingly.

"Is that really necessary?" Luke asked.

"Of course it is," Andrew said. "They've got orders from their bosses to *humiliate* me, you see. No doubt the press has been tipped off and is waiting outside to see me led away in the proverbial chains." The detectives looked away, embarrassed at the truth of what Andrew said. "I told you I had enemies, Luke. This is how they're going to get back at me."

"We'll have you bailed out in no time," Mrs. Keith said, wiping a tear.

"If they grant bail," Weatherall said airily. "Call Mark on his cell, would you?" he asked Mrs. Keith. "I don't want him learning this from the news." He turned to the detectives. "I assume your orders were to call KNN and give them the exclusive?"

"Come on, let's go," the cop said, his face a mask now.

As they hustled him down the hall, he turned back to Luke. "The secret weapon, Luke—ask Kevin what the secret weapon was. Tell him I said it was all right—give him the code word, it's 'octopus.' He'll tell you." And with that, Weatherall was out the door into the waiting arms of, yes, KNN.

Mrs. Keith started sobbing. "I can't believe this! I can't believe it."

"It's okay," Luke said, letting her cry on his shoulder. "We're going to find the real killer. I promise you that."

seven

~~~~~~~

$\mathcal{B}$inky wondered how it was she kept managing to find undercover jobs that actually required her to work. True, on her last undercover job back in Hollywood the work hadn't been so hard, consisting as it had of reading magazines, calling phony reviewers for phony rave quotes, and ringing up Harrison Ford to check his schedule. All the same, it had been *work*, no matter how enjoyable, and on this job, the work was anything but glamorous. Powers had her doing logistics: coordinating convention space around the country for his seminars, booking blocks of hotel rooms for himself and the staff, making sure the sound and video equipment arrived safely at each destination—too boring for words, she thought morosely.

Now she was even working late, or, more to the point, sitting around waiting for the phone to ring to hear whether some hysterical caterer in Chicago was going to be able to fulfill his contract. She filled the time by filing her nails and staring out the window at the New York skyline. She wished with all her heart that she could just be back at Weatherall and Associates, doing what she did best—spending money. Oh, sure, she was spending money here, in the abstract, but it wasn't the same at all. The money she'd been shoveling out the door at Weatherall's had been *fun;* nothing in her previous life had been as exciting and rewarding as going one night to a theater she'd basically funded for the next five years, where they'd treated her like a queen (and put on a performance that made her glad she'd chosen them). She couldn't wait for this mystery to get resolved so she could go back to being Lady Bountiful again. . . .

"Woolgathering?" a voice pulled her back to the present. She turned to find Harlan Mayes standing in her doorway. Harlan was one of the rationalization hotline workers, a pleasantly cynical old duffer who had previously worked in commercial real estate and public relations, and so was used to lying to people for a living. They'd struck up a casual friendship after she'd heard him finishing up a call one day—his desk was near the coffee station (no coffee room, as Powers liked to keep his minions in sight at all times; a coffee room was an excuse to slack off) and he'd just finished reassuring a plagiarist that there was nothing new under the sun. "Which is why they oughta send you to the dark side of the moon," he'd said out loud after hanging up, and Binky had been unable to resist laughing— it was the first time she'd heard someone here who hadn't convinced himself that he was doing a "public service," who hadn't *rationalized* his role in this place. They'd made light coffee chatter ever since.

"Got you on the dead shift, huh?" Binky asked. There was hardly a soul manning the phones and none of them were ringing; it was evening and the ruthless people of the world were out carousing and enjoying their ill-gotten gains—later on at night, when they couldn't sleep from guilt, the phones would be ringing off the hook.

"And what's your excuse?"

"Waiting for this idiot to call me and tell me he can't provide a bunch of rubber chicken for a seminar in Chicago next week."

Harlan chuckled. "Yeah, lucky you. If Herbert Kildare hadn't been killed, you wouldn't have to do this job anymore."

"What do you mean?"

Harlan frowned. "You didn't know? I thought you were plugged into the grapevine pretty well."

"I guess not. What does Kildare have to do with logistics?"

Harlan looked around, then decided to take a risk. He came in and closed the door behind him, his eyes glittering with juicy gossip. "We'd've pretty much all been out of a job in a few months, if Kildare hadn't bought it."

"He was going to shut the operation down?"

"No . . . well, yes and no. He was going to digitize it. The seminars were going to be put on CD-ROM; the rationalizations hotline was going to be turned into a subscription Web site. There was only going to be a skeleton crew of phone bank personnel to handle the people who still needed a soothing voice to reassure them, if the answers they got from the Web site didn't satisfy them."

"So Powers wasn't going to be doing any more seminars?"

"Nope. Too expensive, as I'm sure you're learning, to send him and his light show and his flash cards and his sound system around the country. Kildare wanted to box the whole thing up as software and sell it for the same price. He was obsessed with eliminating labor costs, you know. The fewer workers he had, the less trouble he had, that was his philosophy."

Binky thought about the infamous episode where Kildare had crushed the newspaper printers' unions. "I know. So where would that have left Will Powers?"

"Rich, and out of a job."

"And out of the spotlight," she thought out loud. "No human contact with the CEOs and power brokers of America. He'd just be an image on a computer screen . . . he would hate that."

"You know it. Will's in it for the power, pardon the play on the name, but it's true."

"Yeah . . . yeah. And he would have been nowhere without Kildare."

"Or Randall Reid."

"What?!"

"Oh, yeah. Kildare gave him the money to go national, but he got the seed capital to start the whole thing back when he was in his late teens, early twenties. Didn't you know he'd been a Randall Reid model?''

"No!"

Harlan nodded. "And you know what it took to be a Randall Reid model, don't you?''

"A six-pack, amazing cheekbones, patrician lips . . .''

"And the willingness to sleep with Randall.''

"How do you know all this?''

Harlan smiled. "My partner is a fashion photographer.'' It hadn't even occurred to Binky that Harlan was gay; then again, he'd probably made it in his various careers by keeping it secret.

"Will Powers and Randall Reid . . .'' she said thoughtfully. "Do you think they still . . .''

"Oh, I doubt it. That was back in the mideighties, before Randall got married and had to lay off the boys to keep his image clean. Besides, Will's in his midthirties—a little too old for Randall now!'' Harlan laughed.

She leaned forward. "Harlan, are you *sure* about this? I mean, about Kildare.''

He raised an eyebrow. "Well, yes, I'm absolutely positive. It's not gossip, I got it from someone I know upstairs in Kildare's office. Why do you need me to be so sure?''

Binky got up and grabbed her purse. "Because it's a matter of life and death.''

After Weatherall was taken to the station for booking and Luke had ensured that the lawyers would be there before Weatherall was, he headed directly down to Kevin's basement kingdom. But before he had an opportunity to ask Kevin about the mysterious "secret weapon,'' Kevin jumped out of his chair.

"You were right,'' he said excitedly. "Someone pushed their way through there, disconnected a whole bunch of stuff. We didn't know it because what they'd disconnected were links to Binky's computer and phone, and of course since the murder she hasn't been in there to use them. But someone *definitely* got into her office through the floor!''

Luke nodded, excited to be getting somewhere. "Excellent work. Now the question is, how did they get into the floors? I mean, where did they get into the floor where the cameras wouldn't have recorded them?''

Kevin thought about that. ''Have we reviewed the tapes?''

''No,'' Luke said. ''The cops said they didn't see anybody on the tapes going into Binky's...'' Suddenly it dawned on him. ''They didn't see anybody going through *that hallway* on the way to Binky's office! And that was all they were looking at! You kept copies of all the tapes, didn't you?''

''Of course,'' Kevin said, hurt at the suggestion that he would have done otherwise.

''Good. We're going to have to scan them all, starting around the estimated time of death and working backward. I want to start with the office beneath Binky's. Whose office is that?''

Kevin pulled up a chart on his terminal. ''It's vacant.''

''But it's got cameras?''

''Absolutely.''

''Let's get the tape.''

''It'll take me a while to dig it up,'' Kevin said, moving to the closet.

''It may not do us any good, if it turns out they came through the window, but we have to check it out. I need to get up on the roof and see what I can find up there,'' he reminded himself. ''And, um, before you do that...''

''Yeah?''

''I need to ask you about something else. Andrew authorized me to ask you about the 'secret weapon.' He said to tell you the code word was 'octopus.' ''

Kevin froze and turned around, pale as death. ''Oh, shit. You aren't going to like this.''

''Why not?''

''You're going to be mad at me, and probably madder at Andrew. But it was my idea! I told him it could be done without anyone being the wiser!''

''Kevin...'' Luke said warningly. ''Just tell me.''

Kevin sighed. ''We were going to hack into Herbert Kildare's personal computer. I may have been able to do it from outside, but it would have been best if I'd been able to get into his office and do it right there. That would have been the only way not to set off any alarms in the system.''

''Andrew approved this?''

''No. But he didn't tell me to forget about it. He told me to research it, plan it, double-check it—make sure that if we did do it, it would work perfectly. But not to do it unless . . .''

''Unless something happened that left him no choice,'' Luke finished. ''After I told him about how the *Beast* had destroyed *Edgy Hipster*, Andrew said he had a secret weapon. But he didn't tell you to go ahead with it.''

''He didn't have time, probably. Or he reconsidered. Or then again, maybe Kildare got murdered before he could call me and give me the go-ahead.''

''That's right.'' Luke nodded. ''It was that same night that Kildare was found dead.'' He bit his lip and cogitated for a bit.

''So . . .'' Kevin said hesitantly.

''So,'' Luke said decisively. ''I don't think Andrew Weatherall murdered Herbert Kildare.''

Kevin smiled. ''Well, maybe somewhere inside Herbert Kildare's computer is the answer to who *did* kill him.'' He waited for Luke to reprimand him, but the reprimand didn't come.

Luke thought about that for a while. If the cops were really under orders from some higher powers to nail Andrew, they weren't going to exert themselves in the direction of any other suspects.

''I'm wondering something,'' Luke said.

''Yeah?''

''Whoever did Kildare in Binky's office had to know that there were no cameras in there. Now, you knew that, I knew that, and Binky knew that. I didn't tell anyone; did you?''

''Hell, no.''

''Then who did Binky tell? Because whoever she told . . .''

''Is the key to all this,'' Kevin finished.

''I need a phone.''

As Binky was downstairs learning interesting new information about Will Powers's past and narrowly averted future, Tim was just leaving the same building with Peter Cures for a drink at the older man's club.

For reasons he couldn't fathom, Cures had taken a liking to him. It was curious not just because he was a gay man and a former employee of Andrew Weatherall and, with such a résumé already in place, he had made no bones about being far more liberal than just about anyone else at KNN, but also because Cures was notoriously vicious to his subordinates. "You're all idiots," was Cures's favorite way of ending a meeting, with "You're all assholes" coming in second. While Kildare was alive, the man's paranoia had known no bounds. He'd suspected just about everyone (especially anyone on the business side of the network) of being a spy planted to report on him directly to Kildare.

Kildare's death seemed to have mellowed him; free from his master's short leash, the pit bull had become more of a playful puppy, though nobody had yet tested the limits of his newfound good cheer. Except Tim, that is, who had accepted his surprising invitation and was now sitting in an overstuffed leather armchair, drinking better scotch than he'd ever have bought for himself, as Cures got more verbose with every passing sip of his own drink.

"Now take that episode of *Nightfiring Crossline* the other night. That was damn good TV, you know? Damn good TV. Pasty little Thom lunging for big old Mark Bowers," he said and laughed. "Damn it all if Thom didn't look like he was the sissy on that stage—no offense," he said automatically, not waiting for Tim to exonerate him. "And the coverage!" he enthused. "We even let CNN air it, even though you know how well Herbert got on with Ted Turner, because we knew they'd show it about a thousand times, you know how they recycle stuff on there. Because it would say 'Courtesy KNN' in the corner, and all the people who don't get KNN would suddenly feel like they were missing something and call their local cable operator—'Gimme KNN!' Damn good TV, damn good publicity."

Tim nodded. "It was on *The McLaughlin Group*, too. I didn't know John McLaughlin had it out for Wont."

"Oh, some old feud, who knows." Cures waved it away.

"Better than Mike Tyson biting that other guy's ear off, if you ask me."

"But what did you think about what they had to say?" Tim asked.

"Say? Oh, you mean Thom's old saws about moral principle and legitimate and traditional social goals? Well, he's just prejudiced, that's all! He's just smart enough to cloak his prejudices in a bunch of high-sounding hooey. You know—if it sounds reasonable and considered, then it must not be knee-jerk bigotry. That Bowers made mincemeat out of him! Damn fine ball player, too. Be a shame if he stopped playing."

"So you don't buy Wont's argument about him setting a poor moral example for youth, and so forth?"

"Listen, the man's not an elected official, he's a goddamn ball player! Let him play ball!"

"I'm surprised to hear you say that, to be honest."

"Oh, why's that?"

"Well," Tim said hesitantly. He didn't want to antagonize the man, not yet anyway, but with time running short for Andrew this may well be his only chance to really get behind the man's facade. "It's just that you made some pretty . . . incendiary commercials when you were a political consultant. I mean, they seem like the work of someone who was really outraged that a pro-abortion Congressman might keep his seat. . . ."

"Oh, those. You know what those were? *Good TV.* Damn good TV, if I say so myself. People talked about them, didn't they? Why do you think Kildare really gave me the job? Sure, because at heart I'm a pretty conservative guy, but I'm a conservative like Kildare was a conservative. We want to protect the interests of business; untrammeled capitalism is our game. You want to suck cock? Go ahead! Have an abortion? None of my business! But the fact is, the majority of people who we can count on—I'm speaking as a political consultant now—the majority of people we could count on to vote for us on the business issues had to be pandered to on the social issues. If we wanted them to help us get rid of OSHA and keep the FDA from regulating tobacco and restrain the Department of Labor's activity to compiling statistics, well, we had to give them some red meat! They wanted us to be tough on abortion and queers and immigrants, so there you have it. It was a trade-off. Frankly, I could care less. Same with TV—if the hicks are where the ratings are, well, let's give them Thom Wont and let them think their prejudices are really just 'moral positions.' ''

"Kildare didn't seem to think so that day at the Will Powers seminar. He seemed to think you were a little 'red meat' yourself."

Cures smiled. "Maybe it was in my best interest to let Herbert Kildare think I was a little more tapped into that viewer base than I really am. I mean, I know what they want, but I'm not one of them. Just because I feed the hogs doesn't mean I'm going to roll around in the mud with 'em!'' he laughed.

Tim nodded. "So Kildare's death doesn't really change anything for you."

"Nah. The young Mr. Kildare, who's taking over, he wants ratings, same as his father. If the sitting president were a Republican and he was in hot water with some bimbo, hell yes, I'd run the story if we got the scoop! I don't give a shit! But I'll be honest, it's a hell of a lot more fun to roast a Democratic president over the coals than a Republican. Not that our current president isn't practically a Republican himself!''

Tim laughed along with him. So Peter Cures wasn't a demagogue after all, he thought. If he'd had any reason to bump off Kildare it could only be for the way his boss had treated him—God knows he was a jollier soul now without Kildare's acid tongue lashing him; yes, he seemed almost *happy* that Kildare was dead, but it was happy like a lottery winner's happy, an unexpected windfall rather than a bank robber's anxious happiness, laced with the fear of getting caught. It dismayed him a bit—it meant that his role in the mystery was over, and that meant he was face-to-face with the vacuum. What the hell would he do now?

His cell phone rang; he excused himself and Cures waved him off, used to such interruptions. "Hello?"

"It's Binky."

"Hey, what's up?"

"Can you get over to our place ASAP?"

"Sure, what's going on?"

"We all need to talk. There have been some . . . developments. Luke would just like to have us all together for a confab."

"I'm on my way."

That evening's gathering was the first time Doan, Binky, Luke, and Tim had all been together since the baseball game at Andrew's house. "We never see each other!" Doan complained.

"We're New Yorkers now," Tim explained. "We call each other and say we'll do lunch. Swearing we'll see each other soon takes the place of actually seeing each other." He turned to Binky. "So, what *does* bring us all together?"

Luke began. "If we're going to be detecting, we all need to figure out who knows what. I've got some information to share, and so does Binky. First of all, we've found out how the killer got Kildare into Binky's office without getting on tape." He quickly explained what Kevin had found while crawling through the floor. "I did some investigating up on the roof and found that the HVAC system had been tampered with. Which leads me to believe that Kildare and his murderer came down through the vents, then through the floor to Binky's office."

"Any fingerprints?" Doan asked.

"Not a one. Our killer was smooth."

"How about signs of a struggle?" Tim asked. "Surely he didn't get Kildare down there that willingly."

"A blow to the head before the shot would have knocked him out and made him more . . . malleable."

"You'd have to be pretty strong to hoist a body around like that," Binky thought out loud, wondering if, under his perpetual suit, Will Powers still had the kind of body once requisite on Randall Reid models, back before the days of heroin chic.

"Don't forget we can't rule out a contract killer," Luke added. "The trigger man doesn't have to be the same person we're looking for. The important thing right now is, if Kevin and Binky and I were the only ones inside who knew there was no camera in Binky's office, who else could have known?"

"I racked my brains," Binky said, "and the only people who I told about the camera being taken out were Doan and Chloe, my assistant."

"And where is Chloe now?" Doan asked suspiciously.

"She took a couple days off. I called her at home but I didn't get her; I think she's out of town. Really, I don't think she's involved. I don't!" she said, looking at the doubtful faces around her. "Remember how you all thought Sam Braverman was involved in the Jeff Breeze murder and it turns out he was . . . well, he kind of was, but . . ." she trailed off sheepishly. "I'll keep trying to get hold of her. If nothing else, Luke can talk to her on Monday morning. Anyway," she said defensively, "I have some interesting news, too."

She quickly filled them in on Harlan's news about Kildare's plan to downsize "You Can Rationalize Anything" to download size. "And as far as Will Powers being a former Randall Reid model, I don't know if that means anything."

"Except that New York is a small town just like San Francisco," Doan said.

"It could," Tim said thoughtfully. "They were both under Kildare's thumb, and both had reason to resent it, and they knew each other—in the biblical sense, too, if you believe Binky's source. It's worth checking out."

"That's my department," Doan piped up. He told them about his surprising conversation with Lisa Boston and her injunction to him to get to Rhianna. "If Randall is involved, wouldn't the person who lives with him be the first to know?"

"I thought the wife was the last to know." Tim grinned.

"At any rate," Doan continued, glaring at Tim, "I have an appointment with Mrs. Reid. Well, she doesn't know that, but she will. Lisa Boston had a suspicion she wouldn't share, because she wasn't sure about it, I think, but she knew that Rhianna would know for sure. Whatever it was."

"Umm . . . there's one more thing," Luke said, unsure if he wanted to raise it. "Andrew and Kevin had a plan to . . . well, break into Herbert Kildare's computer and see what they could find."

"Excellent idea!" Doan said. "When do we do that?"

"Well, I don't know that it's such a good idea. . . ."

Binky smiled at Luke. "Darling, if you didn't think it was a good idea, you wouldn't have told us about it. Don't be shy, now, give us the details."

Luke laughed. "You caught me. Guess I'm not a cop anymore, huh?"

"No," Tim said, "you're a detective. A slightly different set of rules to play by."

"Yeah. Anyway, it could lead us to some information on our suspects—and, who knows, could give us suspects we didn't even have before. The only thing is, it has to be done from inside Kildare's office, and Kevin can't even get into the building without a pass."

"He's a genius," Binky said, "couldn't he make one?"

"Yeah, but they're magnetically coded, and to get a code that would work he'd have to hack into Kildare Worldwide's computers from *outside,* and that's just what we want to avoid."

"Whereas," Tim said, one step ahead, "Binky and I have passes to the building. . . ."

"Yeah," Binky protested, "but just to the building, that's not going to get us to Kildare's office."

"You get Kevin into the building and get him access to a Kildare Worldwide terminal, and he can get you the rest of the way."

"That sounds like a pretty desperate measure," Binky said thoughtfully. "Are we that desperate?"

"Well, yes. You see, Andrew's trial starts in a week."

"What!" the others gasped in unison. "I thought trials got delayed for months before they even picked a jury!" Doan protested.

"That's usually the defense tactic," Luke agreed, "but getting this trial rolling is Andrew's tactic. Don't ask me to explain it all, but I know some of it has to do with getting it all over with as soon as possible for the sake of the stability of the Weatherall Fund. Also, he thinks the longer the prosecution has to dig up his past dealings with Kildare, the more he's going to be shown to have motive."

"And the prosecution can't move it back?"

Luke smiled. "Andrew has enemies, but he has friends, too. 'The right to a speedy trial,' is what his lawyers are invoking, and that's what he's going to get.''

"So our time is limited," Tim said. "And that's why you're saying we should go ahead with this."

"I'm just telling you it's an option. It's a risk you and Binky will have to decide if you want to take. If it goes wrong, you could be arrested and charged with trespassing, or worse."

Binky looked at Luke. "You love me, right?"

"What? Of course I do," he said, taking her hand. "Why?"

"Then I'll do it. Because I can't see you recommending a course of action that you think will really get me in trouble."

"Well, I think Kevin knows what he's doing. And he's all ready to take the risk, even though getting caught would certainly mean jail for him. But I think he's got it pretty well figured out, yeah."

"And you believe now that Andrew is innocent, don't you?" Binky continued. "Because you wouldn't take this risk for someone you thought might be guilty."

Luke nodded. "I think Andrew is innocent, yes. But I also think he has a good chance of being convicted. He had motive and opportunity, and in a court of law that counts for a lot."

"I'm in," Binky said. She looked at Tim. "I can probably do it without you, but—"

"Well, actually," Luke cut in, "Kevin's plan would require both of you."

Tim looked at Doan. "Darling?"

"Listen," Doan said. "You and Luke and Binky are all the beneficiaries of Andrew Weatherall's continued freedom. And so is the rest of the free world, for that matter. Who am I to stand in the way of that? Besides, I've been in places I didn't belong in the name of a good cause," Doan said, winking at Binky, "so I'm hardly the one to tell you no."

Tim nodded. "I'm in, too."

Luke got up. "Okay. Tomorrow morning we'll go down to the office and see Kevin."

"I'll take a pass," Doan said. "I have an appointment at Bloomingdale's."

• • •

Doan had not been idle since the advent of Mrs. HMB Jr. and her interesting news—of course, around the studio she was "Lisa" now, though he'd had to restrain Jacob from tossing the Christian name around too frequently and sounding like a name-dropper. A number of calls had been made on a rather circuitous route to get the information he'd needed. His old friends in San Francisco who'd dropped out of the New York rat race were recruited to needle friends back in Manhattan who hadn't, and Jacob made a few calls himself, assured by Doan that it was for a good cause, and eventually Doan had discovered a way to get ahold of Rhianna Reid, if only for a few minutes' conversation.

And so it was that he found himself applying makeup for the very first time since a long-distant Halloween he'd rather forget. Doan was naturally feminine-looking, with his long hair, trim waist, and feline features; pretty much all he had to do to fool the unobservant eye was to toss on a dress to be taken for a woman. However, after his bruising experience at the Armani boutique, he'd felt it best to buy some insurance today in the form of some blush and a little lip gloss—nothing dramatic, just enough to remove the taint of suspicion that might otherwise befall him where he was going.

The lighting in Bloomingdale's is exquisite, as it is in most department stores. The point of this is partly to make the shopper see him- or herself in the most attractive light possible, but mostly to make the clothes look more alluring than they will ever look again, our world being for the most part not a place with flattering lighting. It was this same light that Doan was conscious of when he'd decided to brush up his looks a touch, and he was glad of it as he loitered in the ladies' underthingies department, where he'd been assured Mrs. Randall Reid would soon appear (Mr. Reid having given over his creative heart and soul to making underwear look good on boys, his line for women was not quite as popular, and Rhianna was forced like the rest of us to hit the bricks for the articles beneath the outfits Randall provided her gratis).

Of course, Rhianna didn't just saunter into the lingerie

department and start flicking through the racks; her Bloomie's personal shopper had already come in advance and staked out some likely purchases (one of Jacob's spies at Bloomie's had been the one to tip Doan off about Rhianna's schedule for that day). While the young matron was not required to show up down here with the masses to try on her flimsies, she had been well drilled by Randall that even the best personal shopper often misses finding that elusive perfect purchase (the holy grail for so many who had given up on sex), and it was best to at least make a pass over the racks oneself before settling on something.

Doan spotted Rhianna and her shopper; it wasn't difficult, as the salespeople had been notified of her arrival and were hastening to flutter around her at a discreet distance, not to interfere with the personal shopper in her duties but to simply "attend" in a vague, conspicuous-consumption sort of way, a way that let other consumers know that here was someone *important*. Of course, it being New York, the tourists gawked, not knowing her identity and suspecting her of being more famous than she was, while the New Yorkers, knowing perfectly well who she was, ignored her completely.

Doan didn't dawdle; he picked a few things at random and made for the fitting room before Rhianna, just in case it got sealed off like a floor of presidential hotel rooms after she had been ushered in. Once in a room, he took off his shoes, stood on the little chair, and peeked over the divider to see which room she'd end up in. When Rhianna took a room, Doan got down off his chair and moved quietly across the hall. He knocked on the door of her cubicle and she said impatiently, "Yes?"

"Can I speak with you?"

She was already down to her Wonderbra and panties when she flung open her door and scowled at Doan. "Who the hell are . . . ." Then her mouth opened just as it had that day at lunch. "You!"

"Shh," Doan said. "I have to ask you some questions about Randall and Will Powers."

Rhianna paled. Whatever intention she'd had of calling for help had left her at the mention of Will Powers.

"Oh, my god." She sat down—fell down would be more

like it—and her lip trembled. "Don't tell me you're going to blackmail us, too!" Despite all her years among the elite of New York City, there was still a faint hint of the South in her voice.

"No," Doan said, realizing he'd struck gold and having spent enough time in the detecting business to know better than to give away his hand. "Won't you come with me?"

"Yes . . . yes. Let me get dressed."

Doan held her up by the arm as they walked out of the dressing room. "Did everything fit all right?" the shopper asked automatically before noticing Rhianna's pale, shaky looks. "Mrs. Reid, are you unwell?"

"I'm just going to take her upstairs for some tea," Doan explained. Then he whispered confidentially into the shopper's ear. "And crackers, she collapsed—hasn't eaten in days." Having seen this syndrome in more than one of her clients, the shopper nodded wisely and let them pass.

Doan got her out of Bloomie's and down the street to a café where he medicated her with the formula that had been a cure-all for him for years: strong coffee and a rich pastry.

"Listen," Doan said, taking her shaking hand. "I'm here to help you. I'm not here to hurt Randall, I'm here to find out who murdered Herbert Kildare." This was risky; for all he knew Reid was being blackmailed precisely because Powers knew something about his involvement with the murder.

She nodded and took a bite of the pastry. Doan could see the immediate effects of the food as Rhianna calmed down. "Now," he said, "let's start at the beginning. Once upon a time, there was a young male model named Will Powers, who met a designer named Randall Reid."

Rhianna nodded. "That's right. After . . . after the threats began, when Randall told me everything, he showed me some of the pictures of Will when he was young—he was really beautiful back then."

Doan nodded; last night Tim had gone through the Imminent Publications archives and found some of the old ads. Will Powers today was blandly attractive in that anchor-banker way, but back then, with youth, makeup, good lighting, and Bruce Weber on his side, he'd been astonishing.

"I don't even like blonds that much," Doan had said, *"but
. . . those abs!"*

Tim nodded. *"And a basket even the experts from the
International Male catalog couldn't completely tuck."*

Doan looked harder. *"Oh. Oh! And presumably Randall
saw it before it was tucked for the camera."*

"Anyway," Rhianna continued, "Randall says they
were an item for a while. Maybe three months, that's about
how long they lasted back then, before he got sick of them,
or they got arrogant, or hooked on the coke he'd give
them." Doan raised an eyebrow. Rhianna Reid was nobody's fool after all, it seemed.

"He broke it off but it was ugly. Will said he'd go to
the papers and tell all about the coke and the boys and the
sex parties. This was in 1985, so that kind of behavior just
wasn't done anymore. And," she said with a twist of her
lip, "Randall hadn't made friends with Alex Lebedev yet,
so he didn't have an eight-hundred-pound gorilla in his corner to lean on the press and keep the story out of the papers.
So instead he set Will up with some business, I don't know
what it was, but it wasn't these seminars, those came later.
Late-night infomercials, though, Abcrunchers or imitation
Ginsu knives or the like."

She dug more enthusiastically into her eclair; Doan suspected that high-fat pastries weren't on the personal chef's
approved menu at the Reid residence. "Randall gave up on
everything after that—boys, drugs, everything. It just
wasn't worth it anymore. Then he married me," she said
matter-of-factly. "But a couple months ago Will called
Randall again. Gave him this line about how successful he
was and how he owed it all to Randall. He suggested a
drink for old times' sake, blah blah blah. And Randall," —
she laughed—"hadn't gotten *laid* in about a million years,
and he was curious, too, how Will turned out. So he met
him for a drink."

"And another, and another?" Doan asked.

"Well, I don't think it took that many. Will's got . . .
some kind of charisma. Some weird power over people."
Doan thought of how Binky had described him and nodded.
"And he turned it all full blast on Randall." She rolled her
eyes. " 'Oh, Randall, I've never forgotten you, I've never

gotten over you, you're still so handsome, my dick's still huge. . . . ' '' Doan blinked but didn't interrupt. ''So they started getting together again. He didn't tell me, of course; he didn't tell anyone.'' She laughed. ''And he'd been such a *nun* for so long that nobody even *suspected* he was out having sex!''

''But he told you about it, finally.''

''Yes. Because he said somebody else needed to know, and I was the only one he could trust.'' She narrowed her eyes and regarded Doan. ''Everyone thinks our relationship is just a show, but they're wrong. We don't have sex, but we're partners. We do a lot for each other, and we've spent a long time together. We got married because he needed a beard and I wanted . . .'' She shrugged. ''Daddy, I guess, to protect me and make me his princess. But we're close,'' she insisted. ''Even so, he hasn't told me everything. All I know . . . all I know is that things have gotten ugly. That Will is using Randall for something, something bad. He's got photos of them together this time, and he knows the tabloids would eat it up. Will told Randall he'd take the pictures to the *Beast*, and if they wouldn't print them, he'd take them to one of the supermarket weeklies—they've got no shame, they'd print anything!''

''But you don't have any idea what exactly Will is blackmailing Randall *for*?''

''No. It's not money, though. And Randall won't tell me everything. All he said is that if anything happens to him, I'm to call the police and tell them Will Powers is involved in his death. I told him he was being a drama queen but if you'd seen the look in his eyes . . .''

Doan shivered. Rhianna nodded. ''That's what I did, too.''

''Listen,'' Doan said. ''I work for Andrew Weatherall. Sort of. I mean, I work for Jacob Mannheim, but . . . well, anyway, it's a long story. Never mind. The point is, we think Will Powers may have something to do with Herbert Kildare's death. If Randall knows anything about it, and he doesn't come forward, and we find out the truth some other way . . .''

''Randall can't tell you anything! He can't risk exposure now—don't you see?''

Doan nodded. "I do see. But right now, Randall's only got two choices. One, be exposed as a gay man and face the music. Maybe he loses his invitations to the Upper East Side, maybe he loses some business. But the other alternative is being indicted as an accessory to murder," Doan finished dramatically.

Rhianna didn't blink. "You left out the third alternative. That he decides to come forward and, before he can, Will Powers kills *him*, too."

"In that case," Doan said, "isn't he *already* in danger?"

It was Rhianna's turn to shiver. "Yes, I guess so."

Doan took her hand again. "Talk to him. Andrew is a powerful man—even more powerful than Alex Lebedev. He can protect Randall. And you."

She nodded. "I'll talk to him. But I can't promise anything."

They got up and Doan hailed her a cab. As she was getting in, she turned back and said, "Thank you. I can't tell you how much I needed to tell *somebody*."

Doan smiled. "Just remind Randall that there are worse things in this world than being outed."

She nodded. "I know. And now, so does he."

eight

At the end of their meeting with Kevin, Tim and Binky were considerably more relaxed and confident about the mission to come. The young man had clearly done his research on the security systems of Kildare Worldwide's headquarters, research which, Luke guessed but did not ask, probably included recruiting some of his hacker friends to take dips into the system they were about to assault—dips that could not be traced to Kevin or Weatherall and Associates.

Around eight in the evening, Tim was first into the building, about half an hour before Binky and Kevin. "Too suspicious for the two former Weatherall employees to be seen entering the building together," Kevin had said. Then Binky had come in with Kevin in tow, disguised as a much younger boy. His short stature, along with his skate dude outfit and Thrasher baseball hat, made him look about fourteen, and Binky was able to smuggle him in as a nephew. A desultory search of Kevin's backpack (which held some CDs, a portable CD player, some gum, and some candy bars) and they were in.

The entertainment news offices of KNN were relatively deserted—relatively, as no twenty-four-hour news network's offices are ever totally empty. They'd had to come here, as prime time for the "You Can Rationalize Anything" phone lines was coming up and Binky's office would be swarming with red-tied wonder boys.

Kevin popped a stick of gum in his mouth, plugged the CD player into a port in the back of Tim's computer, and fired up the system. He clicked on the icon that would transform the PC into a terminal accessing the Kildare mainframe, pulled a CD out of its case, put it in the player, and pressed play. He sat back and nodded. "You've got a good setup here. It'll take a few minutes to get in, but the program on this CD is pretty good."

Binky shook her head, amazed. Everything Kevin had needed had been gone over by the security guard, who of course could have had no idea that the CD contained a devilishly clever password-hunting program. He handed Binky and Tim each a stick of gum. "No, thanks," Binky said.

"Chew it," Kevin commanded. "We'll need it later."

In less than thirty seconds, the computer beeped at him twice. "Oh, weak," Kevin groaned, dismayed to have gotten into the system so easily. "Stupid system administrator used a *birthday* for his passcode. Easiest hack in the world," he explained. "365 possibilities for each year, figure in 65 years, in case they used their kid's birthday. 23,725 possibilities—a piece of cake for a computer program to run through that many. And because there are so many *idiots* who use birthdays," he said contemptuously, "it's the first hack the program tries. These guys *deserve* to have their system *trashed*." He made a note of the birthday/password, presumably to pass on to his fellow mischief-makers later on.

"La la la, I am bored, here we go, Binky's number is . . ." he read it off her pass and typed it in. "Tim, your number, and now, let's see what kind of fool we have here. Create a guest pass, there we go, and let's give him, oh, how about 'all access'?" Kevin laughed. "I'm in. Kildare's office, hell, I could get into the *cold room* if I wanted to."

"There'll be plenty of opportunity for fun upstairs," Tim said. "Let's get going."

"Fifteen minutes," Kevin said. "The cleaning crew is

in Kildare's office now. They'll be out of there in fifteen.''

"How can you be so sure?''

''They've got an asshole boss who keeps them on a stop-watch, that's why. If they're not done, they'll just sweep something under the rug to get out in time. Another little way Herbert Kildare showed his contempt for the working classes,'' he said bitterly.

They waited the obligatory fifteen, then took the elevator to the top floor. It was as quiet as the grave. ''Down here,'' Kevin said, having had the opportunity to examine a floor plan of the offices.

He held them at a corner. ''Binky, let me have your gum.'' Binky took out her gum and put it in Kevin's proffered hand. ''Tim, a hand up?''

Tim picked up the slight young man and hoisted him to where he could reach up and over and place the gum over the lens of the camera pointed at the door to Kildare's office.

''Why not just deactivate it when you were hacked in?'' Binky asked.

''Because that would have turned on a red light on some security guard's console. He's less likely to notice one black screen than one red light. Let's go.''

They went down the hall to Kildare's office. Binky slid her pass through the access console next to the door. The door clicked open and she pushed it in. ''Come on,'' she said.

Kevin shook his head. ''Unless you're Herbert Kildare, each person who enters the room has got to put through a valid code. There's a motion detection system that registers the number of people in the room and compares it to the number of people who've just gotten valid access.''

Binky shook her head as Tim slid his card through and Kevin punched in his new code. ''Why doesn't Andrew have security like that?'' she wondered aloud.

''Andrew's not as paranoid as Kildare,'' Tim said.

''Binky, there's a monitor over there that shows this floor. Can you watch it and let us know if anyone shows up on this floor?'' Kevin seated himself at Kildare's desk, pulled a pair of latex gloves out of his pocket and put them on, and hit the power button on Kildare's computer, but nothing happened. "Is it plugged in?" Binky asked.

Kevin gave her a withering glance. "Yes, it is." He pulled open the middle drawer and found what he was looking for. He held up a key. "High security," he snorted. He put the key in the lock on the front of the computer, turned it, and hit the power switch again. The machine beeped and booted up.

"Shit," Kevin said. "It's empty."

"What?" Tim asked disbelievingly.

"The programs are on here, but no files. It's been wiped clean."

"Then let's get out of here," Tim said.

"Wait." Kevin examined the front of the machine and saw the tape backup. "Look around for some tapes. They'll look like cassette tapes, only bigger and heavier. In opaque plastic containers."

As he went through the desk, Tim and Binky ransacked the shelves and credenza drawers. "Are these it?" Binky asked, holding up a box of tapes.

"Yep." Kevin examined them. He laughed. "Oh, these guys are so sad! Here's a backup tape made the day Kildare died." He stuck it in the drive and began the restore process. After a few minutes, he was ready.

"Okay, come look at this." He pulled up the "My Documents" folder and Tim perused its contents.

"What's in that folder?" Tim asked, pointing at one labeled "Master Plan."

"Let's see." The folder contained several documents; Kevin double-clicked on the document also called "Master Plan." Word 97 came up and then a document:

KILDARE WORLDWIDE
MASTER PLAN
Eyes Only: Do Not Print

"That's what we want. Can you print it?" Tim asked.

"Well, Kildare's not around to punish me if I do, is he? We should just take this tape and go. I'll delete the files off here again, and nobody will ever know we were here."

"Sounds good to me," Binky said.

●　　●　　●

Back at the offices, Kevin quickly restored the tape onto Binky's machine. There had been some scraping around looking for a computer with nothing on it, until Binky had, with some redness of face, admitted that her own folders were virgin territory. "Don't tell Andrew," she pleaded.

"If this tape saves Andrew," Kevin said, "he won't give a damn that you can't type."

"I can type. . . ." Binky said defensively, but let it drop.

Kevin restored the contents of Kildare's backup tape to her machine. "I'll print out this 'Master Plan' document so you can all look at it. He's got some other stuff on here, too—like Quickbooks files, which seem to have something to do with his personal checking account. *That* could prove interesting."

Four copies of the master plan were printed and handed around. The first item of business on it was Andrew Weatherall:

> Weatherall is quite simply our Public Enemy #1. It is our *utmost priority* to end his stranglehold on new media technology, especially as it affects our printing and cable businesses. Additionally, it is incumbent that we reduce his profitability by any means necessary to reduce his media visibility—Weatherall without billions is Weatherall without an audience.

"Is that good or bad?" Doan asked. "I mean, on one hand, it makes it look like Andrew wasn't the only bad guy, on the other, it makes it look like he had all the better reason to do in Kildare."

"We already knew it was war," Luke said. "Kildare stole the digital radio technology, and he pounded Bowers to get at Andrew personally. If we had to, I mean, if the lawyers had to, they could use this to argue self-defense . . . if nothing else works, that is."

"If you want to besmirch Kildare's character," Tim said, "how about this part?"

> Our primary personnel goal should be to reduce labor costs to as close to zero as possible. Workers make trouble—they strike, they get sick, they take vacations,

and you have to pay them more every year. The more we can automate our processes, the better our bottom line. Especially since there is, as of yet, no way to replace the costly writers and editors at our papers, or the reporters or readers at the network, we must intensify our cost reductions in the blue-collar and back-office department. If anyone can invent a computer that can write news stories, and a holographically projected "person" to "read" them on the air, I'll make that man rich beyond his wildest dreams.

"Bastard," muttered Tim the writer.

"This was why he wanted to put Will Powers on a disk, too," Binky noted. They skipped lightly over the plans to liberalize KNN, since they already knew about that, though Tim took note of one interesting phrase.

The future belongs to whoever can fill the vacuum. The problem is, the vacuum is invisible. As one of my sons put it to me, nobody in the big media world knew there could possibly be a market for "grunge" music until somebody put out a Nirvana record. Suddenly, there was a mad scramble amongst record companies to sign "grunge" acts. KNN filled a vacuum left by the liberal media networks; but in a few years, that "angry white man" audience will be gone; we need to accept that the vacuum tomorrow will be filled by a network with anchormen from Mexico and entertainment news about Indian singers for homesick programmers from Calcutta.

"Take a look at this Quickbooks stuff," Kevin said. Luke, Tim, and Binky moved around to his computer, while Doan continued on with the master plan, far more secure investigating the world of words than numbers. "Check out some of these payouts."

"I know that name," Luke said. "That's one of the people who does dirty work for Kildare—break-ins and the like. What are all these payments to Will Powers?"

Kevin zeroed in on the checks to Powers. "Here's one

for ten grand, notation says 'Binky project.' '' They looked at Binky, who shrugged.

"He sure as hell didn't spend ten grand trying to seduce me—in the corporate sense," she said quickly to Luke. "I think I got a food basket, some flowers, and a free seminar. I can't imagine he used up the money on that."

"Skimming off the top, probably," Kevin said. "Here's another to Powers, this one says 'Reid project.' ''

"Randall Reid," Tim explained to Kevin. "A designer."

"A creep," Doan said automatically, not looking up from the master plan.

"That was for ten thousand, too. Here's a weird one, twenty-five grand to Powers, for 'Chloe project.' ''

"Oh shit!" Binky said. She looked at Luke. "It was her!"

Luke nodded. "Sounds like we found our mole at Weatherall and Associates."

"She's due back in the office on Monday. What do we do?"

"We let her come in," Luke said, "and then we . . . ask her a few questions."

"Oh, my god!" Doan shouted.

"What?" Tim asked, racing over.

"Listen to this," Doan said, then read aloud from the screen:

> "Our most inadvisable venture was the purchase of Randall Reid, Inc. This was done not with the intention of moving Kildare Worldwide into the fashion industry, but rather to secure some of the social connections that Randall Reid had assiduously cultivated since his 'marriage.' In short, people who would not attend a Kildare event would attend a Randall Reid event, even if Kildare was there."

Doan harrumphed. "Just like a megalomaniac to talk about himself in the third person," he commented, then continued reading:

> "However, the 'marquee value' of Reid has not been worth the aggravation of dealing with a subsid-

iary head who refuses to act like one, and who on several occasions has openly defied orders and taken the company in directions expressly forbidden—perhaps even on occasion because they were forbidden. As a media conglomerate, we are especially sensitive to timing and publicity, so the timing of Reid's removal as head of RRI has got to be handled carefully. Our first media priority is the war with Andrew Weatherall; however, Reid has to be removed soon. We will undoubtedly receive negative publicity for this, especially as his contract allows us to force him to stay on as a designer even after being ousted as company head. However, should the war with Weatherall get ugly, it may actually be the best time to remove Reid, as Andrew's propensity for grabbing headlines will take those headlines away from Reid, especially as Andrew will put up no squawk in defense of a closeted queen.''

"Oh my god, is right," Binky said, somewhat disappointed that the evidence no longer pointed as clearly as it had to Will Powers as a murderer. "If Randall Reid knew about this document . . .''

"He'd have every reason to do in Kildare before Kildare could do him in," Luke concluded.

"But would he have the guts for it?" Tim asked. "I mean, from what I've read, he *is* a big queen. I think even associating with hired killers would upset his appetite.''

"He could get Alex Lebedev to get one for him," Doan said. "Lebedev's got no qualms about crushing people.''

"But murdering them?" Tim wondered.

"I think we've got two suspects again," Luke said. "And a lot of questions to ask Miss Chloe when she comes in on Monday.''

The unsuspecting Chloe wandered in on time on Monday morning, and poked her head into Binky's office. "Hey." She didn't seem to be the least bit surprised to find Luke sitting there, assuming that he was there as Binky's boyfriend and not in his role as head of security.

"Chloe," Luke said, "come in and sit down.''

Chloe hesitated for a moment, but then shrugged and sat down. "What's up?"

"For what purpose did Will Powers pay you?" Luke wisely left the sum off the question; after learning that the motivational speaker had pocketed much of what he'd gotten from Kildare for trying to turn Binky, he thought it best to assume that Chloe hadn't received the full amount on Kildare's check.

She crumpled; that was the only way Binky could describe it later. "Shit. Busted, huh?"

"Chloe," Binky said, leaning forward, "we aren't here to bust you. There are more important things at stake right now; we just need to know the details and I promise we won't prosecute you if you tell us everything."

She sighed. "Can I have a cigarette?"

It was against policy to smoke in the building, but Luke nodded automatically after years of grilling suspects in police interrogations. She lit up and Luke asked, "So how did you get involved with Powers?"

"I applied for the job because my boyfriend told me to. He works for Will Powers."

"His name?"

"Jake Dodgson."

Binky turned to Luke. "I know him. He works on the YCRA phone lines."

Chloe nodded. "Yeah. He said things would be all right if I got the job, that it would fix everything."

"What do you mean?"

She flushed. "Jake's a heroin addict. He doesn't look the part, but he is. I can pick 'em, can't I?" she said to Binky. "Anyway, the deal was, if I got the job and reported back to Jake everything that happened at the office every day, Will Powers would keep Jake fixed up."

"So Will Powers was Jake's heroin dealer?" Luke asked.

"No, no. But he would give Jake enough money every day to keep him loaded for that day."

"But I saw him at work," Binky protested. "He was totally functional."

Chloe raised a jaded eyebrow. "And you think all junkies are homeless and look like shit, right? Well, if you've got a lot of money you can be a junkie and not look like one. It's when you get low on funds and you can't afford rent *and* food *and* drugs, and you have to pick drugs as your first priority, that you end up on the street in rags. Anyway, it didn't seem like a big deal. Jake just said Powers wanted to get Binky's endorsement for the seminars, and that he wanted info on the rest of the goings-on just because Weatherall's operation was so well run and he wanted to see what made it tick.''

"Did you know that Powers was a subsidiary of Kildare Worldwide?" Luke asked.

Chloe's eyes widened. "No. I thought Will Powers owned the show."

"It appears that what you were actually doing was funneling information on Weatherall through Powers to Kildare," Luke said.

Chloe turned pale. "Oh, shit. Oh, my god, I had no idea! I won't tell him anything else, I swear. I mean, I can't, right, because I am so fired."

"Well," Luke said, surprising Binky, "maybe not."

"What?" Binky asked.

"Has Will Powers lost interest in the information you were providing, now that Kildare's dead?" Luke asked.

"No . . . no, he still wants to know what's going on here."

"And the latest you've told him?"

"Well, that you're investigating the murder, trying to prove Weatherall didn't do it."

"Does he know about Binky's involvement in the investigation?"

"I didn't know she *was* involved," Chloe said. "I thought she worked for Will now and . . . oh! You're undercover!"

Binky nodded. "That's right."

"Cool!"

"Chloe," Luke said, "is Will still holding up his end of the deal?"

"You mean keeping Jake medicated? Oh, yeah. But I think he'd do it anyway, even if I wasn't giving him any info, you know?"

"No, what do you mean?" Luke asked.

"Well . . . he's a weird guy, Powers. He's into the power he's got. And he's got, like, total control over Jake. Jake's sweating it out every day—when's Powers going to give him the money for his fix? At lunchtime, at the end of the day, will he have to hang out and wait for it? Just like, totally humiliating him sometimes before giving him the money. Plus Jake's good on the phone lines." She snorted derisively. "Talk about someone who can rationalize anything; nobody better at that than a heroin addict! Anyway, yeah, he's still getting his fix from Powers."

"I have a proposal for you. Say nothing about this interview. And when this is all over, if Powers is busted we'll see to it that Jake gets into a substance abuse clinic, all expenses paid. A good one, too."

"If he wants to go . . ."

"If he wants to go. But the opportunity will be there. We're not doing it for him, we're doing it for you. Obviously he meant enough to you for you to screw up a job at Weatherall and Associates, where you would have been a millionaire in a few short years" (Chloe swallowed as she realized what she'd lost) "so we're willing to help you help him, okay?"

She nodded. "Okay. Whatever you want, I'm game."

That same Monday found Doan at his desk at Mannheim's studio. If Doan had thought keeping up with fashion was hard, keeping *ahead* of it was a nightmare. It was already time for Jacob to start working on a new collection, and the pressure was enormous, and Doan felt responsible for much of that pressure. Jacob had produced an outrageous, over-the-top collection, and there was no topping it with anything more outrageous, and yet, it also meant he could hardly swing back to muted earth tones for the next collection. All he could do now was hope that the brilliant Mannheim could come up with something that would satisfy both the critics who'd loved the last show . . . and the critics who'd hated it. And of course his whole gang of confederates were all on pins and needles now, what with Andrew's trial beginning the next day, and with no time left to find the killer before the great humiliation began.

Mannheim arrived at around ten for their morning meet-

ing. He groggily selected a pastry-wrapped apple from the
pink box (Doan tended to buy half a dozen goodies for the
two of them, just to have the luxury of selection) and sat
down, an assistant placing in his other hand a freshly con-
cocted latte. "You owe me, doll," Jacob said.

"I know," Doan flushed. "The nipple rings sewn onto
the mock turtleneck were a bit much, and—"

"No, no," Jacob said, waving that away with an irritated
hand, scattering buttery crumbs about. "For keeping your
little tryst with Rhianna Reid out of the papers."

"What?!"

"Honey, you do *not* leave Bloomingdale's with a famous
designer's weeping wife on your arm, *and* take her to a
public place, without someone rushing to call *Page Six.*"

"Uh-oh."

"Not to worry. I took care of it. The gossip hag who
was going to run the piece was rather easily bought off
with the home phone number of one of the models from
the show, whom I happen to know is . . . in school and
looking for some ready cash right now, let's leave it at that,
eh?"

"Oh, Jacob, thank you so much," Doan gushed, really
meaning it. God, that was New York for you! he thought.
Everything you do really is in the public eye at all times—
more to the point, in the media's eye, as sometimes it
seemed half the people on the street worked for some media
outlet or another.

"I knew you were going to meet her, but what could
you have possibly said to that ice princess to crack her up
like that?"

"Can you keep a secret?"

"No, not very well," Jacob admitted. "But I can keep
a *really big* secret, if I can run around later and tell everyone I knew all about it all the time, which is even better."

Doan nodded. "Deal. According to Rhianna, Will Powers is blackmailing Randall Reid."

"Ah, the old boyfriend back in the picture, eh?"

"You knew about that?"

"Oh, sure. Will Powers looks like a downtown drone
now, but he was quite a hot cookie in his heyday. Back
when he was modeling, he was *to die for.* Even if you

didn't like blonds, he was something else. That skin . . .''
Jacob sighed. ''Anyway. That was a real fight-and-fuck relationship—loud arguments in public, drinks thrown in
faces, and then they'd make up and retire to some corner
of the VIP room and neck like teenagers. I'll tell you something, I think part of the reason that old queen went back
in the closet was because he wanted to please the money
men, but I also think that after that relationship, he thought
he was better off never falling in love with *anyone* again!
I know what that feels like. But I'm a romantic, I keep
trying!''

''According to Rhianna, Will reinitiated the relationship
recently . . .'' Noting Jacob's bugging eyes, he chided him.
''Now, remember, this is a secret!''

''Mum's the word. Oh, God, this is good. Go on.''

''And has photographs this time, which he's threatening
to send to *Fleet Street*, since he knows they'll print them.
Rhianna claims not to know what Will wants out of Randall
in exchange for silence, but I've told her she's got to try
to get Randall to talk, otherwise they could end up being
charged as accessories to murder.''

Jacob helped himself to another pastry. ''Doan, this is
too much! I feel like I don't even have to watch *Guiding
Light* anymore. Well, except to see Cassie's boyfriend, he's
such a stud . . .''

Doan's phone rang. ''Yes?''

''Doan, it's Rhianna Reid. Randall and I would like to
see you this morning. We have some . . . things to share
with you.''

Doan was not going to face Randall Reid alone. That
Reid was hiding something was already established—something besides his homosexuality, that is. So Doan promptly
called Luke, who picked him up in a Weatherall car at
Mannheim's studio for the trip uptown.

''I just wanted you along, because I think you know a
liar when you see one,'' Doan said in the car. ''I mean, I
know a liar when I see one, but you're a cop, you know a
good liar from someone who's telling the truth.''

Luke nodded. ''Thanks, Doan. That's not always the
case, but I do try. One thing I'd like to ask of you in this
meeting—Randall may tell us things we already know,

about Powers and about himself. Don't tip our hand as to what we do or don't know, just let him do the talking."

They were quickly ushered into Randall's office. Randall and Rhianna were arrayed on the couch, a glass-topped table from the Randall Reid Home Collection between them and their visitors. They looked to Luke like they were ready to be grilled by Mike Wallace; Doan noted with no small satisfaction that this time the delicacies on the table were accompanied by more than two plates.

Randall started, holding Rhianna's hand. "Mr. McCandler, Mr. Faraglione, thank you for coming. Rhianna has told me that you've . . . discovered certain things about my . . . relations with Will Powers, and that you thought that these latest . . . incidents might have something to do with Herbert Kildare's death. Rhianna has convinced me that we are far better off placing ourselves in your hands than we would be in Will's hands, or in the hands of the police later on." He looked at Rhianna, who nodded; he drew a breath and continued.

"Will Powers murdered Herbert Kildare, and he blackmailed me into helping him." He shut his eyes and Rhianna squeezed his hand. Doan snuck a sidelong look at Luke, but he had his impassive police face on.

Randall took a drink of water. "Will is a very . . . persuasive man. He and I had a relationship years ago—before I met Rhianna," he said, as if he were rehearsing aloud to see how it would sound when the time came to spin this story to the press. "He came back into my life a few months ago, and we . . . rekindled our relations." Luke already knew about Powers's persuasiveness, and in the car, Doan had filled Luke in about Powers's assets below the belt.

"Then he threatened you," Luke said.

Reid nodded. "He had pictures of us together this time— negatives, which would be impossible to forge on a computer. He was going to expose me to the world if I didn't help him."

"To murder Kildare," Luke finished the sentence.

"No, that's not how he put it. You see, Herbert had plans to take Will's company away from him. He was going to put the seminars and the 'You Can Rationalize Anything' database on a disk and sell it.''

Doan found it easy to wear the same impassive mask as Luke had on at this point, as he already knew this. It was hard work, he thought, not jumping in and showing off what you knew! At least it was for an inveterate gossip like Doan.

''He'd made some really unconscionably rude phone calls to Herbert, and one very angry visit to his office, after which Herbert wouldn't even speak to him on the phone. He told me he had to get to Herbert, had to persuade him in person that the seminars were worthless without the live element. So I arranged to meet Herbert at home one night. Will accompanied me. In fact, he insisted on driving. Herbert has a house on the Upper East Side, and somehow Will knew what night the house staff had off.''

Luke made a mental note of this, wondering just how widespread Powers's informer network was.

''Herbert opened the door for me, and Will pushed his way in behind me. He and Herbert argued for a moment, then . . .'' Randall shuddered and took a sip of water. ''Then he pulled a hammer out of his jacket and started hitting Herbert in the head with it. When Herbert was unconscious, Will ordered me to help get him into his car. Then we took him to Weatherall's building.''

''Why?'' Luke asked.

''Will wasn't telling me anything at the time, but I figured it out later. He knew that if he killed Herbert in Weatherall's building, the suspicion would automatically fall on Weatherall. Everybody knew they hated each other, personally as well as professionally after that incident with the baseball player. And Andrew had said some rather unpleasant things in the press about Will and his seminars.'' He'd said some unpleasant things about closeted queens like Randall Reid, too, Doan thought.

''So how did you get in?'' Luke asked.

''Will had a pass key to the building next door—did you know it was owned by Kildare Worldwide?'' Luke did not, and he was appalled to learn it, but he kept his poker face. ''We got onto the roof of Weatherall's building, and Will tied Herbert up with a rope. He lowered Herbert down an air shaft on a rope, climbed down the rope, with me making sure it was secure up top, and pushed out one of the grates into the floor under that one office. I don't know why he picked that office; I could tell it wasn't Weatherall's but I was too scared to ask. I thought he was just going to leave Herbert unconscious in the office and go. He told me to come down the rope. Well, I was terrified! I'd never been down a rope in my life!'' Doan resisted the urge to roll his eyes at Randall's femmy horror at having to do something physical outside of a gym. ''But I made it, and he made me . . . he made me pull Herbert through the floor as he went ahead, pushing all these wires out of the way and pushing up into that office.

''We hauled Herbert in there, and then Will pulled out a gun. I thought I would faint. 'You're not going to shoot him?' I said. And he said, 'Hell, yes, I'm going to shoot him. It's him or me now.' And . . . and he did.'' He covered his eyes with his hands and Rhianna put a consoling arm around his shoulder.

''And how did you get out?'' Luke pressed.

''Back up the way we came. Up the rope, and out through the other building. It was easier going up than down because he was behind me and he had that gun; I was so scared and so eager to get away from him I climbed it in record time! Then he said to me out on the street, that if I ever told anyone about this, not only would he leak the photos, but he'd tell everyone *I* killed Herbert. Before I knew what he was doing, he'd put my hand on the gun, and then took it back, and told me the gun had my prints on it.''

At this point, Luke almost lost it—the murder weapon! The one thing sure to get Andrew off scot-free! ''And Will Powers has the gun now?''

''Yes. He wouldn't get rid of it, if he could use it against me. So, you see, I couldn't go to the police—not when it would have meant being charged with *murder.*''

''So why come to us with the truth now?'' Doan asked.

Randall heaved a great sigh. ''Because it's been such a burden to keep it in. Because it's been a strain on Rhianna to be the only other person to know. Because every moment we live in fear of Will Powers! Even jail has to be better than this. But we couldn't call the cops. I don't trust the cops. Will has spies everywhere—why not the police department?''

Luke nodded. ''We will keep this to ourselves as long as we can. But Andrew's trial starts tomorrow, you know. And you may be called as witnesses. In which case you will have to tell everything you know.''

Randall and Rhianna nodded. ''We know. But that's not like going to the cops. We go to the cops, maybe nothing happens. They write it all down and they file it away for the prosecutor and Will finds out and he . . . gets us. But if it all comes out for the first time in a trial, in public, the spotlight turns on Will and we're safer that way.'' Randall got up. ''Thank you for coming.'' Luke took their dismissal; he was not a cop anymore and couldn't press. He and Doan took their leave, without, Doan thought forlornly, ever having touched the tapas.

In the car, they rehashed it all. ''What do you think?'' Doan asked.

''I don't know. I think it all sounded pretty well-rehearsed, though.''

''Of course,'' Doan said. ''First of all, when you're in the closet, you've always got to watch what you say. Lots of indeterminate pronouns, lots of 'that person' and 'this person,' and made-up stories for co-workers about what you did this weekend. When you're a closet queen, your whole life is spent rehearsing so you don't spill the real beans.''

''So true or not, he would have rehearsed it.''

''Absolutely. Because on top of being a closet queen, he's also someone used to being interviewed by the media. And you've always got to have a story ready for them.''

Luke nodded. ''So you don't believe him?''

''It was all rather dramatic. The consoling touch of the wife who stands by him in his hour of trial blah blah blah, but they might have just done that because he's a drama queen, too. Did you see how his eyes lit up at the idea of testifying on the stand? Can't you see him in some Bob Mackie dress with a huge matching Alexis Carrington hat, making all the headlines as he reveals the true killer, just like in some old movie?''

"Well, I hadn't thought of that, no," Luke said wryly. "But now that you mention it, yeah, I *can* see it."

They laughed. "The facts check out, though," Luke said. "He was there, I think. He knew about the HVAC, about the floor, about Binky's office. . . ."

"He could have found out all of that from the cops. Maybe he's got his *own* spies, you know. Jacob is always telling me how in New York, connections and information are a more powerful currency than cash. And if Will *was* blackmailing him, what better way to get his blackmailer to flee the country than to take him by complete surprise by denouncing him as a murderer on the stand?"

Luke chewed on that and nodded. "I think we take Mr. Reid's 'confession' of complicity with a grain of salt. Still, I think it's time to talk to Andrew and his lawyers. Tell them everything we know. See what they want to do—and who they want to put on that stand to testify."

nine

~~~

$\mathcal{A}$ndrew Weatherall had certainly made his share of
enemies before this trial, and he was probably making a
few more during it. Ever since O. J., there has been a large
and thriving industry consisting of people whose job has
been solely to appear as talking heads on TV during legal
tangles, to second-guess and speculate and rehash and an-
ticipate. By forcing his trial to move ahead, Andrew was
depriving the talking head economy of thousands of hours
of airtime and millions of dollars. Which is not to say that
the trial was to be anything other than a media circus—
"PROSECUTION PREPARED FOR POOFTER" was the
New York Beast's headline the day the trial opened.

"Typical," Andrew grunted, tossing aside the paper.
Tim and Doan and Luke and Binky had joined Andrew and
Mark at Andrew's house for what Weatherall had mirth-
fully labeled "The Last Breakfast" on the day the trial was
to open.

"You can sue them when all this is over," Mark said.

"I can *buy* them when all this is over," Andrew replied.

The gang had filled him and his legal team in on Randall
Reid's surprising confession, and Andrew had been in a
vastly chipper mood ever since. The prosecution's case

against him was, after all, highly circumstantial. He had motive, opportunity, and a weak alibi. The alleged murder weapon didn't have prints on it, but that was to be expected. What the prosecution did have going for them was "O. J. rage," the feeling out there that rich people got away with murder because they could afford the best lawyers. This had not been ameliorated when Andrew had hired Jimmy Cutlass as his attorney, a man famous for his brilliant and mostly successful defenses of transparently guilty people. Andrew had agonized over it, knowing full well that to hire Cutlass would be, in the eyes of the media, an admission of guilt. "But," he'd said, "which is worse? To be thought guilty by the people but found innocent by the jury, or to be thought innocent by the people and found guilty by the jury?"

Andrew marched boldly out of his house that morning, braving the camera crews and the shouting reporters. "There is no way I'm going to go into court through the back entrance in a car with smoked glass windows," he'd insisted. And so he entered the courthouse like Caesar going to his doom.

The prosecution's opening statement was much what everyone had expected—an excoriation of Andrew, painting him as an enemy of the people, a willful and arrogant man whose hatred of Herbert Kildare was well known and well documented. The prosecutor admitted that Herbert Kildare had attacked Weatherall where it hurt, but that this was no excuse for murder.

The first witness called that day was Mrs. Keith. She was sworn in and took the stand, wearing the suit of a sedate and efficient corporate secretary and the face of an Amazon princess ready for battle.

"Mrs. Keith," the prosecutor began, "how long have you worked for Andrew Weatherall?"

"Four and a half years now."

"And when you began working for Mr. Weatherall, how much money did you have in the bank?"

"Objection!" Jimmy Cutlass shouted. "Is Mrs. Keith's financial history really relevant, your honor?"

"Overruled," the judge said. "I see where this is going, and so do you, Mr. Cutlass. Please answer the question."

"I didn't have a bank account at the time," Mrs. Keith said, flushing.

"And how much are you worth today?"

She hesitated. "My net worth is approximately seventy-seven million dollars."

There was an audible gasp from the crowd. The prosecutor bit his lip; this was far more than he'd expected, and it made Weatherall look like a friend to the little guy—not a boon to a prosecution based on inciting rage against a rich man.

"And this is all income from your position at Weatherall and Associates?"

"It is income from my position as well as income from investments that I have made."

"That Mr. Weatherall made for you?"

"That Mr. Weatherall advised me to make."

"You were on welfare when you met the defendant, weren't you?"

"No, I was off welfare."

"Because you'd been thrown off, correct? Because you'd been put on a workfare program?"

Mrs. Keith glared at the prosecutor. "Can't you object to that?" Andrew asked Cutlass.

Cutlass shook his head. "Let him try to make her look bad; trust me, it's going to boomerang back on him."

"Yes." Mrs. Keith said, clenching her teeth.

"Where do you think you'd be today without Andrew Weatherall?"

"Probably slaving away in a typing pool for someone like you."

The crowd laughed; the judge banged her gavel. "Order," she said automatically, but she gave no reprimand to Mrs. Keith.

"Mrs. Keith, on the night in question, you say Andrew Weatherall was at your house?"

"Yes. He came over for dinner and stayed the night."

"Stayed the night?"

"Yes, in the guest bedroom. He has done it several times before. We had wine with dinner and it was late and he didn't feel like putting his shoes back on and traveling home."

"I see. So you and Mr. Weatherall are personally close."

"Yes, I would say we are."

"It's very unusual for a secretary and a boss to be so close, don't you think?"

"I'm not his secretary," she said. "He has two secretaries; I am his personal assistant."

The prosecutor nodded. "Personal assistant." He made it sound like a glorified secretary, as if a garbage man had called himself a "sanitation engineer."

"Mrs. Keith, do you remember a day last year when Mr. Weatherall threw a paperweight against a wall?"

"Yes, I do. He was—"

"He was furious, wasn't he? He had just been outbid for a young new media company, hadn't he?"

"Yes."

"And who outbid him for that company?"

"You know damn well who."

"Mrs. Keith," the judge said, "this is a court of law. Please answer the question."

"Andrew Weatherall bangs on tables in the lunchroom, doesn't he?" the prosecutor continued, on a roll now. "He is inordinately fond of shouting the *F* word when things don't go his way, isn't he? He throws a lot of things, yes? Sweeps his desk off with one swipe of his arm?"

"Andrew throws things at other things. He hits his desk, a table, a wall. He yells the *F* word at nobody in particular to vent his rage. I have never seen him hit anybody; in fact, I have never seen him raise his voice in anger against a Weatherall employee," she finished defiantly.

"You have a lot at stake here, don't you? Andrew Weatherall is not only your boss, to whom you are as loyal as any 'personal assistant' could be hoped to be, he is your benefactor, who plucked you off the street and made you rich, and he is your friend, with whom you are so close he stays the night at your house!"

If Mrs. Keith had not been black, it would have been safe to say she turned purple with rage. "And you have a lot at stake here, too, don't you, counselor? You've got your orders from people who want to destroy Andrew. You don't have any proof! This trial is a circus! This trial is

being put on solely to humiliate and punish your masters'
political enemy!''

"Order!" the judge shouted as the courtroom erupted.
"Order!"

"No further questions, your honor," the prosecutor said,
looking as happy as a clam.

Luke shook his head. "This is going to be ugly," he
whispered to Binky.

"Just wait till it's our turn," Binky said. "Then I'll show
you ugly."

The prosecution went on like this for several days, calling
Kevin to the stand and basically giving him the same treat-
ment they'd given Mrs. Keith, insinuating that he, too,
owed his all to Andrew and that he, too, was capable of at
least lying for his boss if not doing the deed himself. It had
been painful to watch the boy on the stand; the brilliant,
acerbic Kevin was gone, replaced by the Kevin who had
developed a phobia about courtrooms after his own brutal
prosecution. He stuttered and umm-ed and took all the humiliation the prosecution could dish out over him, as they
rehashed his crimes and asked him again and again about
why the security camera in Binky's office—the murder
scene—had been the only one deactivated. Other Weatherall employees were called to testify about their boss's
long-running war with Kildare and to recall comments he'd
made on those occasions. It wasn't much of a case, Jimmy
Cutlass reassured Weatherall; certainly they hadn't proven
him guilty beyond a reasonable doubt—but then, it was a
jury trial, and with a jury trial you never knew. . . .

The stress of the whole thing had driven Binky to take
up smoking again. It didn't help that New York was hardly
the antismoking capital that San Francisco was. Out West,
one was practically granted a parade for successfully quitting, and burnt at the stake for taking it up again. In high-
pressure New York, smoking was still acceptable, an alternative for nervous hands in place of strangling somebody.

She was skipping the prosecution's grilling of the last
witness; it was the only time she would be able to get away
from Luke and have a ciggie. While all the attention was
focused inside, she stood on the sidewalk outside the court-

house, simultaneously smoking and sucking on a breath mint. She didn't notice the black limo as it rolled up next to her; as the door opened she automatically moved to the side to let the occupant out. But suddenly she was off her feet, yanked into the car. The door slammed and the car sped away, the only trace of her left behind a still-smoldering cigarette and her Tic Tacs.

She struggled to see who her captor was, and froze when she saw Jake's face. She wheeled her head around and, not surprised, saw Will Powers on the opposite seat. "Hello, Binky."

She swallowed hard. "Uh, hello."

"You've been busy."

"Yes, I have," she said noncommittally.

"You took some time off, which was certainly fair, you've worked very hard. But I got curious when I found that you'd been spending it at Andrew Weatherall's trial."

She swallowed. "Well, it's very interesting."

"Mmm. Yes, it is. I remembered that you used to have a professional interest in crime—as a detective? So I did a little digging. Found out that you'd spent some time working undercover during one of your cases."

"Yes . . ." Oh shit, Binky thought. It's the concrete galoshes for me now.

"And I started thinking, you know, I wonder if that's not what she's been doing at my place all this time?"

"Oh."

"It is, isn't it?" Powers was quite calm, she thought, which made her all the more frightened. Anger is often the outlet of the helpless; people who can make things happen don't have to get angry—they can get even.

"No use lying about it, is there?"

"Not really," he said lightly. "Let her go," he said to Jake, who released her. She sat up and pushed her hair out of her face. "I have a proposal for you. I wish I could have made it in a more businesslike manner and setting, but you see, I've just found out that Randall Reid is about to testify against me in Weatherall's trial." Powers smiled. "He told you a very interesting story, didn't he?"

"Yes, he certainly did."

Powers frowned out the window, angry for the first time,

not at Binky but obviously at Reid. Then he looked at her and smiled. "Well, I have a very interesting story for you, too."

New York may well be the city where people step over bodies in the street, but a woman kidnapped in broad daylight was still enough to get somebody to call the cops. Luke, Tim, and Doan were coming out of the courtroom when a policeman came up to Luke and whispered in his ear. He paled visibly and Tim asked, "What is it?"

"Binky's been kidnapped."

"Oh, my god!" Doan shouted. "I bet it was Will Powers!"

Luke scowled. "That's my bet, too. He knows we're on to him, and he's going to use Binky as a bargaining chip. Damn it!" he cursed. "I should have known we would have to be more careful."

"You couldn't have anticipated this," Tim said. "Don't blame yourself."

The full extent of it started to dawn on Luke. "If anything happened to Binky . . ."

Doan stepped up and took Luke's arm, leading him off, more just to put him in motion and give him the illusion of action than to take him anywhere in particular. "Nothing is going to happen to Binky," he said firmly. "If Will Powers needs her as a bargaining chip, she's no good to him dead."

Luke nodded. "Yeah. That's true. But if he's pushed to the wall, we don't know what he's capable of."

Luke's cell phone rang. He looked at his friends. "That could be Powers." He answered it. "Hello?"

"It's me," Binky said.

"Binky!" he practically shouted with joy. Tim and Doan didn't realize how tense their own shoulders were until they suddenly sagged.

"Don't yell my name," she said. "We don't want everybody knowing what's going on."

"What do you mean? Are you in danger?"

"No. I'm fine. Listen, you need to talk to Jimmy Cutlass. We need to set something up for the opening of the defense. Randall Reid is scheduled to be the first witness, right?"

"Yes, tomorrow morning. It's got the prosecution flummoxed, that's for sure. They don't know what we're doing with a fashion designer as our first witness."

"Well, don't change anything, and don't say anything to anyone but Andrew and Cutlass, but tell them to be prepared for a surprise witness."

"You're kidding. Powers? Binky, what's going on?"

"Let's just say there are two sides to every story. And I want Randall Reid there when Will Powers tells his."

As Doan had predicted, Randall Reid was relishing his moment on the stand. If he was going to do this thing, it was going to have to be in the most dramatic way possible. He and Rhianna showed up at the courthouse in dark sunglasses like movie stars at a premiere, waving away the reporters with "no comment" all the way in.

They took their seats in the courtroom and looked straight ahead, acknowledging nobody. Doan watched them dourly. "Those frosty looks are about to get a few cracks in them," he told Tim.

The defense waived opening remarks. "Our witnesses will tell you all you need to know," Jimmy Cutlass said, to the consternation of the prosecution. And then Cutlass called Randall Reid to the stand.

There would be no point in rehashing Reid's well-rehearsed testimony, which was practically identical to his words to Luke and Doan, even up to the timing of the sighs and the face in the hands. All that was missing was Rhianna's helping hand.

The prosecutor got up to cross-examine Reid. "Mr. Reid, this is an extraordinary story."

"Yes, I can hardly believe it myself. It's like a dream—or a nightmare."

"Mr. Powers has been blackmailing you, is that correct?"

"Yes, it is."

"Then, really, you have every reason to come up here on this stand and try to besmirch him before he can besmirch you, don't you?"

"I am telling the truth, the whole truth, and nothing but the truth."

"Very dramatic. And what evidence do we have that you're telling the truth?"

Randall's eyes widened as he put a hand to his breast. "Do you really think I would do this thing, come up here and destroy my reputation, confess to an adulterous affair with another man, if I didn't have to? Haven't I just gotten up here and confessed to everything that Will Powers was threatening to make public? Why would I do that unless I was in danger of something far worse than losing my good name?"

The prosecutor couldn't answer that one. "No more questions, your honor."

As Randall walked back to his seat with all grace and dignity, like Marie Antoinette to the block, Jimmy Cutlass called out, "The defense calls Will Powers to the stand."

And like Marie, or at least like Norma Shearer as Marie, Randall froze, one hand reaching out for something to steady him. He looked around for Powers, who came into the courtroom only as he was called. Powers walked straight ahead, not looking at Randall, who watched him pass by with a look of perfect horror on his face. Finally Rhianna got up and grabbed him and hauled him back to his seat.

"Mr. Powers," Cutlass said, "did you hear what was just said about you by Mr. Reid?"

"Yes, I did."

"And is it true?"

"Some of it."

"Why don't you tell us your version of what happened that night?"

"Randall Reid murdered Herbert Kildare," he said, and the courtroom rustled.

"Can you prove it?"

"I have handed the murder weapon to the court this morning. They will find Randall's prints on it, and a ballistic test should prove that it is indeed the murder weapon."

"Mr. Reid says that you put the gun in his hand, put his prints on it, to keep him silent."

"Well, he would, wouldn't he?"

"Why don't you give us your version of events?"

Will took a breath. "I had just found out that Herbert Kildare was going to get rid of me. Put me out of a job. And Randall called me—we hadn't talked in years—and he told me that he'd heard about what was happening, and that he was in the same boat, that Kildare was going to be firing him, too."

"The two of you were lovers, then, long ago?"

"Yes, we were."

"And did you rekindle the relationship after his latest call?"

"Well, I wouldn't call it a 'rekindled relationship.' We got together to strategize about Kildare and he . . . offered to service me. He was always good at that, so I let him."

The jurors practically as one all looked at Randall after this statement, but he maintained a perfect mask of outraged indignation.

"He told me he knew I couldn't get to Kildare anymore after I'd . . . lost my temper with him, and he offered to sneak me in on his coattails to Kildare's house, where we could both gang up on him and threaten to go public with his plans. I don't know what good that would do, but it sounded good at the time. When we got to Kildare's house, all of a sudden Randall pulled out a hammer and whacked Kildare in the head. I said, 'What the hell are you doing?' and he said, 'Let's get him out of here.' I couldn't believe what was going on. We got Kildare in the car and Randall told me to drive him to Weatherall's building, that he knew we could do it there and not only not get caught but that Weatherall would take the fall."

"How did *Reid* know about Binky's office not being on the monitor?" Doan whispered to Luke, who shrugged.

"The rest of what Randall said is true: We got Kildare down the air shaft on a rope, got through the floor, got into that office. And then he shot Herbert Kildare."

"And so how did you end up with the gun?"

"He freaked out! When Kildare was down dead on the floor with blood running everywhere, he just freaked out and dropped the gun. I didn't freak; I thought fast, grabbed the gun with a handkerchief, put it in my pocket, and got us the hell out of there, with him blubbering all the way."

"So why didn't you go to the police, if you were innocent?"

"And lose everything? If I come forward, I lose my job for sure, my reputation is shot, I have nothing. If I don't, maybe Randall's scheme works, and Weatherall takes the fall, and I keep my business in my hands."

"So you . . . rationalized it," Cutlass said acerbically.

"Yes. Yes, I did."

"No further questions."

"Your honor, this is all a case of he said, she said, so to speak—" the prosecutor began, but the judge cut him off.

"I am calling a recess, pending the outcome of the ballistics report and fingerprint analysis. Andrew Weatherall is on trial here, and whatever else may not be clear, if these reports come back as the witnesses have both said they will, it will be clear Andrew Weatherall is not the murderer of Herbert Kildare, and this case will be dismissed."

A general jubilation arose from Weatherall's cheering section. Mark Bowers vaulted over the railing and he and the beaming billionaire embraced. The judge pounded her gavel. "Mr. Reid and Mr. Powers will accompany the bailiff to be fingerprinted."

Randall stood up. "I won't be fingerprinted like a common criminal!"

"Mr. Reid, you will go and be fingerprinted or you will be held in contempt of court if not arrested for obstructing justice, and then you *will* be a common criminal. Court is adjourned."

"So we may never know which one of them really did it," Binky said with no small frustration.

"Well, we got Weatherall off," Tim said. "That's the important thing, right?"

Doan looked at Binky and Binky looked at Luke. It was funny, but they knew they were all thinking the same thing—that they were all thinking like detectives, and none of them would be satisfied until the real killer was brought to justice.

"Hold on," Doan said, and he fought his way across the courtroom to where Rhianna Reid was moving toward the door. "Rhianna," he called out.

She turned and saw him but kept walking. Doan and Binky ran after her, Luke a few paces behind. "It was certainly interesting, wasn't it?"

"You set us up," she said coldly, walking faster.

"We didn't set anyone up," Doan protested. "We just wanted to see what would happen. And it was very interesting, don't you think?"

She stopped and wheeled on him. "I think it was appalling. You were supposed to protect us from Will Powers."

"And I have," Doan said. "If Randall and Will are now the prime suspects, there's nothing either can do to the other, is there?" He went back to pressing his point. "It was very strange how Will Powers's testimony was almost identical in the details to Randall's, wasn't it?"

"He heard it in the hall and made up his own version on the spot."

"Oh, no, I'm afraid not," Binky said. "You see, he gave me his version of the story yesterday—without ever having heard Randall's version."

Rhianna paled and started walking away again. Doan and Binky followed her and Doan kept talking. "You know, everything Will said makes sense but one—that part about Randall leading him to Weatherall's offices as the ideal place to put Kildare's body. How on earth could Randall have known about Binky's office not being on video surveillance? How could he . . . unless somebody told him? And who could have told him other than somebody at Weatherall's office—or somebody who knew it because Will Powers had told her?"

Rhianna was running now. "What really happened that night?" Doan demanded. "Did Randall do it with Will as his unwilling accomplice? Or the other way around? *Or were they maybe both there at the behest of a third person?*"

"Fuck you," she muttered, flying out the front door of the courthouse.

Luke stopped a policeman and whispered in his ear as Doan and Binky flew after Rhianna. Binky yelled after her. "You were having an affair with Will Powers, weren't you? Which one of them did it, Rhianna? Only you know—

only you could have told Randall what only Will Powers knew. And afterward, all you had to do was play the part of the troubled wife, who knew something was up and yet who was really in the dark about the details, who only knew what her husband told her. . . .'"

"And a wife can't be made to testify against a husband anyway, can she?" Doan added. "But if one of them took the fall, you'd still have the other, wouldn't you? But now maybe Will Powers might want to cut a deal—now maybe he's going to be willing to turn you in to protect himself."

Rhianna didn't get far. The police stopped her and brought her, struggling, back to the courthouse. "Rhianna," Luke said, "I think you have some questions to answer."

"I want a lawyer."

"Jimmy Cutlass is available, I hear," Luke cracked. "Let's go."

ten

The celebration that weekend at Andrew's house was small and subdued. The participants were all too exhausted for any excessive revelry. Andrew and Mark had invited only our four heroes, Mrs. Keith, and Kevin Stocker—the key players in the drama.

Doan was flopped out on a couch, his head in Tim's lap. "I certainly hope we get a vacation from dead bodies for a while. Detecting is very exciting but it certainly takes its toll."

Binky smiled. "Oh, but it has its rewards." She pulled a magazine out of her bag. "Your fifteen minutes are officially extended, Doan."

Doan bolted up at the sight of the magazine. "It's me!" he said jubilantly as he saw himself on the cover of the latest *New York* magazine. It was a good photo, taken outside the courthouse as the media pressed Doan and Binky for details of their investigation. The words on the cover read, "DEVIL IN A BLUE DRESS: How did this man (yes, it's a man) bring a killer to justice?"

" 'It'?" Doan asked indignantly. "Let me see that."

He flipped through the pages till he got to the article. " 'Not only did Doan McCandler and his friend Binky Van de Kamp (profiled in this magazine recently) absolve eccentric gay billionaire Andrew Weatherall of New York's murder of the year . . . ' ''

"That's the same thing they called me last time!" Andrew said irritably.

". . . but they also unraveled the strands of one of the weirdest love triangles in recent history and found out just who did what to whom."

The article went on to relate the sordid details of the Kildare murder: how Rhianna Reid had initiated an affair with Will Powers; encouraged Powers to reinitiate *his* affair with her husband, Randall; accidentally overheard the information from Powers about Binky's office; convinced her husband to murder Herbert Kildare and use Will Powers as an accessory (yes, Randall Reid did it); and then gave Powers the story to tell in court to contradict Randall's—the goal being not to preserve both men's jobs and freedom but to see one of them convicted as a murderer, leaving her free to hitch her star to whichever one of them got off, still in possession of his freedom, his money, and his position.

" 'Nobody would have thought to credit Rhianna Reid with the brains to organize her way out of a paper bag,' '' Doan read aloud from the article, " 'let alone plot such an intricate conspiracy, but McCandler and Van de Kamp spotted the hole in the men's conflicting stories—a hole only Rhianna Reid's involvement could have accounted for.' They didn't give you any credit, Luke.''

Luke shrugged. "That's all right—best for a security chief to be invisible.''

"And Tim, darling, you helped, too.''

"Uh, I think it's best that the world not know I took a job under false pretenses and broke into my boss's office, don't you?''

"Hmm. You have a point." Doan thumbed through the article. "Oh, look, there's pictures from Jacob's show at Splash! He'll be delighted, all press is good press, he says.''

"Well," Andrew said, "I have to tell you I never in a million years would have thought Randall Reid was capable of murder. I mean, capable of thinking of it, but not of physically carrying it out.''

Luke nodded. "Desperate times call for desperate measures. And he trusted Rhianna implicitly with all his secrets. And if his very own Lady Macbeth told him that he needed to murder Herbert Kildare to keep everything he had, he wasn't going to argue with her.''

"She was a piece of work, wasn't she?'' Tim asked. "She used Randall to get ahead, she used Will Powers to stay ahead—and imagine sending one lover to bed with the other to keep the conspiracy going.''

"Sounds like a good piece for *Manhattan* magazine to me,'' Andrew commented with a smile.

"Yeah, I should pitch that,'' Tim said thoughtfully.

"I don't think that will be necessary. You see, I talked to the new editor and he is very enthusiastic about your doing some articles for them.''

Tim's jaw dropped for a moment, but then he recovered. "Andrew, that is wonderful, I mean, every writer dreams of being in *Manhattan*. But I can't take it as a favor someone's doing for you. . . .''

Andrew raised a hand. "It's not. I asked the editor what he thought of you, and he said he loved you and it was too bad about *Edgy Hipster* and what was going to happen to you, and I said, gee, I don't know—any ideas?'' he finished with a laugh.

Doan squeezed Tim's hand. "Do it, doll. You know you're qualified.''

Tim laughed. "I'll talk to him. No offense, Andrew, but I want to get it from the horse's mouth.''

Andrew nodded. "No problem.'' He turned to Mark and smiled. "There's another new job announcement to be made. Mark has taken a job as baseball coach at the University of San Rancho in California.''

"Wow,'' Luke said, impressed. "Good job.''

Tim nodded. "Excellent school. Great baseball program there, too.''

"You guys are going to be a long way away,'' Binky said.

Andrew shrugged. "Well, thank God this is the digital age and I can do what I do from just about anywhere. And thank God I have my own jet!'' he added, laughing. "Though I think I'll be opening a satellite office in San Rancho, seeing as how I'll be spending a lot of time there.

And even if Mark weren't there, I might need to be spending more time in California anyway," he finished with a smile.

"I'll bite," Doan said. "And why is that, Andrew?"

"Well, I'm thinking of running for president. . . ."

Binky and Doan sat out in the garden that evening as the others watched a football game. "Well," Doan said, "I know one thing for sure—there's no lack of excitement in New York City."

"Excitement seems to follow us wherever we go," Binky noted.

"I don't think excitement could follow us to San Rancho, California."

"It's a pretty nice town, I hear," Binky said. "Uppercrusty, you know, lots of boutiques and gated communities and the kind of parks where you have to show your driver's license to get in . . ."

"I thought that was the kind of place you moved to San Francisco to get away from."

"Well, yes and no. Mostly I was running away from my family. It's funny, but the exact same traits in people you're *not* related to are somehow never as irritating as they are in the people you're stuck with for life."

"How true." Doan nodded. "And I suppose that if Andrew is out there a lot, you'd have to go out there a lot as well, wouldn't you?"

"Well, I should, yes. And where Andrew goes, Luke has to go, at least part of the time. Why?"

"Nothing," Doan said idly. "I'm not *homesick* for the West Coast or anything, but . . . well, I wouldn't mind *visiting*."

Binky laughed. "And if the three of us were out there, Tim would have to come out, too. Doan, do you know what would happen if the four of us ended up there at once?"

"Binky, it's just some sleepy backwater. All that would happen would be that we'd all get some peace and quiet."

"Doan, you want peace and quiet about as much as I do," Binky responded, laughing.

Doan sighed. "That's true. It's a terrible thing to say, but somebody's got to say it—I'd probably die of boredom there if somebody *didn't* get killed!"

CHRISTOPHER WEST

DEATH ON BLACK DRAGON RIVER

Beijing police detective Wang Anzhuang is dedicated to his work, and loyal to the Party. But a visit to his birthplace in the rural village of Nanping threatens to shatter ideals Wang has long held sacred. What was intended as a restful retreat in the country with his new wife, Rosina, turns out to be anything but when the Party secretary is brutally killed. Several paintings that had escaped ruin during the Cultural Revolution are also stolen from his home. Now Wang and Rosina must solve a mystery with links to China's tortured past—a past that has haunted this small community for decades.

❑ 0-425-16783-6/$5.99

RHYS BOWEN

EVANS ABOVE
A CONSTABLE EVANS MYSTERY

CONSTABLE EVAN EVANS WAS GLAD TO TRADE CITY LIFE FOR IDYLLIC LLANFAIR, A WELSH VILLAGE THAT TIME FORGOT. BUT THIS LITTLE TOWN HAS ITS SHARE OF ECCENTRIC CHARACTERS- TWO MINISTERS VYING FOR THE SOULS OF THEIR FLOCK, A LASCIVIOUS BARMAID, AND THREE OTHER EVANSES: EVANS- THE-MEAT, EVANS-THE-MILK, AND EVANS-THE-POST.

BUT BEFORE EVAN-NOW KNOWN AS EVANS-THE-LAW—CAN ENJOY LLANFAIR'S TRANQUILLITY, HE'S CALLED TO THE SCENE OF A CRIME AS BRUTAL AS ANY IN THE BIG CITY. TWO HIKERS HAVE BEEN MURDERED ON THE TRAILS OF THE LOCAL MOUN- TAIN, AND NOW EVAN MUST HUNT DOWN A VICIOUS KILLER—IN A TOWN WHERE ONE OF THESE LOVABLE NEW NEIGHBORS COULD PROVE TO BE DEADLY...

❏ 0-425-16642-2/$5.99

BERKLEY
PRIME
CRIME

PENGUIN PUTNAM INC.
Online

Your Internet gateway to a virtual environment with
hundreds of entertaining and enlightening books from
Penguin Putnam Inc.

*While you're there, get the latest buzz on
the best authors and books around—*

Tom Clancy, Patricia Cornwell, W.E.B. Griffin,
Nora Roberts, William Gibson, Robin Cook,
Brian Jacques, Catherine Coulter, Stephen King,
Jacquelyn Mitchard, and many more!

Penguin Putnam Online is located at
http://www.penguinputnam.com

PENGUIN PUTNAM NEWS

Every month you'll get an inside look at our upcoming
books and new features on our site. This is an ongoing
effort to provide you with the most up-to-date
information about our books and authors.

Subscribe to Penguin Putnam News at
http://www.penguinputnam.com/ClubPPI